I0767909

WHEN REALITY TEARS

ROSS TYSON

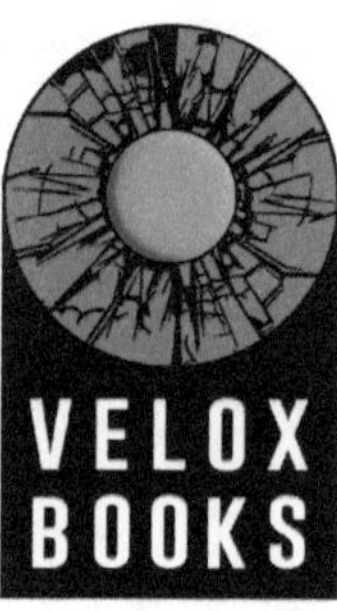

Published by arrangement with the author.

Copyright © 2025 by Ross Tyson.

All rights reserved.

No part of this publication may be reproduced, distributed, or transmitted in any form or by any means, including photocopying, recording, or other electronic or mechanical methods, without the prior written permission of the publisher, except as permitted by U.S. copyright law.

The story, all names, characters, and incidents portrayed in this production are fictitious. No identification with actual persons (living or deceased), places, buildings, and products is intended or should be inferred.

YOU'RE READING ANOTHER TERRIFYING COLLECTION FROM

FOLLOW VELOX TO KEEP THE NIGHTMARES COMING:

CONTENTS

THE KILLING MOON

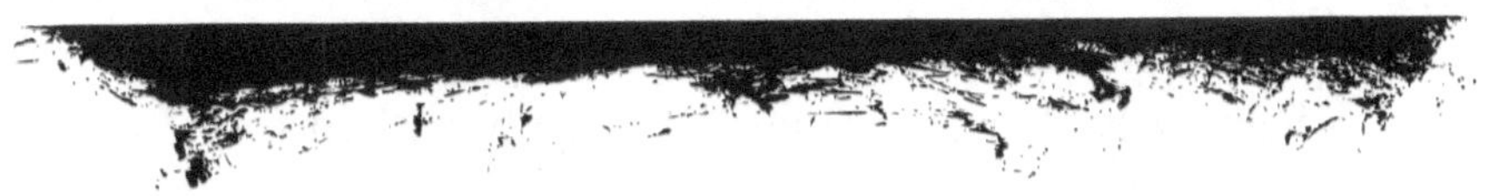

The sun baked the pavement under their feet as they ran towards the waiting sand, trying not to stay in one place too long lest they get burned. It was already hot, and it was only May, but it gave them perfect beach weather to get the summer started. For some of them, their last summer.

"Why the hell did I leave the house with no shoes?" Heather shouted as they finally reached the edge of the pavement, sliding into the sand. "You said it wasn't that long of a walk from the cabin!"

"It's not a long walk!" Alice shouted back, falling over into the soft sand and looking at her friend. She pointed behind them to the cabin only about two hundred feet away.

"That trip is a hell of a lot longer when you're walking on fire," Justin said, covering his feet in sand. He looked around him, taking count of their group. There were only five of them. "Where's Ryan?"

They all looked back toward the cabin to see Ryan walking calmly across the pavement, whistling and swinging a towel around at his side as he walked. His sandles clapped against the soles of his feet as he walked. The rest of the group groaned.

"What? Not my fault y'all are dumbasses," he said, shrugging at them. He walked past them toward the water, swinging the towel around his shoulders as he went. Heather looked over at Alice, who gave her a knowing smile and nodded at her to follow him.

Heather was hoping this was her chance. She had been head over heels for Ryan since they first met in freshman biology a year ago. They had become friends during study group, and a month ago Ryan had told them of his plans to go to his family's beach cabin for two weeks in May, inviting all of them along. They had gotten here early that morning and quickly rushed to get everything unpacked to hit the beach.

It was private land right along the Florida coast. Ryan's family was well off, and the only neighbors nearby were the two other cabins that were at least five hundred yards away from either side of theirs, and even then, those were empty this time of year. The six of them—Ryan, Justin, Heather, Alice, Sam, and Darren—had been able to finish the semester early and get out of most of their finals since they kept a good average. This was the vacation they needed.

Heather ran to catch up with Ryan, then decided to run straight past him and right into the water. She wasn't ready for how cold it still was and quickly did a one-eighty and ran back up the beach into the warm sand, shouting in surprise. The rest of them laughed at her as she ran back to the group.

Darren and Sam spread a blanket out and settled in together to sunbathe, taking in the warmth of the Florida sun. Justin and Alice ran into the waves, not caring about the cold. Alice tackled him into an oncoming rush of water as they went deeper in, laughing as they fell. Heather sat beside Ryan. He was spreading his towel out and setting up an umbrella.

"So you got to come here every year as a kid?" she asked him, looking around. She still couldn't believe how secluded the place was for being at such a prime beach spot. Everything out here was beautiful, unlike the beach near her hometown that looked like a radioactive dump most of the year. The water here was actually semi-clear, where you could see down into it and watch as fish swim by.

"Yeah. Mom and dad never got out here much because of work, but gramma used to bring me every year. Mom gave me the keys last year after gramma died. Guess that was easier for her to do than actually grieve."

"Shit. I'm so sorry," Heather said, taken aback by the honesty he was showing. Ryan was usually the goofball of the group, almost never showing any kind of vulnerability. He looked off into the distance where the sea met the sky, and she could swear she saw a tear in the corner of his eye.

"Eh, mom's always been a bitch anyway," he said, shrugging. "Besides, doubt they would want to come out here after what happened when she was a kid. She didn't even like the thought of this place."

"What do you mean?" Heather asked. She could hear Alice yelling at Justin in the background, telling him to stop splashing her or else she would drown him.

"Supposedly when mom was a teenager they were staying here for a weekend and some of the neighbors were murdered in that cabin," he said, pointing down the beach to the other house in the distance. "Apparently it was pretty grisly, enough blood that the house was basically painted red when they were found.

"Holy shit. That's insane. Did they ever catch the guy that did it?" She was trying to stay cool, but her morbid curiosity got the better of her, and this was the most Ryan had talked to her in weeks, so she wasn't letting it go.

"Nope. There was just a note written by one of the murdered women that said, 'All I see is Red'. Nothing ever came of it, no suspects, no leads... nothing." Ryan shrugged and looked over at her. "Then again, it was Florida in the sixties. Probably a bunch of kids that tripped on LSD and started stabbing each other."

"That's insane," Heather said as she looked over toward the cabin. One of the windows was broken, and it looked like there hadn't been a living thing there in years. She couldn't blame anyone for not wanting to go in.

They sat in silence for a while, watching Alice and Justin splashing around in the waves. After a couple of hours they all went back inside, getting ready for the night ahead, preparing dinner and starting on the booze they brought with them. It wasn't long before they were all buzzed and sitting out by a fire they made on the sand near the cabin.

"Shit. I forgot! There's supposed to be an eclipse tonight," Darren said, laying back in the sand and looking up at the sky. The moon hung high above them, full and large, reflecting the light of a long gone sundown onto the waters in front of them. Heather didn't think she had ever seen the moon look that large in her life.

"Wow. We're going to see a full eclipse?" Sam asked, laying down next to Darren, "That's going to be so romantic."

"They call it a Blood Moon because of how the light reflects off during the eclipse. Causes the moon to be red for a few minutes. Apparently it looks really cool and hasn't happened around this part of the states in a long time," Darren replied, putting his arm around Sam and bringing her closer to him.

Heather looked over at Ryan, giving him a furtive smile. Maybe that would help her chances of getting close to him tonight. They were the only single people here after all, they would need to stick together. She was surprised to see that the color had drained from his face, and he looked worried.

"Hey," she nudged him and said quietly, "are you alright?"

"We need to leave," Ryan said, standing up and nearly tripping into the fire. He had been downing drinks most of the afternoon and definitely wasn't in a position to make rational decisions. The others all looked at him in surprise.

"Woah man, just chill," Justin said, getting up and putting a hand on his shoulder, steadying him. "What's going on?"

"We have to leave. It's not safe here." Ryan slurred his words. He was obviously drunk and not in the right state of mind. Heather took his arm.

"I'll take him up to the cabin. I think he's just had too much quickly," she said, looking at the rest of them. They all agreed, telling Ryan goodnight and to get some rest. Heather hoisted his arm over her shoulders, trying to support him. They began the march to the cabin.

Ryan mumbled most of the way there, and when they got through the door, she hurried to get him over to the couch and set him down. He continued to protest that they needed to leave. Heather gave him a stern look.

"Ryan Hollison. It was your idea to come out here for the next few days. Why do you suddenly want to leave?" she said, looking at him.

"I'm so sorry," he slurred, only half awake. "I'm just drunk. Just drunk, thinking about old stories gramma used to tell me."

"Like what?"

"The Red," he said simply, looking towards the nearest window. The moon shone bright outside, illuminating the beach beyond. "The Red comes out during the Blood Moon."

"Yeah, the moon turns red. We know that." She gave a small chuckle. He was unbelievably drunk, and she actually found it kind of cute how concerned he was about all of them. He actually cared. She turned in the direction he was looking, seeing the shadow of the earth begin moving across the moon. "Oh! It's starting. I didn't think it would be so early."

"God help us," Ryan said, then leaned over the side of the couch and promptly vomited on the floor.

"Oh shit. Hold on. I'll get a towel!" Heather ran to the trash can, pushing it under Ryan as he heaved once more. She went into the linen closet, grabbing the first towel she saw, and threw it over the puddle on the floor. "Alright. You're cut off for the rest of the trip after this. It's only day one."

A scream came from the direction of the beach. She looked outside but couldn't see anything but the red moon hanging over the ocean, making it look like a sea of blood washing ashore. She assumed it was one of the guys scaring the girls, their usual pranks.

Ryan finished emptying his stomach and sat up, looking over at her. He suddenly looked completely sober, giving her a serious look as he attempted to stand, pointing to the cabin door that was still open.

"Close that and lock it," he said seriously. The edge in his voice could cut through bone. He was scared, but she didn't know what he was so frightened of.

"Why? What's wro—" She was cut off before she could even ask by Sam, Justin, and Alice running into the cabin and slamming the door behind them. She saw a red handprint on the door where Sam had grabbed it.

"Oh my god. He's dead. He's fucking dead." Alice screamed wildly, a manic look in her eyes. Heather looked at them all, trying to size up the situation and figure out what the hell was going on.

Sam was shaking, her eyes looking forward but not seeing anything that was there. Heather noticed that the front of her clothes were smeared with red. Jesus Christ, what was happening?

"Lock the door," Ryan said, looking at them all in turn. He stood up, walking over to the kitchen and rummaging through the drawers, finally pulling out a large chef's knife and a meat cleaver. "Lock. The. Fucking. Door. Alice, take the knife. Justin, you take the cleaver. Sam, Heather, there are bats in the closet. Grab them."

"What the fuck is going on?" Heather looked at Ryan with fear in her eyes and a tremble in her voice. "What happened to Darren?"

"We were all just sitting around the fire. We looked up to see the eclipse, then we felt something spray on us. I looked back and there was a man standing behind Darren and... oh fuck. There was so much blood." Justin was babbling at this point. Heather ran over to lock the door and looked out toward the beach as she did so. She could see a crumpled frame laying by the fire and a large figure walking toward the cabin.

She slammed the door and turned the deadbolt, then hurried away and behind the kitchen counter next to Ryan. She had never been this scared in her life, not even when she had been in a car crash in high school. This was a new kind of terror she had never felt. She knew she could die tonight.

"Fucking hell, Ryan. You goddamn idiot." Ryan was muttering to himself as he rummaged around the kitchen more, looking for any other weapons they could use. He was stone cold sober at this point, a totally different person than the boy slurring his words ten minutes ago. "Alright. We've got to get out of here."

"Ryan, what the hell is going on?" Alice screamed, sobbing. She was breaking, almost hysterical. Tears streaming down her face left tracks in the spray of blood, running their way from her cheeks to her neck.

"It's the eclipse. Gramma always told me stories growing up about how we should never be out here during a Blood Moon. Said there was something evil about this place that only showed up when the moon was red as the blood of its victims," Ryan responded, finally finding what he was looking for. He grabbed the car keys from the corner of the kitchen where they had been thrown that morning, motioning for everyone to gather around him in the living room and looking at them in turn.

"I'm sorry. I thought they were all just stories. I wouldn't have come here if I knew what tonight was. It's the one thing that gramma constantly made sure that I knew. I think it's what happened to the people in the cabin next door," he said, "Now, we're going to run to the car. Whatever this thing is, it isn't human. It may have been once, but right now it's only focused on killing. We have to get out of here."

Heather's mind raced. This was it. This was The Red that the note was about. They were going to die here. She snapped out of her thoughts when there was a loud thump on the door.

"It's probably Darren!" Sam said, running to the door.

"He's fucking dead, Sam!" Ryan screamed, chasing after her and attempting to tackle her to the ground. He wasn't quick enough, and she opened the door before he could get there.

Darren's lifeless body fell through the door, his head almost severed from the large gash in his neck. In the doorway stood an imposing figure, at least six and a half feet tall, dressed all in black. It wore a plain wolfs head mask over its face. It was a deep crimson, but they couldn't tell if it was painted or if it was from layers of blood that had been spilled on it.

The Red lunged forward, grabbing Sam by the throat and pulling his other arm back. Heather saw a large, twisted blade, almost like a sickle that had been forged then twisted around. It lifted Sam into the air and drove the blade through her stomach and up into her chest. She screamed for a moment, then silently gurgled. Blood poured to the floor, splashing their feet. Alice screamed once more.

"Back door. Run," Ryan shouted, pushing Heather in front of him toward the back of the cabin. "Get out there, then circle around to the car. GO!"

They ran, Heather first, Ryan right behind her. Justin and Alice brought up the rear, clinging together as they ran, almost dragging each other. Alice had stopped screaming, and instead was sobbing maniacally, alternating between begging for God's mercy and saying they were all going to die.

Heather barged through the door, almost tripping on the threshold as she burst outside. The warm night air hit her, the stinging smell of saltwater coming off the ocean not far from them. She ran around the corner of the house and toward the driveway where Ryan's SUV was parked. She looked behind her to see Ryan right on her heels, while Alice was just coming through the door. Ryan tossed her the keys.

"Get it going. I'm going to try to buy time," he shouted. She nodded and kept running, throwing open the door and jumping into the driver's seat. She turned the key in the ignition, but was only met with silence.

"SHIT! Ryan! It won't start!"

He let out a swear and ran back over to her. She scrambled over to the passenger seat as he climbed in, looking around and trying the keys again. There was still no sound from the engine. He leaned down to see if he could jumpstart the car and saw the wires slashed. Frantically, he tried grabbing them and attempting to jumpstart the car.

"Alice! Go!" She heard Justin screaming from behind the house. Alice turned the corner, running full on toward the car. She saw Justin round the corner right after her, then get violently jerked back behind the house. There was a sickening splash and a spray of crimson onto the sand nearby, then an object came sailing through the air.

Justin's head landed squarely on the windshield, sending a spiderweb of cracks through it. His eyes were still staring, and Heather could swear his mouth moved a bit, almost as if begging for help. Blood leaked from the mangled stump of his neck.

"NO!" Alice shrieked, stopping in her tracks. She was almost right in front of the car, the red light reflecting off the moon bathing her in an eerie glow. She broke down and fell to her knees, letting out an agonizing scream that tore through Heather's very soul—a sound she would remember for the rest of her life.

The Red was slowly coming towards her, a determined lumbering. It lifted the blade in its hand, hefting it high above its head. Alice turned, screaming at it, telling it to leave her alone, to go to hell, to give her Justin back. Her screams fell on deaf, uncaring ears. The only thing The Red cared about was seeing blood.

"Jesus Christ," Ryan said, furiously tapping wires together. After a moment the car sparked to life, headlights illuminating the killer just as he brought the blade down on Alice, stabbing her between her shoulder and neck, driving it down into her lungs. Heather saw the crimson tip of the blade poke through her side.

"How long has it been?" Ryan asked, looking at Heather. She didn't understand what he was saying. He cranked the car and looked back at her. "How long? How long since the eclipse started?"

"I... I don't know," Heather said. They had been inside when it began, so she wasn't sure of the exact time. It had to have been going at least a few minutes now. "Why does it matter? We need to get out of here."

"When the moon is red, it will come for the dead," Ryan muttered, "Beware the Blood moon for death will follow soon."

"Ryan, we have to go!" Heather shouted. The Red was standing in front of the car, basking in the glow from the headlights. It was struggling to remove the blade from Alice's body. Her head bobbed back and forth as it tried to twist the weapon free.

"That's what gramma always told me growing up. I think it will go away once the total eclipse is finished," Ryan said, looking around them. "Listen. I've always liked you. I'm sorry I've been distant. Things haven't been easy since she died."

Heather stared at him, mouth open in surprise. Of all the times he could be confessing his love, why now? He leaned over and kissed her lightly.

"I'm going to distract it. Maybe I'll survive long enough. You need to get out of here and go find someone. Bring them here. If I don't make it, make sure this entire fucking place is burned down. Make sure nobody ever comes here again. Please."

Before she could protest, he got out of the car. The Red had finally gotten the blade free from Alice, lifting its boot and planting it on her face as he pulled the blade free. Heather realized she was crying as Ryan screamed at the thing, telling it to come get him. He backed off toward the beach, attempting to make it chase him out to the water.

Heather moved over to the driver's seat as The Red turned toward Ryan, cocking its head to the side slightly. She wasn't just going to leave him here. She couldn't. She reached down to the gearshift and threw it into reverse, backing a few dozen feet toward the road. She quickly moved the car into drive and revved the engine, waiting for The Red to line up perfectly with the front of the vehicle. Once it was there, she throttled the gas, gaining as much speed as possible.

She hit the thing with a sickening thud. It was thrown almost thirty feet to the sand, rolling to a stop just short of the waves. Ryan looked back at her, amazement on his face. She got out of the car and ran to him.

"I can't just leave you. Not after you pull that shit," she said, screaming at him as she got closer. He hugged her close, thanking her. She looked back towards the water, scanning the tides for the body.

"We have to call someone. Do you have a phone?" she asked, looking at Ryan.

"I have a cell in the center console of the car," he replied, looking around them. They began running back towards the car, keeping an eye out for the killer. The moon still hung low above them, but it was now more of a rust color than the crimson it had been before. Heather jumped back into the driver's seat as Ryan went to the passenger side. He immediately opened the console and pulled out a phone.

"Alright. I'm calling the cops," he said. "I think the eclipse is almost ov-"

He was cut off by the blade flying through the windshield. It impaled itself into his left eye, his right eye going wide as he choked on his last words. His brain attempted to fire off any unmanaged neurons, but all it did was overload him. He convulsed for a moment before falling forward, dead.

Heather looked forward through the shards of broken glass. The Red was standing there, right where the waves reached their limit. She could swear it was smiling at her as blood dripped from it, leaving crimson tendrils where the waves took the streams back out into the ocean. She felt emotions overtake her.

She didn't realize what she was doing. She felt rage at the thing that had just killed her friends in such a short amount of time. Grief over the loss of Ryan, of everyone. She had loved him, and just found out that he felt the same about her, only for that to be taken in an instant. She didn't realize she was on the accelerator until she was barreling toward the red, the light from the moon reflecting off the water, turning it to a sea of blood.

She was almost upon it when the moonlight turned to silver once more, almost blinding her with its bright and sudden change. The Red exploded, leaving behind a shimmering mass of crimson blood where it once stood. She drove through it and into the waves, causing water and viscera to mix and splash through the shattered glass. She was thrown forward by the impact of hitting the water. Her head hit the steering wheel, and the world disappeared.

STRAYS

HELEN'S STORY

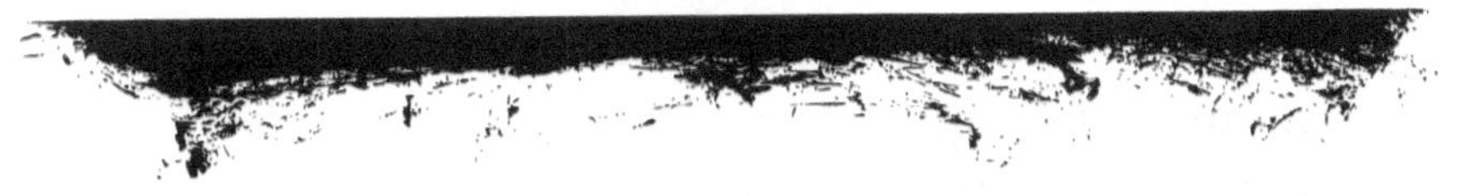

We're not first. By that, I mean we're not the first attempt at human life, at least that's what I'm putting together. If you're going to listen to my crackpot theory, though, you're going to have to hear the backstory.

My name is Helen. I'm thirty, unhoused, and scraping by on the streets of NYC. Despite what you might think of this, I'm in a sane mind and have others to corroborate what happened, or at least some of it. A few of the others I was living around and I were going to a nearby soup kitchen, hoping for at least a warm meal. I don't think I've actually eaten real food and not just scraps in three days at this point, but that's the least of my concerns after this morning. We were on our way, getting ready to cross the street, when a car came speeding through, whipping around another at the stop light.

I'm not really sure why I reacted how I did. There was a girl in front of me that I'd just met, Phoebe. She was younger, down on her luck, but a really talented artist. She just needed to find some sense of stability, you know? That's hard these days. The car was heading straight for her on the crosswalk, no way it was going to slow down or even try to. I just jumped forward, pushing her out of the way and taking the full force of the sedan barreling toward me.

At least, I should have felt the full force. Instead, it just kind of knocked me back into the pavement. It still hurts, but more like when you run into a pole or something when you're not paying attention. Here I thought it must have stopped or slammed on the breaks, except when I finally opened my eyes and overcame the daze of the hit, the street was suddenly empty.

I mean totally empty. Not a goddamn person, vehicle, or even animal in sight. There are five pigeons for every square foot of this damn city, yet at this moment, everything was silent and still. Then the humming started. It was low, reminding me of the old, giant TV that my grandma kept in her living room. That sound of low, static humming when a channel was on with nothing to watch.

Eventually, I picked myself up, not quite sure how long I was laying there though. Opening my eyes made me think I was officially dead though, or had some major, major brain damage. I'm going to describe it as best I can, but bear with me if it sounds a little odd. Everything was the same, geography-wise, with the familiar layout of the city I grew up in. Except it was... I don't know, low-res?

It reminded me of when I fucked up a Grand Theft Auto game and glitched everything else out. The empty world was more angled than real life, with fewer curves and more edges on everything. It wasn't until trying to actually get up that I started to really feel the ground under me. It was smooth, a slight static just breaths away from the surface. The asphalt looked as if it was painted on, giving the appearance of poured concrete. In reality, it just felt like a smooth, marble surface. Cool to the touch, too.

As I stood, the rest of the world came into focus, and I could see the buildings looked much the same. Windows and doors as if they were crudely textured over. Everything reminded me of an old Playstation 1 game, looking around, but how the hell I was inside it, I don't know. The sky above looked fake too, with clouds painted on with angled powers. Just looking up started to make my vertigo go crazy, though.

After a few minutes of gathering myself, I started moving down the street, trying to figure out what this place was. The streets were empty still, with not even a breeze moving the still air. When I walked up to one of the windows, a blurred display with a sign that said SLICE with pictures of pizza that made jpeg compression look like Da Vinci, there was nothing I could see through the windows. Hell, it was like just solid color, painted like glass to give the appearance of a front. Might as well have been a cardboard cutout.

"Hello!" a voice shouted from around the corner. It froze me at first, realizing I wasn't as alone as I believed. I had to find a way out of here, though. Maybe they knew something? I don't know, it's not the least rational thing about today. Because when I finally reached the intersection and got a clear view around me, unobstructed by the tall buildings around, I almost lost my fucking mind.

The World Trade Center was standing tall against the sky. Not with much detail on it, but the Twin Towers were punching into the sky for the first time since I was a kid. The world grew louder, my mind racing, trying to just find some comprehension of what I was seeing. God, I just wanted to get a hot meal and now I'm in pre-Y2K hell. With no fucking idea how to get the hell out of this place.

I almost resigned myself to death at this point because everything was so fucking overwhelming. Then the voice came again, a small "Hello?" this time from behind me. Everything in my body screamed not to turn. Don't look, don't face whatever nightmare was probably right behind me. Despite it all, I still looked.

A kid was walking toward me, maybe a couple blocks down, this time though they gave a much louder "Hello?".

This is on me, not going to lie. I grew up homeless for a lot of my childhood, so I've got a soft spot for kids who need help. That was almost the end of me.

"Hey, are you okay?" I shouted down the street. The child only gave another "Hello" in return, nothing else. They were moving toward me still, but the light didn't let me make out any features. Cautiously, I started walking to meet them. They repeated hello again, this time louder. It wasn't until I got closer that I noticed the humming growing louder, static cutting through the silence.

"H-h-h-h-ello?" It said again, this time stuttering it out, resetting to the beginning every time. When it came into view, I took a step back, realizing I made a huge mistake.

The smiling, cheery face looked pasted onto the angular head. Their shoulders and arms were oddly sharp, just floating at the side without movement. Legs were moving, but not actually touching the ground. This thing was gliding like a ghost, closer and closer to me.

Features grew clearer as it got closer. The smile was too wide for the face, stretching ear to ear, showing far too many teeth. Empty eyes stared forward, crudely drawn onto the skull. I honestly don't know if it could see me, but it felt like it *wanted* me.

"H-h-h-h-h-h-h-h-h-h-h-h-h-h" It started glitching harder, the words stacking on top of each other without getting out the first word. In only a few feet it became one long sound, a scream of binary technology missing a one or zero. It got overwhelming, causing me to fall to my knees in the middle of the street. Gliding ever closer, the figure was now bending, contorting, and stretching itself in every direction. There was a singularity in the middle, with every fiber of the thing screaming, trying to escape it. I could see the ground around it beginning to pixelate, popping in and out of existence.

Once the stretching got to its face, everything went to hell. The sound grew even louder, more static and loud, mechanical errors deafening me. Static charge filled the air, crackling around as the hair on my arms raised. I was being electrified, growing more intense as the glitch grew closer. It wasn't similar to being tased yet, but god I could feel it ramping up.

Pretty sure I started screaming, which may have been what saved me. Whatever god there was in this fucked up digital prison must have taken pity on me. I felt something grab me by my shirt collar, stretching the fabric as it did. That was it, I thought I was going to die. This thing was trying to eat me, and I would die here, forgotten on the streets just like in the real world.

"You can stop screaming now," a voice said, pulling me along the road toward one of the storefronts. The contorted glitch of a person was still following behind us, but at a much slower pace now. Looking up, there was a person in a sloth mask pulling me by my shirt collar. "Anyway, bye. Try not to come back."

Without a second thought, he threw me into one of the painted doorways with ridiculous strength. Bracing myself for the impact of a wall, I instead stumbled out, the heat of the city streets hitting me like an inferno. People were bustling around, bumping into me and going about their day. I was back in the real world, just down the street from where I was when everything started.

Cop cars were down the road near where I got hit, as well as an ambulance. When I walked up, I couldn't even say anything. Phoebe was standing there crying by the ambulance, a large scrape going down her forearm. Seeing me must have made her think she was being haunted, because she started to point at me, crying too much to get anything out.

Talking to the others that were with me, I'm still not sure what the hell happened. Everyone says they saw me push Phoebe, the car make contact, then I was just... gone. An hour passed and everyone thought I was still on the grill of that truck, being taken along on a high-speed chase. They still haven't even caught the driver, apparently.

I'm tired. Everything is still blurry. I feel like I saw something I wasn't supposed to, like something taboo and ancient. Even though the look of it was relatively recent, it just felt... old. There was something there that wasn't right. Not to mention whoever the fuck rescued me. God, I have a lot of fucking questions but right now I'm just glad to be alive.

Maybe someone in the homeless camps knows something. I'll reach out to a few of my shelter buddies too, to see if they've experienced anything similar. To be honest, surviving on the streets in the real world seems a little trivial now after seeing all that. I don't feel like I'm real anymore. I keep hearing scientists talking about living in a simulation, but I think I just saw the demo. God, I hope I don't have to go there again, though.

I'm still really unsure about the things I've seen, but I do know there are others who have seen it now. Did a little digging and found some random message boards suggesting a 'Demo" like a first attempt at humanity. Except now I'm finding out that visitors to the Demo don't end up sticking around long after they return.

From the few threads I've seen, and bear with me—I'm fucking homeless and using library computers—the few of us who went in and made it back all had somewhat similar experiences. Emptier, more low-res version of their surroundings at the time, and a voice luring them closer before glitching out on them. Most ran, and everyone assumes there were plenty more people who didn't get away, but everyone who found a way out says it was by complete accident. No mention of anyone in a mask, Sloth or otherwise. I appeared to be an isolated incident.

There wasn't even a common theme in how they got there in the first place. Things were seemingly at random, whether it was just a random doorway while urban exploring or just being in the wrong place at the wrong time. One person described their experience of just falling through the floor one day, emerging in the

Demo version of their school. I couldn't find any correlation, even among the small handful of people who had shared their stories.

I just found out one thing that's consistent between all of us though, and I'm not sure how much time I'm going to have left. The glitch followed me. Others mentioned some strange happenings, seeing glitches in real life, technology acting strange, and a feeling that there was something watching them, waiting. I've felt that since the first encounter, just a few days ago, but I feel like my heart is still racing. Mechanical, constant screams echo in my head, static building on my skin like wearing a fleece coat fresh from a dryer. Except not comforting at all, leaving me with cold sweats.

I stayed in the library overnight to avoid the rain and damp outside. I hadn't been myself the past couple of days, pushing everyone away who tried to check on me. EMS told me I was a damn hero for pushing Phoebe out of the way, so why do I feel like I'm being hunted? I did a good deed, right? That deserves some sort of reward, you would think, not a fucking curse.

Everything settled in the library around midnight or so, with workers, librarians, and janitors finishing up their duties. Years of experience taught me where to hide and avoid anyone checking around, though the janitor was extra thorough tonight for some reason. Must be an event or something tomorrow.

I curled up on one of the couches set aside for reading, nestled in one of the back corners where a small light cast shadows. It was comforting, one of the only places I've ever known that felt like home. Guess that's why I finally ended up drifting off to sleep, but it was only minutes before things got weird.

A loud series of thumps from a few aisles down, books hitting the floor in quick succession. Pages were turning like a hurricane was blowing right through, threatening to tear them apart. In the shadows I could see the shelf wavering, ready to topple over at the force before a figure emerged, gliding from the aisle like a damn ghost. It turned, looking toward me. The same small child I saw in the Demo was standing there, a faint glow coming from it as the sneering, plastered on face focused in on me. Then that loud, mechanical scream again, like voices sounding out briefly before being silenced, becoming a chorus of glitching, digital hell.

My reaction time was much better, maybe because I knew where I was or because I didn't have the initial shock at whatever this damned thing was. When the Glitch started moving toward me, bending and stretching like gravity was tearing it apart at the seams, I took off down another aisle.

Well, that pissed it off apparently, because it started getting even louder, the storm of gravity around it pulling everywhere. Where to go or what to do was secondary in my mind to just get the fuck out of here. I ran the maze of aisles, judging where the Glitch was by the tornado it was whipping up. Whoever came in there to clean in the morning was probably pissed, but when I came back this afternoon, everything was in place. Whether it was the work of all the employees or another bit of the Demo's fuckery, I have no idea.

I'm ahead of things again, sorry. At some point it occurred to me that this thing wasn't just going to go away. It meant I was going to be out on the streets in the rain, but it was better than what the Glitch might do to me. I still don't know what the hell it would do, and to be honest, I'm not keen on finding out. Took me a second to look around, figure out where I was, and make a break for the doors.

The adrenaline is what I'm blaming for this one, because it totally escaped my mind that the damn doors are locked. Not my smartest moment, I know, but something worked out for me anyway. I dashed through the detectors that kept the doors separate from the rest of the library, hitting the doors themselves HARD. I was still bruised from that truck hitting me, so hitting the metal push bars was incredibly unpleasant to put it lightly.

I was scrambling once I realized they were locked, and the Glitch was screaming like a dial-up modem in a fucking blender behind me. It was almost on me, and I still wasn't able to get the top deadbolt undone, my hands slippery with sweat while trying to pull the old, rusting lockout.

The Glitch charged at me then, mouth wide in a smile that looked like it was going to chomp down on me. It hit the detectors set up to prevent weapons from being brought in, suddenly compressing down to a small singularity as the parts of it stretching in every direction were absorbed, infinitely folding itself into oblivion before it could pass through the other side. Wasn't stopping me from getting the hell out of here, though. I finally fumbled the deadbolt open and burst through the doors faster than the devil running from a church. I ran maybe four blocks before I finally stopped to catch my breath, a few other pedestrians on the street giving me an odd look.

Found an alley to curl up in that was somewhat dry. It wasn't easy to fall asleep, though, with me on constant high alert thinking it could appear again at any point. Not to mention my mind fucking running marathons trying to figure out what made it disappear. I'm hoping I can figure it out to keep myself alive, at least. God, I've been just surviving for so long that I kind of forgot what it feels like to actually be relieved to be alive.

Thinking about it, writing it all out now, when it hit the metal detectors it was almost instantly done for. Whether it killed it or just sent it back to the Demo is a whole other thing entirely, but there's something there...

Oh fuck. Magnets. Holy shit, why didn't that click earlier? They're digital, everything looked like it was from old, digital media discs. I still remember when my dad got mad at me as a kid and decided a "punishment" was taking my copy of Final Fantasy VII to a refrigerator magnet. Still never got to the final disc after all this time, but I guess he got karma since he fucking died a few weeks later. Maybe you shouldn't have drunk and driven, Robert.

Sorry, little trauma dumping. I ended up falling asleep in the alley until about noon, when it became too uncomfortable. The sun was hitting the trash back there just right to really bake some old dairy. Made my way back to the library instead to scour the internet more, maybe find some answers, and write all this up.

I think I need to find the Sloth. He definitely wasn't a part of that world, with much more clearly human features even just by his build. Until then, I'm going to see if I can swipe a few magnets from the library desk. If anything, I might be able to find the stuff to make a small electromagnet. Maybe I can find something lying around the trash. Until then, I'm definitely not sleeping here, so guess it's back out on the street along with all the other strays.

———

It's been a rough day. I mean ROUGH. Let's dive in.

I found Sloth. It wasn't how I would have wanted to do it, though. Instead, things went a little rough. I found my way back to the Demo. or at least the Demo found its way back to me.

Let's see... so things were pretty chill the rest of the day after I made the last update. I swiped some magnets from the desk at the library and tied them around a small bar I found in an alley. That way, if the glitch managed to come back for me, I had it ready to go, giving it a good whack and taking it out. If only the plans went right.

I don't know where it came from or how it just found me, but I was trying to sleep in an alleyway last night. Figured I would be safe there, not much tech around to worry about anything. I have a stupid theory it came out of the computers at the library, but I have no idea if that's how it works.

Feels like I had just drifted off, sleep finally overtaking me despite trying to stay alert. The sounds of the city around me were loud, but I've been able to tune them out for years. Maybe that's why I didn't notice it at first. The sudden static, a hum beginning quietly before roaring to a constant, crashing crescendo of chaos. That was around when I woke up, seeing the Glitch standing at the end of the alleyway as I sprung up from the makeshift bed of garbage I was sleeping on.

I barely had time to grab the magnet pipe before it was on me, faster than it had moved before. Closing my eyes, I gave the hardest swing I could toward it, hoping it was enough. The magnets stopped it momentarily, the singularity coming to a complete standstill. The parts bending out from it began to shrink in again, once more folding in on itself.

If it managed to grab me or if it was just the force of it disappearing, somehow it took me along, screaming for my damn life. My eyes weren't closed, but all I could see for a moment was darkness, before dropping into a blinding, white light. When it finally faded, I could see I was in the alleyway, stripped of any of the clutter. Walls looked painted on, with fire escapes were simply drawn on top of them without structure. For a minute I was losing my mind, wondering how in the hell I got back here again. Then the Glitch started screaming again. Louder this time.

Glitch was obviously feeling some hurt from the magnet, but at this point, it was starting to become something different. The painted-on face stayed the same, grinning malevolently with empty white eyes wide open to see everything. The body was bending and morphing more, though. I was barely able to catch myself before the magnet pipe was torn from my hands, hitting a wall. When it impacted, the magnets left pixilation briefly before it was covered by the texture again, briefly popping out of existence first.

The only option I had was to make a break for it and hope for the best. Ducking around the Glitch, heart pounding, I ran out of the alleyway into the street, hoping to whatever god made this fucking place that the layout was still the same as the city I knew.

Made the classic mistake while I was running and looked behind me to see if it was following. Yeah, stupid me. It wasn't the same Glitch that had been hunting me. This fucking thing had evolved, the bending limbs stretching out into dozens of legs as it crawled toward me on all of them. Arms were long, propping the torso up like some fucked up centaur, face now glitching in and out, changing faces and voices as the "Hello?" grew louder and more frantic. Thankfully, despite the appearance of it just gliding along, it must not have been used to the new movement style. Either that or it just got a major downgrade on speed in return for becoming a nightmare.

By the time I got a few blocks down, I was out of breath. I could hear the Glitch far behind me, but wasn't sure where the hell it was. The one thing I was sure of was I knew this part of town much better. Wall Street. Where all the rich people live and we on the street pick up the scraps. I've done a lot of pickpocketing here, even more time just begging for scraps, hoping people would take pity on a woman. Except the people here didn't have any pity, only greed. I got spit on and propositioned more times than I ever got a cent.

While I was catching my breath I took in my surroundings, seeing everything familiar as if it hadn't quite loaded in yet. Most of the buildings were still the same, though many had different, more outdated signs. A banner on one of the bank doors caught my eye, huge letters with fireworks all around in celebration.

HAPPY NEW YEAR! SEE YOU NEXT CENTURY!

Memories snapped back into place for me, suddenly, clearly, with a force that would put that truck the other day to shame. I still remember begging out here that night. Dad kicked me out again, not for the first time. A seven-year-old out on the streets alone, I did what I could to try and eat. Always heard that Wall Street was where anyone could make money, so I made my way there thinking I could earn a few dollars for a Happy Meal or something.

I was seven, cut me some slack. I learned how things worked pretty fast after that.

It was raining. New Year's Eve 1999. I was huddled under a little awning, one right across the street from me right then actually. I remember a man walking up, showing the first hint of kindness

I had seen in the seven hours I had been there. That same banner that was blurry and pasted on in the Demo was right there.

"Are you alone, son?" Those were the first words he asked me. When I nodded, all he said was, "Well, I could buy you some food, if you'd like to play."

I was hungry, but even seven-year-old me had alarm bells. I ran as fast as I could, though I don't think he even tried to follow me. He was older, balding, and wearing a freshly pressed suit. Considering the cigar stink radiating off of him, I'm assuming he wasn't much of a runner.

Sorry, still dealing with a lot of these memories coming back. I... I've been running from shit for a long time, y'know? My mom died when I was still a baby. Dad apparently realized pretty early on that I wasn't going to be the pro-athlete son he always wanted. Don't think I've even spoken to him since I was twelve, so God knows how he would react seeing I'm not his son anymore. Hell, as far as he's concerned, I probably never was anyway.

The Glitch roaring jerked me back to my senses, getting closer at a much faster rate than when I had left it. I looked back and realized why—it was growing larger. The number of legs filled the entire street now, with faces changing even faster on its head. The same, terrifying smile was always there, but the teeth and inside kept changing, taking on different textures and colors, from sharp teeth to just a blue void. The eyes remained solid white, while the entire skull kept stretching and growing, enlarging the pasted-on face so it looked even more grotesque.

It was close. Closer than I wanted it to be. I don't know when I started screaming, but at least I was trying to find somewhere to get away. The doorway of a bank nearby caught my eye, appearing different than the others, almost completely white. I swear it wasn't that way a few minutes before, but I was also having a pretty bad flashback, so my mind is pretty messy.

I swear I ran faster than I ever had, going for the door with every fiber of energy I had left in me. When I tell you I was nowhere near prepared for what was next, I mean it. I thought my life was about to end here, forgotten. Nobody in the real world would give a shit, anyway. I was a stray, one of millions of Americans living on the bottom just scraping by. Not a single person would go looking for me.

I hit the doorway with all my might, hoping to bust the door open. Instead, it busted me. I was knocked back hard, thrown across the street right on my ass. A little luck had my back, though, sort of. At least the pavement wasn't actually pavement, just a slick sheet of hard static with the look of a paved street painted on. I slid across, over the painted curb, and into the wall.

I was a little dazed after that. It. hurt, I think I may have hit my head at one point. When I opened my eyes though, the Glitch was screaming closer, ready to bear down on me. Everything hurt, and I tried to force myself up to run, but the strength just wasn't there. I was so dizzy I could barely tell up from down. I don't know what bounced me, but it hit me hard enough to completely kick my brain for a good minute.

Over the screaming I heard another voice, this time a little familiar.

"What in the hell are you doing here? Didn't I throw you back on like... Monday? Wasn't it Monday?" The Sloth was walking up, quickly slipping the mask down over his head while looking at another figure standing alongside him. This one was tall, lean but muscled, dressed in all black with a Raven mask over his face.

"How the fuck should I know? Who is this?" The Raven asked Sloth, gesticulating a hand toward me. "I thought living people couldn't get in here? Did you let her in?"

The screaming of the Glitch grew louder, only a couple of blocks down the street now. Its growth seemed slowed down, with fewer legs growing from the torso. The face was still changing, more rapidly while sometimes blinking completely out of existence, leaving an empty black void where it was. All I could do was point to it and scream for help as it got closer.

"Oh shit. I've never seen one like that. Have you? That looks mean," Sloth remarked, turning to look at the Glitch as it moved closer. Raven stepped forward, raising a hand in front of him and centering it on the creature.

"We don't have time for this shit." Raven briefly raised his hand above his head before slicing it downward through the air, a chopping motion in the direction of the Glitch. A wave of solid light extended from his hand as he made the movement, extending far enough to slice the Glitch directly in half down the middle.

I'll be totally honest here if you're looking for answers—I don't know. All I could really say at the time was that the Glitch was what brought me here, that it had been after me since the other day. Sloth and Raven just stood there and listened, never taking off their masks.

"Can we finish up? Only three days until we do this," Raven said, crossing arms in front of him. I was still in shock after seeing the thing that's been chasing me for days just get sliced in half like paper. Now I was finally able to ask questions to the one that saved me the first time and I could barely fucking speak. Raven gestured to a nearby doorway. "You gonna open it for her?"

"Hold up, hold up, hold up! The Glitch was in the real world? Like our world?" Sloth asked me. My heart was still racing, but I was getting the feeling they knew about as much as I did about that thing. "You're not even supposed to be here."

"How are you here, then?" That was all I could get out. Sloth actually started laughing at that question.

"I fucking died." He laughed even harder. "You mean you didn't have some near-death experience or anything? Meet anyone who gave you a talk? None of that?"

"I pushed my friend out of the way of a truck, and it hit me. I ended up in here." Things were making less sense than before. "They told me I disappeared until you threw me back like twenty minutes later."

"I'm sorry, you've spoken to her before? In here? What does she know?" Raven was asking as Sloth still laughed, starting to cough now from not being able to catch his breath.

"Oh my god, chill. I literally just threw her through a door. Holy shit, this changes a lot of stuff. We had no idea you could just get knocked in here. Hell, you might've had the least terrible experience out of all of us. God, wait until we tell Tam. They're going to be so pissed." He was laughing again, clapping Raven on the shoulder. "Sorry, a friend of ours. His trip here was SUPER unpleasant, even compared to all of us. Don't know if the universe just likes fucking with him or what but... woo, too long of a story. Anyway."

Sloth turned toward the door nearby, raising a hand and flipping his palm from face down to upright in its direction. A black void overtook the doorway, blotting out any of the markings on it.

"Look, this isn't a good place to be. You're gonna want to stay out of here if you can help it," Sloth offered.

"Please go, we're on a time crunch," Raven said. Even through the mask, I could feel his eyes rolling as he spoke.

I was pretty hesitant to walk toward the door, trying to gauge if it was okay to go through or not. Sloth waved me along, telling me to get out of there before more Glitches showed up. I closed my eyes, stepping through the doorway and out into the dark street, the sun barely starting to break over the horizon.

Weird as it sounds, I haven't had any of those dread feelings since I got back. Maybe they really were able to get rid of the Glitch. At least, I hope they were. Things are still shitty, hard not to be that way when you're living on the streets. I still don't know who they were, but I'm keeping my eyes out for anything that seems out of the ordinary. Might be back on the street, but we'll make it through. I can feel a change in the air, and I've learned to trust my gut after living so long as a stray.

HOUSE OF THE LORD

Considering how crappy everything pays right now, I was beyond hyped when I found an opening for a night janitor paying forty dollars an hour. In the rural ass, backwater swamp of Georgia, FORTY FUCKING DOLLARS AN HOUR?! TO CLEAN A CHURCH!? My little agnostic heart was ready to pull up for an altar call once they finally hired me. Good god, I see why they pay that high now.

It's an easy enough schedule, too. I go in after church services or meetings, do some basic cleaning, and dip out. Takes maybe two or three hours every night and I do an afternoon clean on Sundays between services. So Mondays, Wednesdays, and Fridays I do a couple of late nights and it's all good. They told me they wanted a more thorough clean once a week, whatever day I chose, so I just decided to make my Wednesday nights the long ones.

For forty bucks an hour, I'm not going to skimp either. I go over every goddamn inch of god's good house with a fine toothcomb. I'm in here flipping more tables than Jesus to make sure they're clean. It takes maybe seven hours or so to go through everything and it's the easiest money I've ever made.

The place is old, from what they told me when I started it's at least a couple of centuries, built in colonial times and renovated/rebuilt over the years on the same land. There's a little cemetery out behind it too, though many of the graves are too worn down to read at this point. They haven't had a new resident since the 1800s, I think.

One big sanctuary makes up most of the place, with a couple of little rooms in the back behind the main altar. A little door on the right side led back into a small hallway that smelled of mildew, with two doors on the left and one at the other end of the hall. Normally it would look like just your average old Protestant church in the south. Except it gets a little weird.

The first door on the left is painted blue. Not like a regular blue either, but like a bright cerulean. It's both padlocked and dead bolted from the outside though, and only the pastor, William, has a key to it. When I was talking to Anita, the treasurer who hired me, she told me she had no idea what was down there, but it was probably just old storage or something. I had to ask her again when she said "down there" because we're in the heart of Georgia swamp country. If someone tries to make a basement around here, they're just going to get a room of crumbling mud and humidity. She assured me it was a cellar, though she only was told this by Pastor WIlliam.

My first Monday night clean went off without a problem. Went in and just ran a vacuum over the floor after a prayer group meeting. Tuesday I was off, so I just stayed home and played Shadow of the Erdtree. Wednesday night after service, I went in around eight-thirty to start my cleaning. The only person left there was William at this point, but even then we only briefly passed each other as he was heading out. There was not much to say of the interaction though. We just explained pleasantries and he said he was off to get some shut-eye. I was just desperate to get into the church and out of the swamp heat.

I got in, walked to the little supply closet in the back of the sanctuary, and pulled out the vacuum. Wednesday night service wasn't very crowded usually, just a few grandmas and the really devout couple of middle-aged men with their thick study bibles, so nothing was really dirty. I figured I could just milk the clock a little by dusting around and just fucking about in general. Might as well get some money while I'm here.

Vacuumed the sanctuary with no problem, and went to go get in the back hallway next. Probably a good time to mention the sanctuary has two sets of lights, one for the front altar area and the other for the actual pews and seating area. I only had the altar area lights because they were pretty damn bright. Until you get into the hallway at least, then you can barely see because the light only extends a few pews out.

Headphones in, music going, I just kept doing my cleaning. Ran down the hall, into the office next to the blue door, and even got to the pastor's office while I was at it. I didn't really notice anything until I looked up and out the door from the end of the hallway. I could see straight down the beige hall, blue door glowing bright in the fluorescent, into the sanctuary. I don't think I've ever felt goosebumps like I did when I looked down that hall.

At least seven or eight people were sitting in the pews just out of the light's reach. They were all dressed in black, heads bowed so faces couldn't be seen. I had to squint to see them almost, but they were definitely in the first two rows outside of the light. I don't know if there was anything behind them... it was much darker, but I was already shook. I briefly closed my eyes and reopened them, but they were still fucking there.

Then there was a loud THUMP on the blue door. Like something being thrown hard against it, but there wasn't a sound of it falling down either. I took my attention from the sanctuary to the blue door for just seconds, but it was long enough for everyone in the sanctuary to suddenly vanish. Nothing was there when I looked back, with it looking just like I had left it, not a soul around.

I kind of just shook it off as having like a late-night heeby-jeebies moment, you know? Except I finished up right there and started locking up. I've never really believed in any kind of supernatural, was religious in my younger days, but had since really drifted off.

I've always liked horror stuff, but the idea of ghosts and shit in the real world? Please. Then I realized I had to turn the lights off at the altar and leave through the main sanctuary door. Swear I'm not scared of the dark, but I'd be lying if I said I wasn't creeped out a little.

I turned off the light, saw the moon shining through the stained glass, and immediately got a chill again. It's been nearly a hundred degrees with full humidity the past few days, and it felt like I was being dunked in ice water. There wasn't even anything there. I looked around, but nothing. Pulled my phone out and turned on the flashlight, making a quick pace toward the front doors. I swear, to whatever god you want to hold me to, that there was the sound of footsteps thudding along behind me. I swung the door open and practically dived through. Never felt so fucking good to feel swamp heat on my skin. Slammed the damn thing behind me too, started to walk to my car, then realized I didn't lock it.

I thought about just not going back. Leaving it be until the next person got there on Friday for a prayer group. Then I realized the money I would lose if I didn't do something right and lost this job. Look, rent is fuckin' high right now, and I've gotta pay bills. So despite everything in me telling me to get the hell out, I turned around to go lock the door. The keys were in my hands jingling like wind chimes because I was shaking so damn hard. I finally got the key in and started to turn it when sound started reverberating from the sanctuary, a chorus with an organ swelling to a crescendo. I turned the key and yanked it out at the same time, almost taking the doorknob with me, and ran the hell out of there.

I could still hear it in my car when I started it and whipped out of the little dirt parking lot. Pretty sure I hit the ditch on the way out too, but I sure as shit wasn't just going to stop. It wasn't until a few minutes into my drive that my hand finally loosened on the steering wheel, and I realized what they were singing. I remember it from going to an old Baptist church with my grandma. They only did old hymnals and refused to use anything but a piano, but I remember the damn words.

"Nothing can, for sin atone. Nothing but the blood of Jesus. Naught of good that I have done, nothing but the blood of Jesus."

I asked Anita about it on Friday night when I went in. Made sure I was out by nightfall this time, though. She said that she'd always thought there were angels around this place, keeping watch over the flock. Don't know how angelic that sounds, but I guess she hasn't been here alone after dark. When I told Pastor William about the thump coming from behind the blue door, he had the briefest flicker of something on his face. Then it was right back into smiling preacher mode, like fuckin' Baby Billy. Told me there was a problem with possums digging into the basement and not finding their way out.

I don't know that I really believe him. That sounded bigger than any possum I've ever seen, even the one that gets into my garbage every night I started calling Round Ronald. No way a possum was going to get that fierce with a door.

They canceled service on Sunday so I was off. Going back in tonight after the prayer meetings and doing a little cleaning, so I'll update if there's anything that happens. I want to chalk it up to just being in a strange place at night, but there's no way those chills were based on nothing. This shit keeps up, I might start praying while I'm there...

Yeah, not gonna lie, I've worked some really awful jobs but next to nothing has had me feeling this kind of anxiety before going in. Hell, I remember puking every morning before going to my call center healthcare job. Getting screamed at and told you're the reason some boomer is going to die, all because their heart medication was denied by the insurance and they had to pay three dollars. It's really not fun, like at all, but I would honestly take it again at this point. If it paid the same as this place.

Went in last night to clean after the prayer meetings. Except I went in a little early to see if I could actually catch William, maybe see if I could get through the blue door. Didn't work, mind you. Think he's being a lot more secretive about something than he lets on.

I approached him after the last of the older men left, giving a hearty wave and "see you Wednesday" along with it. Pastor William started to walk back to his office as I was starting to get my usual cleaning supplies out. The sun was still up, so I was planning on hitting this place QUICK and getting the hell out before it got dark again. Never thought I would be thankful for the sun staying up until nine in the summer, but here we are. Before he could walk into the hall, I got his attention, asking if he wanted me to clean up the room behind the blue door.

He just kind of... smiled. There was this look I just couldn't quite place. Maybe concern? Then he gave me some bullshit answer about how he had done a spring cleaning back in May, so not to worry about that. Just focus on the areas where people move through and keep things nice. That's all I need to do. A little weird, but whatever.

Then he dropped the goddamn bomb that they're hosting a wedding tomorrow, so I'm going to need to do a deep clean. Fuuuuuuuuuuuck I was NOT prepared for this. I tried making up some excuse about not being able to do it tonight because of a family event or something, and he just told me to come back after the event was over. Said he absolutely needs it cleaned by tomorrow.

I didn't have anything with me. I wasn't going to drive the thirty minutes to get back home either with my busted-ass air conditioner. There wasn't much choice, so I just started doing whatever I could and doing it fast. Swear to god I've never cleaned that fast in my life. Dusting corners, scrubbing down filthy baseboards, they wanted me to pull out a whole damn carpet cleaner. Before I knew it, the sun had gone down without me realizing. The church lights were so bright with the stained glass that it was hard to notice when it got dark, but now it felt like the lights were a haven. Phone said it was around nine-thirty, so not much time since sundown. That's when I realized I forgot to bring my phone charger, which was just really fantastic. The cherry on top of the whole thing, y'know? At least it still had about half the batter.

Put it in power saved and just hit work even harder. It wasn't until I was cleaning windows that shit started getting weird. Maybe thirty minutes later, I was up on the stepladder, going down the stained-glass windows with a soft rag and warm water, getting UNGODLY amounts of dust may I add, when something suddenly thumped hard against the window. Honestly with how hard it hit, I don't know how the window didn't break. Sounded like a whole cinder block, but it must have hit just right on the window trim to absorb the impact. Almost made me fall off the ladder, though. Hell, I was barely saved thanks to the clumsy recovery reflexes I've honed all my life.

It took me a minute, but I steeled myself and went out the front door, looking right around the corner to where the window was. There was a streetlight that illuminated the entire side, giving me a pretty clear view. Nothing was there, though. Only the small, worn-down graveyard a few feet away from the church, made even creepier by the shadows being cast from the saturated light of a sodium bulb. That was about the time I noticed one of the shadows longer than the other. When I looked back toward the cemetery, there was a tall, dark-suited man with a wide-brimmed hat, just kind of standing in front of one of the graves.

I'm gonna throw this out there—if you want intricate details of the rest of the night, you're not going to get a lot. Things are still a massive blur, and I'm completely fucking freaked out. This is all from what I can remember in the very rapid escalation that came next.

Obviously seeing the goddamn Undertaker making his WWE return in the middle of a graveyard was NOT on my agenda last night. I ran my ass inside so fast I should be on a plane to the goddam Paris Olympics right now, okay? I need you to understand just how little I am willing to fuck around with whatever is going on here. I got right back in there and locked that door, deadbolted it, whatever I needed to do. Whatever the hell was in here might just be some spooky spirit shit, but that thing out there could very well be an irl murderer. Look, if I'm going to die let it be by some instant Thirteen Ghosts mess. I'm not chill with being murdered by a human, they can be *really* fucked up.

Locked, deadbolted, didn't stop there. I flipped every light switch on and ran down the hall into William's office. Shut that door and deadbolted the fuck out of it too. Then I grabbed my phone and started to make a call to whatever officer they would send out here.

Except I'm in bumfuck NOWHERE. No damn signal and somehow, even though I put power mode on, I'm at fifteen percent on my battery. I tried calling the cops again and my phone died right then and there.

At this point, I am decidedly not chill, and am debating whether it's my best move to just hide in here or risk getting to my car. It took me a few minutes, but I started to kind of calm down and try to rationalize everything. It was probably a gravestone, right? Like a taller one with one of those weird sculptures on it? I've never looked too close at it to be able to tell, to be honest. Not especially planning on it unless it's high noon and the sun is shining. This was not that time, so I decided that for now, we're safe in here, and we're just gonna chalk all this up to being a big misunderstanding late at night.

Nerves going a few fewer miles per hour, I decided to go back to cleaning windows. That was about all that was left other than cleaning the baptism pool, and that was as simple as a quick scrub since it didn't seem to be used often. All good, we're getting through this. I'm sorry I start talking in the plural when I'm freaked out.

Washing the windows was going okay, but I still kept the deadbolt and everything on the door and every light on. All good, all fine. No worries just wiping the window. Then came the screaming.

Ice in my damn veins. It was a woman, I think? All I know is it was guttural, like the sound of grief in the rawest form. I don't know what the cause of the scream was, but I could tell it was in the building. It took me a minute to get moving again, but I had to know if I was right. It was still going too, with few stops in between the loud roars of anger and despair.

I was right. I wish I wasn't, but it was coming from behind the blue door. It kept going too, but it sounded so fucking far away down there that I'm not really sure how it could. Unless there's some massive concrete bunker under here, I don't know how anything more than a crawlspace could be under there. Then it stopped.

I was in the hallway at that point, in the middle of trying to rip myself in half so I could run away. There was that one nagging little feeling that this could be someone who was in trouble. I can't just leave someone here if something is going on. That would make me just as responsible, wouldn't it? I swear to god, if my momma hadn't raised me, my ass would've been gone faster than my dad.

I knocked on the door, giving a second to see if there was any response. It was only a moment until there was a faint answer, like a "hello", I think? I kind of chased down my courage and shouted through the door, asking who they were. No answer. I knocked on the door again and still nothing.

I gave it one more good knock, figuring the third time was the charm. Turns out, that's bullshit. Right as I let the third knock go, things went to hell. The lights flickered, briefly at first, but they kept going sporadically. Never actually goes off for more than seconds at a time, but always flickers on just enough to fuck with my vision. My eyes were doing that thing where you can't see in the dark after coming in from the bright sun, making everything in the dark vague. I turned around, ready to find my way out of the church and just say hell with this for the night. Except I turned back toward the sanctuary to leave and saw an entire congregation standing there before the lights flickered off again.

I'm proud to report I did not, despite popular reports, soil myself in that moment. Instead, I screamed like a damned Looney Tunes character and started running for my keys sitting on the first pew. Thankfully, the lights came back on steadily and it was no longer occupied by whatever ghostly churchgoers were there just seconds before. I thought I had caught a break. Thought I was going to grab my keys and make the run to the car. Water started splattering behind me. The baptism pit was running, quickly splashing as the tub filled. I took a gulp, turned around, and that's about when things went totally fucking Shining on me.

Deep crimson was pouring out of the faucet, interspersed with intense blasts of a rusty, dirty black-like swamp water. I wanted to throw up right then and there, seeing all the crimson splattering everywhere against the white backdrop. I'm not really religious, but a baptism pit filling with blood seems a little... sacrilegious I guess? I wasn't waiting around to debate the ethical implications of a bloody ghost bath though. I turned around to grab my keys, which were still sitting on the pew. Mistake number two.

FACE TO FUCKING FACE. I don't know who it was, I don't know what it was. All I know is that I was face to face with one of the dozens of good church patrons that now filled the sanctuary. The sound that came out of me was like a car hitting the brakes at seventy miles an hour. I'm certain every dog in the tri-county area must have perked up, because this thing still haunts me. Like it's burned into my mind because it was right there in my face. Almost nose to nose, if it had one.

The face was waxy, almost like eggshell white skin. Not scary by itself, but the dark, hollow sockets instead of eyes were what really got me. I expected to be staring into thin air but I'm seeing into the back of this thing's skull. That was when it opened its mouth, rancid, decayed breath blowing into my face. If I had eaten anything since yesterday morning I might have puked then and there. When it opened its mouth I snatched my keys off the pew and tore off down the middle aisle.

Sounds from hell were what started all around me. The organ came to life, screeching and out of tune. Then came the singing, that same goddamn hymnal as the last time. Started wishing I hadn't deadbolted and chained the door when I was too shaky to pull it open, but somehow I got out of there and tore the hell out of the parking lot.

And here we are. I've been up for hours on end because I can't get that face out of my mind. Not to mention I still don't know what the hell was going on behind that blue door. That scream sounded human, and I could swear I heard someone saying hello after the first knock. I don't know what to trust anymore though after this morning.

I got a text from William. Know what it said? Because I expected it to read along the lines of "What in the hell happened here?" Nope. "Wow. Cleanest I've seen this place in years. Amazing job, thank you!" What. The. Fuck.

I'm going to do some research, maybe see if I can find anything on the cemetery or the church. Hell, I'm about to look into William himself. Something doesn't sit right about him. And yes, I know, there are going to be some people asking me why I don't just quit or break the lock. Number one: I am so damn poor y'all. Like I get why the job pays so much now, but the chances of me finding anything else right now are slim. My landlord is chomping at the bit to evict me so he can raise the rent again. Honestly if it gets down to it, I might. I don't know what the hell is past that door, but if things start looking like there may be someone, I'm not past some vandalism.

Anyway, I'm off until tomorrow night after Wednesday's service. I'll probably try to do an early clean again in the daylight, so I don't deal with this again. I'll update if anything happens, but I really don't plan on being there overnight again until I absolutely HAVE to.

———

So that was fucked up.

I don't really know what to say? Like I genuinely am still... I don't know what's going on. I mentioned a while back I've been agnostic at best since leaving evangelical Southern baptism over a decade ago. I was the Reddit Atheist back in the beginning. Now, I don't know if I can ever live my life the same. I want you to know that what you're about to read may shake your faith a little.

I went in early on Wednesday evening, hoping to catch William before anyone else got there. Sure enough, I pulled up and he was already there, car in the parking lot. I hurried in out of the heat, thankful that at least the AC worked if this place was haunted as shit.

Found William in his office. He was... surprised to see me at the least. There wasn't really much else that I could do at this point. The encounter on Monday night fucked me up. I can still smell the stench of that thing... the decay from its breath. I want to gag. That's not to mention I keep hearing the sound of blood splashing in the baptism tub. Did you know blood splashing sounds different than water splashing? Think it's because of the consistency of it. It's really gross, I've been wearing earbuds most of the time since because it just keeps ringing.

He must have known what I was there about. Not that he looked scared or anything, just concerned. Before I could even get a word out, he asked me what happened. Kind of took me off guard, to be honest. I was honestly going in expecting to be gaslit as insane. Take the little wins where I can, I guess. So I told him everything. The congregation, the swelling music and hymns, the shadows in the cemetery, and blood pouring from the baptism faucet. Everything was out in the open, and he acknowledged what I was saying, though didn't say much as I was going through my story.

Until I told him about the screaming through the blue door. That one got him. Something changed on his face. Worry maybe? I couldn't entirely place it. That was when I really leveled with him, just one question to ask— "Am I safe or should I quit?" Yeah, it seems like a stupid question, I know. Nobody is safe in a haunted fucking church, what kind of bullshit is that? It was all I could think of though, and the crux of what I needed to know. I grew up watching horror and shit, worked in haunts for a while, and I can deal with horror-type shit. As long as I know it can't hurt me and won't kill me. Haunted church? Sure, I'll just take an edible before I go in, me and the spirits can be chill. Hell, I'll bring some for them. Maybe they'll shut the fuck up. I was expecting him to tell me the opposite, though.

So imagine my surprise when he tells me that I'm physically in no danger. He probably realized I didn't believe him, too. I'm still not entirely sure if he was trying to get me to quit then and there too. The story I got at that point in the day already seemed like bullshit, or at least not the entire story. Unfortunately, I was right, but I couldn't settle for just leaving it at that.

In short, William told me that what I was experiencing were former parishioners. He says he's had experiences too. Hell, said he was terrified by almost the same thing happening to him as I had Monday night, way back when he first came here. Even apologized that he hadn't told me before, saying it was not okay and offering me a bonus for my troubles. Yeah, this was starting to sound like there was a lot more at play here.

From his story, the church was hit badly by a strange plague back in the early 1800s. Nothing surprising there, considering we knew bumfuck all about diseases and spread them everywhere.

William said most of the congregation perished, with the only survivors being the single pastor and his family, who somehow made full, prosperous recoveries. Totally not shady at all, right?

What he tells me from here is all conjecture, because supposedly he can only theorize. The churchgoers would apparently gather often, even staying at the church for days, worshiping and praying for a cure. Meanwhile, this obviously would spread the disease among the flock, just damning them all one by one. Still, the preacher insisted they stay steadfast in the lord, praying for forgiveness even as bodies began piling up out back. His family were some of the first sick, with his son even supposedly thought dead at one point, though looking back, it must have just been a very deep coma. Yet they're the only ones that survived. Everybody in that cemetery was once a member of this church who perished in that plague. The amount of death in one building would definitely be a magnet for weird shit, but William insists that the spirits are still looking for the preacher, believing he sacrificed them for his own family to live.

I was honestly on board with that explanation. He assured me that the spirits wouldn't harm me, simply trying to get me to do what they wanted. Except then the question of "What the fuck does a congregation of ghost Christians want me to do for them?"

Open the door. That's what they wanted me to do, according to William. According to him, the ashes of the preacher and his family are stored down there. He was superstitious after losing his entire flock to a plague. They found him and his entire family dead down in that room one day, door and room freshly painted with a bright seafoam blue. From what William told me, he picked up on some Gullah Geechee superstitious customs when he started getting paranoid. They said spirits couldn't cross through, mistaking the blue for water, so he would be safe.

Out of respect for the dead family, the church has kept the door blue since. William assured me that I was safe, but that there was nothing behind that door. It was simply a small room, sealed off out of respect or adherence to the dead, whatever I wanted to call it.

The story was kind of believable when he was telling me. Maybe it's just my willingness to buy in thanks to just having my experience validated. Either way, he reassured me, and I took my leave for the afternoon, telling him I would be back after service. Was I going to have to be here for a while after dark? Yeah, but the bonus was six hundred dollars, so who are you to judge me?

It wasn't until I was back home that I really started thinking about it. There was no way there was a room there. It didn't make sense with the outside of the church. So, it started bringing me to other questions, like if he was so willing to tell me that, why not just show me? Spirits couldn't slip in behind that easily, right? Should just be an empty room, right?

Then I thought about the screams I heard. They were definitely behind the door, but if spirits aren't allowed to cross in then why the hell are they there? Is my haunting logic broken? Look, something wasn't sitting right with me about how he was acting. Something about what he was saying was giving away that there was more to everything. So... I decided to solve this shit once and for all.

Wasn't there some movie where the ghosts were trying to give hints about how someone needed help? Like they were doing terrifying haunting shit but really just trying to help? Crimson Peak maybe? Either way, I thought that was a legitimate possibility. I'm not going to stereotype or anything, but we've had a number of evangelical preachers doing shady shit in the news lately. My conscience wouldn't let me pass. So, I ran into town before I was due to go back after Wednesday's service. Bought a set of bolt cutters and a crowbar. I'm finding out what's in that damn thing, even with a little vandalism.

Kept everything hidden in my car until William left. He gave me some platitudes about still being there and being a dependable employee that he could count on. It sounded like a very veiled warning, though, like telling me to tread carefully with whatever I do tonight. That kind of reinforced my feelings about what I was going to do that night. He finally left around nine, right when the sun went down, and I was finishing up vacuuming the sanctuary. I waited, made sure he was gone for a few, just sitting in one of the pews waiting so I could make sure nobody saw me getting bolt cutters out of my car.

Made it to my car fine, but turned to walk back into the church when a line of dark figures were suddenly standing among the cemetery headstones. None of them moved, just staring me down. Definitely upped my speed to get back into the church and slammed the door behind me, even if he said they couldn't harm me. Hell, that could have been a lie, too. Who knows at this point?

I ran in, made sure every light was on, and started going at it. Cut off the padlock, cut the chain, and started hitting at it with the crowbar when things began going to hell.

Lights went out, and gospel music began. I could look out into the sanctuary and see that the congregation was already there. I don't know if it was the adrenaline or what, but I suddenly got some Hulk-level strength and braced my foot against the door-frame, pushing the crowbar in harder. It finally gave, crashing in hard to the wall as it swung in. Deep blue light was pouring from below, showing faintly at the end of a long staircase.

First off, I don't know how the hell there was a basement this deep in swamp-ass Georgia. Nothing about a lot of this makes sense, to be honest. But I could hear the screams again, this time louder, full force, drilling into my brain. I kept making my way forward, though, determined to find the source. There could be someone hurt down here... or by the sounds of it, multiple people. The scream seemed to layer on itself, like a host of people all crying out in unison. It drowned out the gospel music, which started growing fainter behind me.

Whatever was in there didn't even register for me at first. I had no idea what I was looking at, even more unsure about if it was something real. Maybe William was trying for a budding SFX career in Atlanta, I don't know. I was trying to rationalize a lot of things until it hit me.

I'm describing it from memory, so bear with me. My eyesight isn't great and I sure as hell didn't get close. The bright blue light was actually emanating from the thing, almost like a fucking anime aura. I have no idea how else to describe it, but the light was just radiating from it in waves, washing over me as it did. I could FEEL light, not like when you sit in the sun for too long and start to burn though, this was like water washing over me. Sort of like floating down a lazy river, feeling the current flow past you toward the sea. I think back on it, and I should have felt more terrified, but the aura of it was peaceful, like it was speaking to me through it.

Be not afraid.

If you're a former Christian of any sort, you've heard that. Hell, even I feel like it's stereotypical, but I heard it. Not with my ears, but through the waves. I suddenly felt my heart rate relax, my muscles loosening as the aura continued. I felt at peace here for the first time in ages, and I knew it wasn't my antidepressants.

That was when I took a full look at the creature in the room. Bright skin, shining like the sun, was giving off the aura. For a moment, I thought it was a massive bundle of limbs at first, which wasn't totally off base, but this thing looked like multiple torsos all conjoined, like they were sewn together, all standing back to back in a circle. Each one of them had different features, but each was covered in eyes, blinking every different color I knew of, and some I couldn't quite comprehend. Every single one was fixed on me, though. That's when I noticed pieces of them missing.

Arms and legs were cut off, leaving bleeding stumps that were gushing as if cut recently. There was a steady trickle of bright red falling from the creature, chained to a wall in the small room. The bodies looked frail, malnourished, and emaciated. Despite that, they were still pristinely clean, even bleeding. Its eyes remained fixed on me, a pleading in them.

"Help us."

It spoke to me again, this time more frail than the first. It must have known that I wasn't the same as whoever put it here. I don't know if it could sense something or just went off guesswork, but it was asking me for help.

That was when William spoke from the steps behind me. The angel changed, an aura of anger and fury taking over the blue, turning it to a crimson red. My sense of peace faded, turning to confront William, who was walking toward the angel, pulling a small pocket knife from his coat. I was still holding the crowbar, though I didn't even realize it until that moment when the entire atmosphere shifted. He stepped toward the angel, flicking the pocket knife against one of the outstretched hands, slicing a finger off and catching it before he turned to me.

This motherfucker had the audacity to offer it to me. Like a fucking snack. I felt my stomach turn harder than it did smelling death's breath, with zero fucking idea of what was going on. I literally asked him if he was trying to get me to eat it. Meanwhile, there was this thing howling in pain in the corner. The screams were back, with every face distorting in terror as sound pierced the air. He waited a moment for them to stop before he started in again.

If I ate that finger, he said, I would have prosperity beyond belief. All I had to do was believe in him and eat of the flesh. He even said he's willing to supply me with more if I find I'm not quite happy yet, with the other effect being a major extension on my life. The only question I could really think to ask was how.

I'm sorry if the details are vague. I get overloaded incredibly easily with information, and this was... if you really want to put it literally, a biblical amount of fuckery. His explanation made me even more sick. I grew up on the internet wild west of Liveleak and Limewire, and this might be the first time I've really gotten a comprehension of man's depravity. This motherfucker was evil.

He popped the finger in his mouth more casually than Yuji Itadori could ever hope to. Said he was a devout man his entire life, believing God would send salvation for him and his flock. Until the disease came. William told me how his son, Peter, fell ill first, having trouble breathing before slowly degrading, coughing blood from his lungs, and soon after going into a deep, death-like sleep. That was when he started taking a different route than prayer and praise.

William gathered his flock in the church one day, bringing them all together in a marathon of praise and worship to God. Then he began convincing them it was time to be rebaptized in the blood of the lord, cleansing them of their illnesses. He brought in water, lining up all the parishioners to bring through the baptism tub. He baptized them, one by one, making sure they were thoroughly drenched. Once everyone was soaked, back at their pew ready to begin another hymn, he took his place on the pulpit and let loose the plan.

He set up a rope ahead of calling over everyone, tagging up sacks of lye in the rafters. From there it was just pulling on the rope, slicing the bags open with nails in the rafters, causing a caustic snow to fall down on the soaked congregation. He said it was a glorious sight, everyone quickly realizing their baptism in the waters of heaven led to burning as if by the fires of hell. It took minutes before they all passed, killing everyone in the church except William. That was when the angel appeared.

According to William, it was sent as punishment for the blasphemy he just committed. This jackass literally said, "I'm not going to confuse you with the details, but I studied a bit of dark practices," and trapped the fucking thing with whatever it was. That's why it was still chained down here, letting him just pick pieces off wherever he wanted. He said he cut off a foot for each of his family, making a stew for them while they were sick. Just pouring some into his son's mouth brought him out of a coma in hours. The angel's flesh is quite literally made of miracles, he said.

And then he gave me the ultimatum—leave, and have no job, with my entire mental state totally fucked by this encounter and nobody to believe me. Or I could die. Two options, neither of which were great for me. He lifted the knife, getting ready to strike if need be.

Fight or flight came in HARD. I don't know how I swung the crowbar as fast as I did. Maybe adrenaline again, but it bashed the side of his head. William crumpled quickly, falling to the ground in front of me with a thud and knocking his head on the hard floor. Dead.

The chains holding the angel snapped, freeing it immediately. I don't even know what the hell happened after that. There was a bright flash, I could hear a voice saying, "Thank you" and suddenly I was standing out in the cemetery. In front of me the church was ablaze, a full inferno already. The heat coming off was intense, immediately drying any of the humid air around me. It raged up, with the sound of rising alongside the smoke, before totally incinerating in the dark night, flames dying out just as quickly as they began. Where the church once stood was nothing but a pile of ash, not even one board left standing.

Look, I'm not talking to anyone unless they come to me asking what happened. Even then, not like they'll really believe me. William has got to be gone for good now, so maybe they'll just think he torched it for insurance but the deed went wrong. Who knows, maybe I'll get arrested. At this point, I'm out of a job, so it might be the preferable alternative to finding a job in the current economy. Things are going to be rough. I'm still shaken up and the anxiety about what's going to happen is fucking killing me.

I don't know, maybe after this I'll have an angel watching out for me. Fingers fucking crossed at least.

IN BLOOM

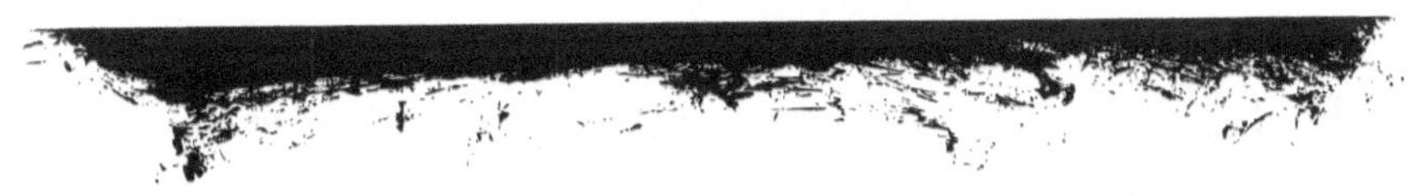

POP! Tara was awake suddenly to what sounded like a firework exploding right next to her. She felt the car skid as Matt lost control, desperately trying to keep the car on the car away from the steep ditch filled with swamp water.

"Shit!" Matt screamed as he lost the battle, another pop echoing from Tara's other side. Gravity slapped her to the side as they went down into the ditch, throwing her face-first into the dashboard as she desperately put her hands up in vain, crashing hard into the dash on her left cheek. They came to a stop as Tara held a hand to her face, looking to the driver's seat.

Matt sat there, skin pale, with a thousand-yard stare looking straight ahead. He had a small trickle of blood coming from his nose but kept a tight grip on the wheel.

"You okay?" Tara asked. Matt let out a shudder before everything suddenly hit.

"Holy shit. I'm okay. Are you? Jesus, I don't know what happened..." He was speaking fast and breathing shallowly, a panic attack setting in. Tara put an arm on his shoulder and brought him close.

"It's okay. It's okay, hey..." she stroked his hair as his breathing leveled, coming down from the anxiety threatening to overwhelm him. "Everything's gonna be alright. You hurt?"

"Hit the wheel with my nose. Are you okay?" he started searching for his phone in the floorboards, finding nothing.

"Neck hurts a little. Dash came right at my face, but I'll be alright. Here..." She pulls up her beaten old phone, scratches and a small crack along the screen. "Shit. Of course..."

"I think we blew a damn tire," Matt muttered.

"Well, I don't have a signal," Tara said, tossing the phone down in her lap and pulling the visor mirror down. A bruise was beginning to show on her left cheek. "It's getting late, too. Jesus Christ, can't one fucking thing go right?"

Matt was composed again, the panic attack behind him and adrenaline kicking in.

"Hey, we're going to be okay. I'm gonna take stock, you just take a minute. Breathe." Matt took charge. Tara nodded as he pushed his door open, grunting with the fight against gravity.

"Be careful, please!" she shouted after him as he jumped out, the door screeching down after him. Tara rolled her window down. "How does it look?"

"Fucked!" he shouted back. "Back tire on my side is blown. Can't even see the other side, but the front tire is flat now too."

Matt screamed at the sky, kicking the car's fender.

"Oh, hell," Tara said, suddenly feeling something on her foot. Looking down, she could see dirty water trickling in, pooling on the floorboard from the flooded ditch. "There's a leak!"

"Seriously?" Matt said, putting his hands to his face and groaning. Tara grabbed what she could, looking at her reflection in the rearview as she clambered over to Matt's side and pushed the door open. A bruise was already beginning to show, though she wasn't sure if it was from the crash or not. "Can't have one goddamn thing go right in my goddamn life..."

"Any idea where the hell we are?" Tara questioned, pretending not to hear his mutterings.

"I don't think anyone's mapped this place yet," he replied. The sun hung low over the road, mixing their shadows into the dark pecan trees off the curb. "Gas station was about five miles back. Might as well head that way."

He barely had the words out before headlights appeared in the distance, racing toward them. Matt hesitated before Tara started jumping alongside him, arms waving. As he slowed to the stop, they could see a massive lifted truck, a round old man behind the wheel looking like he was headed to a tractor pull.

"Yes sir! We blew a tire and uh... well, you see it," Matt said, his voice shaking. The adrenaline was gone, and aches had set in for both of them, fatigue starting to follow quickly behind.

"Either of y'all hurt?" he asked next, looking them over. Tara looked like a mess, with makeup running down her face and red hair wild. Matt was shifting from foot to foot, nervous. "You can hop on in, least I can do is get y'all off the road 'fore it gets dark."

Matt glanced at Tara, raising eyebrows as if to say it was a bad idea. He noticed the shadows bathing them both, obscuring half of Tara's face as the driver kept looking. She spoke before he could.

"That would be amazing, please!" she said, holding her hands up in thanks. "Things just haven't gone right today."

"Hell, ain't nothin' any decent human wouldn't do," the man said, unlocking the truck. "Y'all hop on in."

Matt opened the back door for Tara, helping her into the lifted cab and squeezing her hand tight. Once she was in, he climbed into the front passenger seat, pulling the door closed behind him.

"Thank you," Matt said to the man, buckling. "I thought we were trapped out here. Wherever here is."

"Awe, don't worry about it. You're right outside of Red Shades, Georgia. Y'all from around here?" He chuckled, "Hell, it don't matter where you're from. Matters you're here! On the right day, too!"

"Uh." Tara let out a small sound before choosing to stay quiet instead.

"Dammit, Jerry. Where the hell are your manners? I'm so sorry miss, I invited y'all in my car and ain't even told you my name!"

Nervous laughter, he took his hand off the wheel and offered it to Matt. "Name's Jerry Tillson. Nice to meetcha."

Matt's hand was shaking as he raised it to meet Jerry's, cold sweat making it even weirder.

"I'm Matt. This is Tara," he said, the shaking seeping from his hand to his voice.

"Well, bad as breakin' down is y'all couldn't have picked a better place." Matt drew back as Jerry laughed loud, "We got the swamp stomp tonight! Just a little festival we do in the spring, y'know. Food, music, little games for the kids and all. Y'all can stay and have some food while we get your car!"

"Oh, gosh no. You've already been so nice to us," Matt said, looking toward the window as the sun's last light died.

As Jerry laughed. Tara looked from her window, now seeing thicker trees and the moon reflecting off dark water. Something about it was mesmerizing, almost alien.

"I insist. Y'all look like you've had a rough day of it." He looked in the rearview at Tara. "Apologies, miss. You're very pretty, just look like you're exhausted."

"Oh, you're fine," she says, looking back through the window. She could see a large, clear expanse of water suddenly with only a small island breaking the surface in the middle. The moss was shining, moonlight dancing off the water around it in little waves. She could see the moon reflecting on either side of the little island and lights across the water.

"It's beautiful out there," Tara says, still transfixed by the dual moon in the water. She couldn't break her gaze, as if the swamp was challenging her to a staring contest. It wasn't until they passed a tree that she seemed to come to her senses.

"Yes ma'am!" Jerry exclaimed. "Out here on a clear night without all that city light, you can just about see every star in heaven. Hell, that's why we do this in the spring. Between the sky and all the fireflies coming back to the swamp... looks like you're walkin' through stars."

Matt glanced back over his shoulder at her, eyes wide and questioning. Tara shook her head at him, unsure why he was so worried.

"Alright, we're just up ahead here," Jerry said, slowing the truck and putting his blinker on. "I know there ain't anyone comin' up behind me, but those State Troopers will get you for the darndest little things."

Tara giggled a bit in the back seat, looking at the lights ahead as the truck turned down a dusty dirt road. Matt noticed crowds of people milling about, probably fifty or sixty at least hovering between trees and under lights.

As Jerry reached the lighted area and slowed, they could see tables and chairs set up all around a small dance floor. Some younger children were already chasing each other around the wooden platform, laughing as they ran.

"Alrighty. I'll introduce y'all to Sam, then go get Earl. Me an' him'll go get your car for you," Jerry said, freeing his seatbelt from holding his gut back. "Now, y'all are gonna love the food. We're doin' chili this year and I've heard Cecilia got some good stuff up her sleeve."

Jerry hopped out of the lifted cab, grunting as he hit the ground and closing the door behind him. Matt looked back at Tara again as they both unbuckled, still visibly shaking.

"It's definitely human meat," Tara joked, trying to get him to lighten up. "I'll eat anything at this point, though."

Matt shook his head, following her out of the truck and over to Jerry, who was already bouncing along toward one of the bustling food stalls.

"Samantha! Hope y'all ain't dug in yet!" Jerry hollered across as they walked. "I got a couple hungry mouths coming your way!"

An older woman appeared behind one of the stall tarps, dark skin shining with sweat against solid white hair.

"No, but we should have before you go gettin' your paws all up in every dish," she shouted back as Jerry laughed, embracing her as he closed in. Tara and Matt exchanged surprised looks as Jerry and Samantha parted, kissing each other on the lips before separating. Jerry notices and laughs.

"I promise we don't just go kissing each other like that around here." Jerry smiled, "We know a town like ours is kind of an outlier 'round these parts. This is my wife, Samantha, and this is Matt and Tara."

"We're just all about love," Samantha said, leaning on Jerry's arm and looking at him with love and almost relieved that he was back.

"Oh my god, you two are so cute." Tara held a hand over her chest and gripped Matt's with her other.

"Well, thank you darlin'! Now, how did my goof of a husband manage to pick y'all up?" She motioned them along into the little booth, set up with bubbling pots and trays of cornbread.

Matt and Tara awkwardly moved to the side as someone bustled past, bringing in another large pot to Samantha filled with various cups and bowls. Matt starts to talk before being cut off by Jerry.

"They blew a tire back on the highway. I'm about to go find Earl and get the tow for 'em," he said, scanning the crowd beyond. "Now where is that old bastard?"

"I saw him out by Cece's booth," Samantha chimes back, stirring a pot. "You gonna be back in time for the ceremony?"

"That's why I'm gonna make Earl do it," Jerry said, moving over to a pot next to her and pulling a spoonful of chili out, holding it up to his lips before taking a huge bite. "Ow, goddamn that's hot. Needs a little salt."

"Now this is exactly what I mean. Get out my kitchen!" Samantha swats him away, snatching the spoon. Jerry tiptoes off, picking a dinner roll off a nearby tray as he walks from the stall. Samantha sighs, "That man would eat everything here if we let him."

Tara giggled as a rumbling came from Matt. Samantha looked back at them and gave a little laugh.

"Sounds like y'all need some food." She turned to the table in front of her, grabbing bowls and plopping a square of cornbread from nearby down into each before drowning it in a huge spoon of her chili. "Now, y'all are gonna have to work for it."

Tara exchanged a side glance with Matt, putting a hand close to her purse.

"Yeah, we can do dishes and help clean up," Tara offered.

"Oh no, y'all ain't gonna be cleaning up," Samantha whispered, sticking a spoon into each bowl and handing them to the starving couple.

Tara was getting a little uneasy now, with Jerry gone and just her and Matt in the small booth. Everyone outside seemed to be settling now instead of just mingling. Matt noticed a large kitchen knife right next to Samantha on the table.

"When it comes time," she said, smiling and handing them the bowls. "Y'all need to vote for my chili. Damn if I'm gonna let Cecelia win again. Not this year, hell no."

Tara laughed, relaxing again as she took the bowl, the spices stinging her nose as they steamed up. Samantha gestured them after her, eating as they walked towards a table where a young couple was sitting across from each other.

"Y'all, this is Matt and this is Tara. They had a little accident out on route 87, so we're keeping 'em fed and entertained." Samantha motions to the man, mid-20s with chestnut skin and a bushy beard. "Now, I expect you to make sure they feel welcome while your pa fixes their car."

"Yes, momma," the man responded, looking at the two newcomers. His eyes rested on Tara for a moment before looking back to his mother. He seemed shocked. "I'm Blake, nice to meet y'all."

Satisfied, Samantha walked away as the couple took a seat across from each other at the table. Matt, next to Blake and Tara, sat opposite, next to the now smiling woman.

"I'm Jess." The woman extended a hand to shake. Tara took it awkwardly, feeling Jess squeeze a little too hard.

"Tara. Nice to meet you." She was eating fast, almost inhaling the food. "I'm so sorry, I haven't eaten all day, I don't mean to be rude."

"Darlin', don't you be sorry for a thing. We're blessed to have you here," Jess said, waving her off. "Y'all sure got some good timing, though. This swamp's gonna look beautiful this spring."

Jess trailed off, looking intensely at Tara, giving her goosebumps as she felt studied. She shifted as to cover herself, even though she was already wearing long sleeves.

"Oh my god I'm so sorry, I didn't mean to stare like that." Jess suddenly snapped back to reality, grabbing Tara's hand in her own. "You are just so darn pretty. I've always wanted my hair that shade of red and never could get it. Now, how long have y'all been together?"

Tara looked to Matt, avoiding conversation despite Blake's attempts. His dark hair was rustled in every direction at this point, looking like a bird had nested in it. He glanced at her briefly before going back to eating.

"It'll be ten years next month," Tara answered, turning a little red. "We uh... we met in college and we've been together ever since."

Blake smiled, squeezing her hand back. Tara noticed Matt shooting little glances around.

"Can't imagine what y'all have been through. Things must have been tough," Jess said, trying to start more conversation. "Y'all probably haven't gotten too many warm welcomes 'round these parts."

Tara's complexion switched to deep, blushing red, prompting Jess to backtrack hard.

"Oh my god. I'm so sorry, I shouldn't have said that. I didn't mean to offend or anything. We just don't see many of y'all out here." Jess was tripping over words before they even made it past her lips. "Ah dammit, I didn't mean y'all like that like... ah hell I'm gonna just shut up."

"You're totally fine, it happens a lot more than you think." Tara waved her off, laughing a little. "Yeah, traveling the south has been a little up and down for us. Some places are safe... some not so much.

"I'm so sorry you have to go through that darlin'. You are absolutely a beautiful woman, don't let anyone tell you anything otherwise." Jess took a moment to compose herself, wiping a small tear away. "Well, y'all been together over a decade, but I don't see a ring."

"Oh, gosh. We haven't really talked about that yet. I just met his parents..." Tara trailed off, remembering the morning's chaos. "We're fine how we are, I think."

Jess offered a smile and patted Tara on the shoulder, giving her reassurance. Tara grabbed a napkin, wiping smudged mascara from her eyes, before looking back.

"It's just a piece of paper, anyway. Though, I think you would out-pretty the flowers out here in a wedding dress." Jess smiles and stands up, motioning over to Blake. "Come help me grab drinks for these two."

"For sure. Want a beer?" Blake stands, and Matt nods in return, staring into the distance as Blake and Jess walk off. Tara could see the wood dance floor paneling close by now, noticing intricate carvings and patterns on the floor.

"You seem really nervous," Tara said, snapping Matt back to reality. She put a hand on the table, open for him to take.

"I just don't like this," Matt said. "Somebody's gonna find out..."

"What? About me? I don't think any of them will care. Jess doesn't." Tara, confused now, "You've never had a problem being seen with me before."

"No, Tara, about my parents," Matt replied, still staring off into the distance, distracted.

"Why? They made it obvious they don't like me." Sighing, she picked at her remaining food before pointing one finger at the bruising becoming more visible with makeup giving way to sweat. "Pretty sure your dad did when he gave me this and called me 'a corrupting sodomite.'"

"No. After that. When you ran out..." Matt was suddenly clear-eyed, looking at her, "I think I killed him, Tara."

Tara stopped, air catching in her throat.

"Sorry, what?" Tara could only remember meeting his father briefly before being punched when he made the connection. "No. You... you came out with me and put me in the car. You hugged me and told me it would be okay."

"No, Tara..." Matt's voice was breaking, choking on spit and snot as his breathing quickened. "He hit you, so I hit him and... he fell by the fireplace. You were dazed and I was angry. I didn't fuckin' mean to... I'm sorry. I'm so fucking sorry I'msofucking-sorryilove you..."

Everything suddenly slowed, the world dragging and sounds growing dull. Tara could feel her pulse in her ears while the lights suddenly flared brighter. She didn't feel the table suddenly meet her bruised face.

———

"We sure they're gonna work? I just don't want shit backfiring just to have your kids put back up there or all o' us fucked." A man's voice echoed all around as Tara came to. She tried to move but couldn't, her muscles working against her.

"Fuck's sake, Earl. I don't know how many times I gotta tell you it don't matter so long as they love each other." Was that Jerry? Tara felt heavy, the weight of planets pushing her into the earth. She tried to open her eyes, fighting against her haze. "Ah, hell. They ain't s'posed to be awake yet, Samantha!"

Finally, she cracked an eye open, almost blinded by the single light left on in the small gathering, hanging over the small dance platform. Someone was standing right under the light, head nodding forward.

"Matt!" Tara tried to scream, seeing that her boyfriend was tied to a stake erected in the middle of the platform, still in the dream-space between sleep and waking. Her voice came out as a garbled half-moan, her muscles refusing to do what her brain was screaming for them to do.

"Well, it ain't like I had a whole lot of warning. Couldn't even tell me about this damn crazy plan you have. All I had to work with was a bottle of Benadryl Cecelia had!" Shouted Samantha, from the far side of the crowd. Matt groaned as Tara tried to call to him again, still not making the sounds she wanted. Matt's head nodded to the side, catching sight of Tara.

"Alright, alright, it don't matter. What matters is that they're here, and they're going to help us tonight," Jerry said, walking in front of Matt and quieting everyone down. "Now, since she is awake, it's only fair she knows why this is happenin'."

"Awe, we ain't gotta tell him shit. Just kill the boyfriend and let me go home!" A voice from the crowd. Tara could hear small murmurs and quite a few boos among the crowd.

"Frank, I'd put you up there instead a' her if anyone loved you enough," Jerry replied, drawing cheers and laughter from the crowd. "Now, call her that again and I'm gonna throw you in as at-for-one. Y'all have some damn respect for what this young man and woman are doin' for us."

"For you." Another voice, "Awfully damn convenient all things considered."

"Shut the hell up, Earl." Jerry again. He walks over to Matt, grabbing him by the chin, and tilting his head up, slapping his cheek lightly with his other hand. He mumbles something inaudible to Matt, leaning in close so nobody else can hear, then wraps him in a brief bear hug before stepping back and pulling Matt's head straight up, exposing his neck.

He pulls a large hunting knife from his waistband, holding it up to Matt's neck, making sure it was placed just right before pulling the serrated edge across fast. Tara tries to scream his name again, only for pained sobs to escape in short breaths.

Jerry steps away as blood pours from Matt's throat, soaking the platform below and all its intricate runes. Tara could see them more clearly now, symbols and rituals she remembered from a book long ago, something from her more witchy days. They glowed vaguely familiar as his blood flowed through the connected etchings, eventually completing the entire circle.

Rot filled Tara's nose, stinking of putrid swamp water and decaying flesh. As the final light flickered out above Matt's head she could see thousands of small dots illuminating the darkness, playing off the water of the swamp. Tara saw the two twin moons on either side of the island, sparks of fireflies making them look in motion. As her eyes adjusted, she noticed clouds in the sky, blinding moon and stars from her sight.

Tara stared transfixed as the twin moons rose above the water, the mossy island rising with them to tower over the swamp. Waves splashed against the small clearing as it moved toward them, gliding smoothly across the dark water. She couldn't tell what the hell it was in the dark, only noticing the soft, pale yellow of the two bulbous, pockmarked orbs she assumed were eyes. Before she knew what happened it had glided onto the land, skittering loudly closer and then setting upon Matt, whatever blood left in him flying.

The thing turns, Tara making out Matt's dangling, mangled body being slowly pulled into a wide, vertical mouth lined with small feelers. She screamed again.

"Take this love, we bleed for you," Jerry said, bowing his head. The crowd echoed him in a fearful chorus.

As it leaves back into the water, smearing the viscera and swamp scum behind it, Tara can't scream any longer. The moon comes out again just long enough to catch a small flash of a leathery, translucent exterior before the thing vanishes, taking Matt to the depths along with it.

Tara simply sobs as a light comes on and four men step forward, one holding each of her limbs. Together, they lift her over to the edge of the water, setting her gently on the shore.

"Why?" she manages to choke out as Jerry comes toward her,

"I am sorry," Jerry says, kneeling next to her. "I want you to know that it was nothing personal. You were just the first car that came by."

Tara sobs again as he pulls the hunting knife again, trying to shrink back and hide her neck, but barely managing to nudge herself toward the water.

"No, no I won't use this on you. You don't deserve any undue pain. You're helping us. I just... I couldn't do this to them. Not to my own. I'm sorry. I hope you understand." He places a hand on her cheek, brushing calloused fingers gently over her bruised face. Jess walked up from behind him, kneeling next to her as Jerry washed his knife in the water.

"I meant what I said. I'm sorry, you didn't deserve any of this. You'll bloom more beautiful than I ever could," Jess whispered to Tara, gently kissing her on the same bruised cheek before standing up.

Tara felt something coarse and slimy work its way up her feet, dragging her further down into the water. Screaming in vain as water filled her lungs, fireflies becoming stars in the space above her.

Her last fading thought as her body settled to the bottom, moss and algae moving along her arms and legs, was that the two moons in the murky depths near her were oddly tranquil. Their moonlight glow through the blackwater lulled her into a dreamless sleep as her breathing stopped, the living greenery finally enveloping her completely into the warm embrace of earth.

MAY FALLEN STARS GUIDE US HOME

"Alright, off the wagon. I ain't taking any animal o' mine through here." The rough voice came through my dreams but didn't quite register. There was a light approaching in my dream, something beautiful, a star maybe? "I said off!"

Pain started in my shoulder and my stomach dropped as I hit empty space. I barely had time to register my dizziness before my fall. I briefly saw the hanging lantern spinning in a rush before I crashed to the damp ground below, taking a face full of grass and soil. I pulled myself up, spitting out dirt and trying to ascertain my whereabouts. Water was splashing in the distance. Were we finally there?

"You're on your own." The driver didn't even look at me as he climbed back up on the wagon, barely giving a thought as he started off and left last words trailing back to me, "If your brother was there, he's probably dead. You do have my condolences."

Stop. Stop thinking about it. I couldn't let myself believe him dead. He had signed up without hesitation, leaving me back home with the choice to stay or follow. I felt the twinge of pain in my ankle where it had been broken, keeping me home and apart from him. We had been a team since I could remember, storytellers from the beginning...

I was brought back to the present by a howl coming from the nearby forest. The small port lay ahead, lanterns burning low, barely illuminating the encroaching darkness as their reflection played off the dark river ahead, making eyes in murky water that followed me as I walked. I could see a glow coming off Tybee, dim against the dense forest of the island.

Whether he was here or not, that would be my last stop on this journey.

I started walking after grabbing my belongings off the ground, though it wasn't much other than some dried beef and a canteen in my bag alongside the small bowie knife he had given me three Christmases ago, still shining bright as the day it met my hands. I gripped the cold leather on the hilt as the small tavern overlooking the port neared, hesitating as the hand under my long coat gripped the knife hilt while I pushed the door open.

Sound hit me in waves, as the smell of beer and tobacco hit me harder, overpowering my senses and almost knocking me over like the breakers crashing below. My grip loosened as I moved, stepping into the tavern's warm embrace. The smell of roasting meat and baking bread overpowered the alcohol finally, and I relaxed my hand on the dagger. There was a friendly-looking girl standing at a nearby counter, filling a glass from a massive bottle of dark liquor.

"Be right with you, sweetheart!" she shouted to me, taking the glass over to a table where one man sat alone. He gave her a nod and smile as she walked back to me. The first thing I noticed was the blue army coat he wore, buttons fraying off. The second thing I noticed was the massive scar running down his face, only separated by the eyepatch covering what I assume was his now vacated socket. The barmaid was in front of me suddenly, flashing a bright smile and giving me a warmer welcome.

"Alrighty, darlin', you lookin' for food, booze, a room, or the whole deal?"

I snapped back, trying to pretend I wasn't staring intently at the man. The squalor around us made a decent enough cover as I took a seat at the bar. She couldn't be older than fifteen and looked to be running this place herself. Don't know how she managed, but she was standing at attention with a hand ready on a spatula behind her, waiting for something on the stove to finish.

"Uh, drink, please. Cider if you have it," I said, though she didn't catch me at first. I tried yelling it louder when she finally understood me, moving back with a fresh glass from the nearby shelf to a cask at the far end. A soft, pink-orange liquid poured into the glass and foamed up. Peach cider... hadn't had that in a long time. Not since meeting him here in the city, all those years ago...

Lost myself again for a moment before she handed me the cider, looking expectantly at me for any other questions.

"I need to get over to the island. Do you know if a boat is running in the morning?" I shouted across at her again. I saw her face pale, turning the shade of a new moon. Looked like one of those ghosts in the stories he would tell me...

"Hell, sir. Ain't nobody wanted to go to the island in years. Not since Sherman at least." A general hush fell over the nearby patrons when she said that, bringing them to glare at whoever had said the name before realizing it was the girl supplying them booze, overriding their cares about the Union with love of alcohol. "Chamber's takes people on occasion, but he usually ends up comin' back alone. There's still bodies out there that just couldn't be brought back. My papa's probably one of 'em. S'what mama says at least."

She pointed toward the scarred man in the back, wearing the blue colors that seemed to be so prominent around these parts. I didn't see many back home displaying their blues out in the open, even back home in the swamps. Hell, nobody wore their grays when we were back in Boston just a few years ago. This guy was either a hero or an absolute bastard and I wasn't ready to find out. She spoke, even though I already knew what she was going to say. "He might be willin' to help you."

I nodded to her in thanks before taking my cider, walking over to the man as he trained his eye on me. I had seen the waters down past Florida once when I was young, where the water was the bluest thing on earth I'd ever seen. That's what was in this man's eye as I waded into its unknown depths. He swore under his breath as I approached.

"Dammit, Millie. What?" he asked in a voice like the shale outside was scraping his throat. I saw the beard growing gray under his sunken blue eye now, teeth missing and nose awkwardly cut short at the tip. Two cavalry sabers sat on the seat next to him, uninviting anyone nearby. I took a gulp of my cider before sitting across from him.

"I need your help." I started out before he waved a hand and cut me off. He took a sip of his liquor, not showing any sign of tasting the pungent alcohol even I could smell coming off of it across the table.

"You want on Tybee? Go fuck yourself." He started, still training his eye on me before going in again. "I've stopped taking you assholes there to 'survey the land'. You never pay up front, then you fuckin' die before you can pay me. The government can either bring in some actual troops to figure shit out over there or just do what Sherman should have and finish his damn march."

He finally left off, taking a deep breath before chugging more of his drink in a quick gulp.

"I'm not looking for anything like that. I need to know if someone was there." I started in before seeing his face change from anger to... pity.

"Shit..." He sat back in his chair, raising a hand and rubbing his scruffed hair back. He stroked his beard and looked at me, sizing me up. I looked back at him, never moving my gaze from his eye. "My condolences. Who was it, if I might ask?"

It was my turn to hesitate, wondering what I should tell him based on the coat over his shoulders. He must have noticed my apprehension, because he patted the coat fondly before dropping it down his back, letting the tattered grays show under it.

"I ain't a traitor to the Union, if that's what you're wondering." He gave a half-hearted laugh as I eased back a bit in my seat. "No, I picked this off a particularly nasty bastard I had a grudge with, and one coat ain't keeping me as warm nowadays. I'd stand up so you could see where I took my grudge, but we all bleed red in the end. Someone in the war, I take it?"

"I... I know it's a lot to ask," I hadn't expected such a level of observation, nothing I could have ever imagined in this barnacle-soaked coast outside Savannah. I had to steady myself, preparing to tell him the truth. "I'm looking for a soldier, he was-" I bit my tongue almost rather than say it "-is a negro, sir. He fought for Sherman; the last message I got from him was that he was stationed on the island until things were settled. He never came back after..."

"If'n he was one of Sherman's, he's a brother of mine. I was part of the march, too." He took another drink, throwing his head back and draining the glass. "Fuckin' ceasefire was barely a week old when the stars fell."

"I know he's probably not alive. I've heard the stories about the island..." I started mouthing off whatever I could to tell him I knew the risks. I had to go. "I made a promise. Even just borrowing a boat..."

His face softened as he looked at me. I tried to concentrate my gaze on the cider but couldn't stop tears from dropping in, making ripples as the cider fizzled. There was a boulder, sitting right behind my tongue and threatening to let loose a landslide if any pebble of a word slid through.

"I was there," he offered up. Looking me in the eye, he nodded as if to reinforce his point. "I know what you're going to find, but I owe the dead there some respect. If that means bringing peace to one of their friends, that's a start."

He stood now, hoisting the two sabers off the other chair and tightening their belt around his waist. He looked at me expectantly, still sitting with my cider and looking at him. I couldn't believe he had agreed so easily to take me, much less that he had empathy for my plight. If he was out there... he was smiling at me when I entered that tavern.

"I didn't get your name, sir?" I choked out, at least hoping I could thank the man who would be helping me. He simply smiled, crooked and gap-toothed, back.

"Call me Chambers." He held out a hand to shake, which I accepted before realizing he was missing the ring finger on it. He laughed as he shook my hand, noting my surprise.

"Alan," I said back to him, still choking back words while trying to hide behind my cider. He finished tightening the belt, picking up a blunderbuss alongside it. He looked at me as I stood, sizing me up.

"You bring a weapon with you, Alan?" he asked, slinging the blunderbuss over his shoulder. I noticed a pouch of gunpowder and some silver beads in his belt, opposite the sabers. He was prepared for something that I wasn't. I simply brought my hand up from my coat, revealing the shining bowie knife. He gave a hearty laugh. "That won't get you very far. If you know how to use this, I'll give it to you."

I shook my head. He motioned me after, leaving money on the bar for the young lady working, who shouted a thank you to him from across the room. He waved back as the door swung closed behind us. Now he and I stood alone in the pale lamplight from the single, lonely flame above the tavern door. He pulled a canister from his pocket, striking a match on the tavern wall and lighting the wick he had just produced.

I gasped, light shining in a bright circle from the canister, casting a beam to show our way. As Chambers adjusted a nozzle attached to it the light grew brighter, better lighting the greenery and surrounding coastline. "I don't think I've seen anything this bright since the sun went out."

Chambers laughed at me like a father watching his child discover something new. He pivoted quickly, waving a hand at me to follow him down the narrow steps toward the docks.

"So, you've heard about the island?" he asked, the rough cobblestone trying to twist my ankles as we went. My hands were shaking as the docks began to shine below us, a few lonely lanterns keeping the darkness from the bay.

"I heard one landed there," I replied, remembering the horror stories I had heard from those that went through the fall. "Some said they fell where blood was shed. Others said it was god's judgment. I know the places where they fell got overrun with something before long."

"Something ain't the half of it," Chambers chuckled back. He had oddly grim humor about going to the island. I could see the glow brighter now, though not enough to determine color. We finally reached a small boat on the docks, a smaller sailboat with a few oars attached at the sides.

Chambers went up to the small lamp posts at either end of the boat, lighting them from his torch and bathing the docks in bright light from the flames now burning high in the night. He adjusted knobs again, bringing the flames down slightly while moving small mirrors around them, adjusting their light in different directions. "Most of the bastards are 'fraid of light, so they'll leave us alone as we cross. Come on, now."

He climbed into the boat after I did, wavering a little as the water rocked us. It had been years since I'd been on any kind of water, but it came back naturally after a moment. He settled in and hoisted the sail above us, lighting a lantern atop its mast. Chambers settled in on the aft with the till while I took a spot near the mid, looking back at him as he met my eyes with his single one. The deep blue caught me again, even in the dim light, as his face hardened in the flickering lantern's glow.

"Star's done a lot around here since it fell. You're going to see a lot that ain't natural." He picked up a small pistol from a cabinet on the boat's side. "Assuming one of them gets you and doesn't kill you right away, I will deliver one shot from this directly to your skull, no hesitation. I'm saving you from something worse than death."

"What exactly are they?" I couldn't comprehend what would be a worse fate than death, other than the horror stories of the war, and how some lived injured on the battlefield for days. I had tried to stray around any of the Starfall areas on the maps I had and typically had safe passage all the way here, so I hadn't come across anything the other travelers spoke of.

"Dunno," Chambers grunted, guiding them along in the water, leaving the docks behind as wind caught the sails. "Know I used to have some friends when I was younger and frontiering. Natives. Warned me 'bout some of their old legends, and I'd rather have those than what's on this island."

I shivered. Cold wind blowing through the humid air brushed long, unkempt hair from my face as we crossed the gap from the mainland. Something breached the water nearby, letting out a small wail as the light illuminated it briefly before disappearing back to the depths.

"Pay it no mind. We're almost there. Now, if you look in that compartment on your right, you're gonna find an old axe. I want you to hang onto that while we're in here. That thing got me off the island in the first place." He glided us smoothly along the water, the island approaching ever closer in the dark. Now the glow of the island was brighter, a color somewhere between that deep blue ocean I remembered and the old lavender bushes that grew in our garden back home. "Now, you gotta tell me some things before we get in."

I nodded.

"Who are we looking for? What was his name?" He looked at me, setting that same blue eye that managed to stare into my soul better than any two ever had. "And are you prepared to see what he might be now? I'll help you look, and I will do my damndest to protect you, but we will go no further than the crater's edge."

"Yes." I gulped, steeling my resolve as we coasted toward the shoreline, water splashing around as something peeked out at us from the waves. "He was lighter skinned, said his mama was a slave and daddy was... well, you know. He uh... he kept his hair short, though I imagine it's grown out plenty since he's been gone all these years. Hazel eyes, like uh... like a pecan that ain't quite ripe yet. He..."

I stalled, stopping before I was too far into the small details. The little things I could recognize immediately upon seeing him. The little, beautiful details...

"He was missing half of his left pinky finger. Happened in a milling accident when he was a kid." I kept going, not noticing the change in Chambers' face. "His face... the right side of his face is scarred. Pretty terribly. He told me it was because he tried to take a whipping for his mother and his dad just went at him wherever he could get. He has them all down his arms and legs too, they're darker than the rest of his skin so he looks like he's got a net or something on all the time. He can't grow a full beard because of it either, so he has lines running through it where the scars are. Looked pretty comical when he was first growing it, but now... I'm sure it's all over."

"Ezekiel," Chambers muttered, snatching me back from my memories with the sound of his name.

"Do you know where he is?" I was immediately back to the present, adrenaline pumping with the most hope I'd felt in months. "Please tell me you do."

"Shit." Chambers sat back against the boat as they began scraping onto the beach. "Shit, kid... shit! I'm sorry. I... I can't let you go in there. We're turning around."

My chest seized, breath refusing to move into my lungs. I couldn't control it when it suddenly broke out in heavy, short bursts as I tried desperately to breathe. Despite everything he had already told me, despite the now rapidly spiraling screams in my head telling me otherwise, I still wanted... needed to know if he was alive. "What happened to him?"

"God damn it all." Chambers sighed as he stopped trying to steer the boat, allowing it to simply rest on the shore. "Ezekiel was one o' my Privates. I was a Lieutenant under General Sherman, in charge of the regiment with him in it. I was with him when the damn stars fell. We barely made it out in time, or we would have probably been killed when it hit the fort. Left a damn big crater in the ground. Things didn't change immediately, you know? Sure, sun disappeared in the blink of an eye but, at least we didn't get them right away."

"The creatures?" I asked, still unsure of what to say to him. I was desperately waiting for an answer to my first question, but he wanted to avoid it. "Did they kill him?"

"I wish they had," Chambers said back, giving me a solemn look of pity as tears welled in my eyes. "Least then I could give you a straight answer. Should've gotten them out of there after the damned thing fell... they wanted us to stay and make sure nothing happened around it. Guess it was natural to be suspicious after Lincoln was killed, but goddammit this wasn't the time. The damned star cracked about a day after it landed. Cursed things came pourin' out o' it. Not like anything I ever seen, like it sprung a damn leak and was sprayin' out everywhere. I don't know how we missed it, but that thing, whatever was coming out of that thing... I've seen cannonballs hit people and it weren't that bad..."

I gulped. He looked at the tree line up the beach briefly as a shriek rang through the night, coming from further into the island overgrowth. About then was when I noticed the smell that quickly overpowered every other sense I felt. Death, a hundredfold. I had smelled rotting carcasses of farm animals most of my life, discovered a few that had died before sitting in the hot Georgia summer for a few hours, and that would be like the finest lavender compared to this. It didn't phase him, still telling me of the horrors.

"I didn't see 'Zekiel being hit, but the ones that were became somethin' else when whatever it was went back to the star. Then it just started glowin' and soldiers started turnin' into damn nightmares all 'round. We got out of the fort, escaped the worst of them and was able to kill a few smaller ones with that there axe."

He pointed to the one I was holding now, giving a small smile when he looked at it.

"That thing cut quite a few down. Ezekiel was pretty handy with a sword too, took down as many as I did..." Chambers grew quiet again, focusing his eye on mine once more, not wavering for a moment. "Runnin' through the woods... it was worse'n any hell I heard preached about. Them boys, the ones that got hit, they just lost most of their color, started getting these little wisps to them like they were... it wasn't smoke, not burning, but... Steam comin' off of 'em, even if they were barely held together after the hit... they started twistin' and stretchin' every which way after that, saw some have bones splinter through, some just tore... but their faces kept smilin'. Not a care in the world, happy as a pig in shit, smilin' teeth and all. That's what stays with me. That's what Ezekiel held off when we got to the beach."

I let out a shaky breath, gulping back the pain welling behind my tongue and piercing deep down into my chest. "So he held them off while you ran."

"I tried to grab him, kid, I really did. He just kept pushing more people in front of him onto the boats and when there wasn't room... well, he stood right there, planted his blade in the sand, picked up a damn repeatin' carbine that someone dropped on the beach, and started going at it. We might've been dead if it hadn't been some fuckin' miracle of timing. They were loading up excess ammo from the forts, so there was a whole damn barrel o' the tubes the Spencers use. I saw Ezekiel reload the damn thing twelve times before they even got past the trees. He picked up his sword and just started goin' at 'em. Never seen a man use a rifle with one hand and a sword in the other, but goddamn he was a fighter. The lights receded too much and last I saw was one grabbed him." He stopped here, locking his eye with mine again, "I don't know if he died, but they took him. I been on this island a few times since, cleanin' up bodies and scavengin', but I ain't seen no sign of him, not a corpse nor one o' them bastards."

"So you don't know that he's dead," I asked, feeling a small pang of hope. I grabbed onto it, holding tight and not letting go, no matter how hard it clawed to get away. He just sighed as he stood up, bringing the sails down and opening a small compartment alongside his seat, pulling out a small canister he tossed to me along with a matchbook. I looked in the flickering lanterns at the matchbook, looking at him in surprise, "Thought you couldn't get white phosphorus anymore? It had some bad health effects."

"Son, I'm more concerned about keepin' my insides in me, alright? Now, you see where that twists at the bottom? This is a replacement." He tossed me another, smaller canister, about half the size of the one I already had. "Screw that in when that one runs out. You keep that lit at all times, hear me? Axe out too. I didn't see him die, and I figured out enough with you by now to know you ain't gonna leave until you know."

I stood up quickly, eager and hoping to find him hiding somewhere out there in the dense brush. I struck one of the matches quickly after ripping it from the book, lighting the small wick on the canister he gave me. The match was bright as is, but whatever was in the canister burned brighter than the sun right in my hand. I almost dropped it in the bottom of the boat out of surprise as he reached back in and took it from me, popping the small casing around it up to focus the beam ahead of us. He handed it back to me as I got out of the boat, leading the way up to the tree line as waves crashed behind us.

"I'm gonna ask you one more time, but I already know what you're gonna say. Are you sure you want to go in here?" I could only nod as Chambers nodded back to me, situating his lantern canister in a small pocket on his chest before drawing his cavalry swords, one in each hand. "Stay right with me and do not stray. We're going to try the star. If they dragged him back, that's where he'll be."

I followed him into the dense forest. Nettles and branches whipped at me from every direction with even the slightest movement. Chambers hacked away at some, but not many gave way to his swings, rather bouncing back before coming back on me. "How do you know he'll be at the star?"

"They all go to the star," he grunted. His bright light was illuminating the way in front of us, but the lights from the boat had long disappeared through the trees. I could hear something off to my left cackle, shrill and breaking like an obnoxious drunk. It quickly turned from a cackle into a scream as it rushed closer. "Shine your damn light around us, keep them off!"

I did as he commanded immediately, fearing for my life as I swung my light in the direction of the noise. I briefly caught a glimpse of pale, stretched skin unfolding from a slender body before its mouth opened wide and sharp teeth let loose a screech. I could barely comprehend what it was I saw before swinging my ax, missing. It leaped upwards, off into the higher branches and away from exposure. My heart caught in my chest as I began wildly flashing my light all around us, gripping the ax tighter.

"What the hell was that?"

"A damned judgment from god if I ever seen one," Chambers replied, leading me into a small clearing in the forested area and pulling the canister from his belt, sliding back the shade and letting the light bathe our surroundings. A calamity of hisses, shrieks, and screams of anger and pain poured forth from every direction around the clearing, branches rustling as terrors retreated from the light's burn. I could barely tell now but there was a low glow through the trees, coming from a ways on from us, maybe another five minute's walk?

"I'm gonna ask you again. Are you sure? Because you seen what's out here and I can promise if he's one of them... you don't want to see that."

"He could be one of those?" I felt like I was going to throw up thinking about that now, picturing him over that pasty, white-eyed thing that had briefly been seen in my light. I had to steel myself again, catching sight of something else staring at us through the tree line. This one was on all fours, crouching behind a fallen tree as it... I think it stared at us. The eyes were just slits, almost like the middle of a snake's eye, but glowing purple. It licked its lips when it noticed that I had picked up on it, smiling a mouth with only four sharp teeth before curling fingers in a wave. I shivered, almost losing my nerve again before nodding to Chambers. "I need this."

"He loved you," Chambers said to me, looking toward the pale light. I looked in surprise, taken aback at what he said while terrified he had figured it out. He just looked back at me. "I can tell you Ezekiel mentioned you a few times in passing, while we would all talk about what we had back home some nights, he would tell us about you."

I felt my heart drop, hands shaking more now in the bright light than they had when I was sitting in the dark with whatever creatures were looking at me. "He told you."

"Son, a love that strong ain't somethin' I'll shame you for. We could all be so lucky," he said, picking up the lantern again and setting the shade back to guide us again as I adjusted mine to give me more feeling of safety. I was still shaking, but that was the best thing I could have heard. At least I knew he wouldn't leave me here on the island. Unless... he broke through my thoughts again, "Black, white, man, woman, it don't matter. Shit, we had more love the good lord might not've rained the heavens down."

"Still think it was a god that did this?" I asked, moving forward along with him through the underbrush and trees, the glow growing brighter with each step, even overtaking his lamp's bright white light. "I don't know if I ever believed in him before all this."

"If it weren't God, that scares me more," Chambers replied as we came upon another small clearing, the fallen star in the center now visible to me in full glory. The star was nearly taller than the trees around it, giving off the same glow I could first see from the water of purples and blues mixing and almost breathing from the star. It didn't come out in beams like regular light, but more like steam from it, floating in luminescent whisps through the air as the light dispersed, turning from the deeper hues to lighter as they ascended before covering the surroundings. It was beautiful, a celestial body right here, a mere stone's throw away. I didn't notice the things around it at first, almost invisible as I could see straight through them, their ethereal shapes outlined as the glow pulsed over them.

"It's…" I whispered, still gazing at the star open-mouthed as the comprehension of the beings hadn't hit me just yet. "It's like something from a dream."

"A damned nightmare," Chambers replied, pulling a small scope from his pocket and holding it to his eye, singling out the ones gathered all around the star, worshiping at its altar as it breathed there.

He continued looking as I gazed on, transfixed at the layers of cracks that had spread through the star intricately, almost fearfully carved in the surface of the celestial body as it breathed the faint light in and out. As I tore my eyes away from it and looked to the surrounding beings, I noticed the faces and re-membered Chambers' warning. I knew that smile from any-where, a gap between his two front teeth that always caused a small whistle when he talked while overexcited. His eyes and skin were the same translucent as all the others, almost like he was an old ghost from a story he told me one night. Chambers must have noticed him at the same time.

"Ah, shit." He let out a sigh of resignation, putting the scope away and redrawing one of his swords. "Kid, I'm not letting you throw your life away. I know you've lost a lot, but I promise he's not Ezekiel anymore. Let's make it back to the boat and I'll buy you some drinks at the tavern. You can tell me how he was before the war."

I felt him bump my shoulder but didn't notice, still transfixed on Ezekiel's smiling face bathed in the stars' glow. He was so joyful, just like I remembered him from before he left to fight. Before he left and became this thing. I saw that same smile as he told me stories, me writing them down on paper so we could take them to the presser nearby and share the adventures we created together. He, the jovial creator, me the enraptured recorder. I had to see that smile up close again. I turned to Chambers, handing him back the ax and canister he had given me as he tried to turn me back to the trees, back to safety.

"I'm sorry. I can't. I know. I know he's gone. I just... there's no point if I go back without him." I was crying as I said it, Chambers relaxing his grip and letting me take the tense steps forward, toward my beloved who was taken from me before I could ever say goodbye. He smiled at me as I got close. I looked back to Chambers, nodding.

He sighed and waved goodbye solemnly, making his way back into the trees, fleeing the accursed island and its inhabitants, soon to be one more. The purple eyed creature leapt at him from a nearby tree as he walked away, but he turned in time to slice it clean through. He kept walking, adjusting light as he left.

Ezekiel was still smiling as he came to me, an iridescent hand taking mine with warmth and embrace just as I remembered. I smiled at him as he led me to the star, all the way up to a small opening almost at eye level. He smiled back at me before guiding my head to the opening in the star, to gaze inside at what was causing this magnificence. I felt excited now, with the prospect of being with Ezekiel once more alongside the beauty of the star that had me enraptured. I gladly looked into the small opening, gasping as vast fields of stars and suns stretched. bright dandelions of light for an eternity before me.

All time seemed to stop, and my smile wouldn't fade. Nothing would. I pulled my head back to the open air of night, meeting Ezekiel's smiling eyes with mine. As I embraced him and he did the same for me, I felt the infinite stars from within suddenly burst forth into my conscious, the most intense feeling I had ever experienced as every emotion overcame my body before being overcome by nothing but intense warmth. Love. Ezekiel is here.

I am Ezekiel. Ezekiel is me.

We no longer had use for a name in the great field of stars, twin nebulas burning bright in each other's glow forever now, with no worry as to who may see in the infinite sea of the cosmos. Far away from their life before, but never more at home with each other.

HELL HOLE

“**C**ome on, do it!” Aaron yelled, shooing me closer to the old porch steps. “Go in! Don’t be a wuss!”

“They won’t. They’re too much of a bitch,” Danielle said from behind him. Her arms were crossed, and she was giving me the look that said she was right and I wasn’t.

“Not by myself I won’t,” I replied. This place was old as hell, no way I was going in alone whether it was haunted or not. “If I’m getting asbestos exposure so are one of you.”

“This place has asbestos?” Aaron asked, confused. Danielle just sighed, rolling her eyes at her idiot brother.

“This place hasn’t had a living soul in fifty years. They can’t sell the damn thing, and nobody wants to tear it down,” she said. I was still hesitating on the steps, staring up at the rickety two-story. One of the upper windows was busted, and it looked like a wooden step to the porch would crack under the weight of a leaf, much less if we tried to climb it. This place was a safety violation more than it was a home.

“Kind of hard to sell a house after a group suicide happened in it,” I muttered, seeing the front door was slightly open. A cold breeze blew by, cutting the still October air with chill. This place has a bad history behind it, going back almost a century at this point. Everyone’s been saying it’s haunted, and it’s usually one of those rights of passage for kids on Halloween to walk through the door and prove their courage.

"They say if you go in the basement you can see the blood-stains," Aaron said, sounding far too excited about the prospect.

"Then you go in," Danielle nudged him further. He just shrugged, stepping up to the stairs beside me.

"I'll go down to the basement if you go, too," he said, looking over to me with his eyebrows raised. I had to hesitate a moment before finally sighing, putting a foot on the first step.

"How are there blood stains? Didn't they do the Jonestown thing?" I asked, looking over at him as we walked up the steps carefully. They creaked hard, and I could briefly feel the boards bend under our weight. I stood back for a moment. "Might want to take stairs one of us at a time."

"Don't chicken out on m-" Aaron was cut off by a loud crack as his foot went right through the frail porch step. I reached a handout and caught his arm, keeping him from putting his entire leg through. He let out a low whistle and straightened himself up. "Shit. Thanks."

As we reached the door, both of us hesitated. I put out a hand, nudging it open slowly before another hard wind blew by, slamming it the rest of the way open. The long, yellow hallway was peeling off wallpaper like sunburnt skin, slowly tearing off the walls as the breeze came in. It looked ominous enough outside, but the inside was a strange, liminal space locked in time.

"You know, the cuckoo clock and wallpaper make for a really great haunt aesthetic," Aaron wisecracked. All I could do was roll my eyes. It was already getting dark outside, and in here was even more shadowy. I pulled out my phone and turned on the flash-light. The yellow wallpaper was even more dingy in the light, with smudges all over and the occasional graffiti. Someone attempted a pentagram near the end of the hall but made it sideways and one side was bigger than the other. Pitiful what the state of Satanic graffiti has come to.

"So where's the basement?" I spoke as we ventured into the hallway, both looking back to see Danielle waiting for us on the sidewalk. When I turned back to the long hallway, I froze. "Aaron..."

"Yeah?" He turned too, freezing when he did. We both saw a massive, tall figure standing around the corner at the end of the hall, barely peeking around. I wouldn't have been able to tell if not for the shine in the eyes, almost like when headlights catch an animal late at night. "Holy Shit!"

We both ran, bolting out of the front door and down the steps toward Danielle. Aaron just narrowly avoided going through the step again as Danielle stared at the two of us, puzzled.

"That was fast." She gave the snarky comment as Aaron and I looked at each other.

"You saw it?" I asked, to which he nodded. There's no way we could have imagined it. Those eyes were staring us down from around the corner, studying us. "There was something in there."

"Please. You two are just messing with me. Probably came up with this while you were standing there." She rolled her eyes, hugging toward the porch.

"No, really. There was something around the corner of the hall. It was staring at us," Aaron said, pleading with her not to go in. "Seriously, we should just go."

"Nope. I'm going to show you both that you're wimps." Danielle was holding her head high as she walked up the steps and right in. We could see her phone light click on from the sidewalk, watching as it swept the area. "Wrong, nothing here."

"We know what we saw, Dani!" Aaron was yelling again. Suddenly a scream cut the air, and Danielle's light disappeared through the entryway. "God damn it."

We both ran back up the steps and in, switching flashlights on again and looking around. I raised my voice as much as I dared to, "Danielle?!"

The thing at the end of the hall wasn't there anymore, with the peeling wallpaper in its place. We kept walking, slowly as we tried to find her. There was only one door to pass on our way through, and the small room inside was mostly an inky black, with a single, final ray of sunshine coming through a cracked window. It almost looked like it was falling on a person in the corner, but when I shined my phone light over it there was just a chair. I almost smacked myself for falling for the obvious haunted house cliche, but my heart was pounding hard enough to justify it.

"Dani!" Aaron shouted again, louder than I did. We reached the end of the small hallway, hesitating a moment before peeking around the corner. "Are you th—SHIT!"

Something flew at Aaron from around the corner with a scream, taking him back against the wall. I jumped back, trying to avoid whatever it was as laughter suddenly cut the air.

"Dammit Dani!" Aaron was shouting now, leaning back against the wall, peeling wallpaper curling over his shoulders like fingers. She was standing back in the hallway, holding a mask on a little mannequin head, eyes glowing green in our flashlight glare. "The hell is that?"

"Guessing this is what scared the crap out of you two." She was still laughing, holding her new head up high. Now we could see it was just a mask propped on a stick basically, with a huge wad of tape near the bottom that must have been holding it on the wall. "I've gotta say, it's not a bad idea."

"You're the worst sister on earth," Aaron muttered at her, turning to head back toward the front door.

"Uh-uh-uh, I thought you were going to the basement?" she teased him. I could only roll my eyes, not able to take any of their sibling pissing matches seriously. "I'm going."

"Can we please just go home?" Aaron was groaning, turning back to his sister. She tossed aside the mannequin head, leaning back against the wall, crossing her arms, and staring down at her brother.

"Guess you're just not brave enough. I could mention to Kelcy Barry how you screamed when a mask flew at you..." she threatened. Aaron turned red, rolling his eyes and looking up at the sky in exasperation.

"Fine. Where the hell is it?" he asked. Danielle just shrugged her shoulders, trying to push herself off the wall she was leaning on. The wallpaper still looked like it was curling around her, peeling off the walls. She tried again, making a larger effort to get further from the wall, pushing hard. Aaron just shook his head again, moving toward her. "Seriously? Don't you think you're playing your cards too close together?"

"I'm not screwing around." She was sounding a little frantic, still trying to push herself off the walls. Now the wallpaper was sticking to her, like it was pulling her back in, looking more and more like cruel, jagged fingers trying to take her. "It won't let me go! Aaron! Help!"

Aaron grabbed one of her arms, trying to tug her off the wall. No good. He looked back at me, and I grabbed her other arm. Now it was like we were playing a tug of war, us versus the house, with Danielle on the line. We lost.

I don't know if I saw the wallpaper suddenly yank her into the wall, but I swear for just a moment it looked like dozens of hands came out to grab her. She let out part of a scream before it was cut off abruptly, with no echo hanging in the still air. Aaron and I felt ourselves hit the wall hard as her hands left ours, bringing us into collision with the wallpaper.

"Where did she go?" He looked at me, the dim lights from our phones highlighting the fear in his eyes from below. "We have to find her. Where did she go? She couldn't just be gone, right? Like that's not possible..."

"Hey, chill the hell out. We're gonna find her, she's got to be around here somewhere. Maybe she just fell through, is there a rip in the wallpaper?" I started feeling along the wall, trying to see if it pressed inward at any point, but only hitting solid wood and drywall.

"Aaron!" Her voice echoed faintly from deeper inside the house. We both turned, flashing our lights down the hallway, this one leading off to branching stairs.

"Dani! Where are you!" he shouted back, the two of us rushing to the stairwell.

"Aaron!" she yelled again, still not responding. Her voice was coming from the second set of stairs though, leading down.

"Guess we found the basement…" he says, hurrying down the stairs toward a small door. Aaron slammed through it fast, almost collapsing on the concrete on the other side. "Danielle!"

I was right after him, bursting through the door, stopping as I saw what was in the room. Danielle wasn't there. At least, I don't think she was. Maybe she was somewhere in the mess… How long had all this been down here?

"Those aren't blood stains," I said, looking over to Aaron. He was still on the ground, frozen in fear at the sight before us. There was a massive pit in the middle of the concrete floor, shadows from our flashlights playing off the side as Aaron slowly inched toward it. Around it were what looked like… corpses. But not fresh or preserved. They were bloodied, like the corpses you see in movies after getting dunked in an acid bath. Eyes were hanging loose from some while others were screaming silently with mouths wide open. I wasn't sure if they were real or not, but the way they shone in the light wasn't promising. "Aaron… what is this?"

"Aaron!" Danielle's voice, but more faint. It was coming from the pit, though, and Aaron looked back at me like he was expecting me to look in. I shook my head, eyes wide. He took a deep breath, slowly picking himself up and shining his light toward the pit, inching over to it. Her voice rang out again, fainter now. "Aaron!"

"Dani!" he shouted back, getting closer to the edge. "Are you in there!"

I could hear another sound now. It was more faint, but it was coming from the pit, just like hers. The sound was rising though, getting louder. I could hear a shrill, piercing whistle at first before finally it became clear. In the circle of gory corpses, a massive pit was now emitting the sounds of hundreds of screams, if not thousands or millions. They were all screams of agony, pain, suffering... all in one dissonant harmony with each other. Ice stabbed through my chest before I was able to move. Aaron was moving closer to the pit, ignoring the screaming and shouting louder against it for his sister.

"Dani! Dani, are you down there? We can get you out!" He was screaming again, trying to make himself heard above the noise. The screams became overwhelming now, and I swear some of them were coming from the bodies around the pit. Aaron got as close as he could to the gap between him, like it was an entrance to the hole in the ground.

"Do you see her!?" I shouted to him, the screams starting to hurt my ears. He looked back at me, shaking his head in disappointment.

"Danielle! We're going to call someone to come help—" He was cut off again, all I could see was a brief bit of movement before the corpses close to him suddenly sprang to life. They grabbed onto him, the others circling around as their bones crunched, somehow cutting through the screams. Skin and guts sloughed off of their bones, some with intestines hanging out. Aaron's screams joined the discord of others, joining as the bodies converged on him, lifting him above their heads with rotting arms. "Help! Help!"

He was trying to fight against it, but just couldn't get free. I heard him scream for help one more time before he disappeared; the bodies tossing him over the edge before turning back to me, starting to make an advance. My flashlight was shining in their faces, showing their eyes, not lifeless, but burning. Burning with the flames of torture, hatred, and suffering that's only felt after being the target of so much of it. I snapped out of my frozen state then, turning tail and running through the basement door behind me. I went up the stairs two at a time, hoping to God I didn't trip before making it up. As soon as I did, I almost drifted through the hallway, turning toward the escape.

The last turn was in sight, with rays of sunshine floating through it from the dying evening sun. I could turn the corner and see it right there. Run. Just run, dammit!

As I passed the doorway from earlier a hand darted out of it, grabbing onto me by my coat collar.

I pulled, not able to get out of the grip it had on me. Finally, I had the briefest moment of bright thinking, turning around quickly to see the corpses beginning to shamble around the corner behind me. I slipped my coat off, seeing the mottled skin on the hand that still had it grasped tight. Finally free, I ran like hell.

Don't think I've ever been as grateful to eat sidewalk, but busting my nose open and falling off that front porch almost made me cry from joy. Whatever the hell was in there, I was out. Looking back toward the door, it was totally shut now, with a rental lockbox over the doorknob that definitely hadn't been there before. I looked up toward one of the windows, trying to see if there was anything different about the house or if Aaron and Danielle were just playing a prank from somewhere.

Instead, I saw both of them in the upstairs window. They were both smiling down at me, faces twisted. They both put bloody palms on the window, leaving prints on the glass. I could just barely make it out in the dimming light, but their eyes stuck with me. No pupils, no irises, just solid white eyes like they were rolled back in their heads. Both just stood, staring down at me while seeing nothing at all.

All I could do was run away. Run until my breath was ragged, stinging my broken nose.

They still haven't found either Aaron or Dani. I told my parents as soon as I saw my mother, blubbering out what happened and probably sounding mad. She called the police, I think more to calm me down than anything.

When cops finally went in the house, they said it was stripped bare for renovations. No wallpaper, no pit, just bare walls and torn out electrical. Said they were going to contact the current owners, but otherwise there wasn't anything else they could do. Not even declare them missing until after three days.

I don't know if they're really missing. I still see them when I close my eyes, smiling with vacant stares from white eyes. I can hear the screams still, smell the sulfurous fumes and burning flesh. They want me to come back.

MEETING GOD IN A TIN CAN

It's been a year since Gramps died, and the lease on his storage unit was finally up. Me and mom went to take care of things there, going through the various items, picking what was good to keep and what was garbage Gramps kept. A lot of old photo albums, and various relics... the guy was old, and he had a mountain of stuff to prove he'd been here a while.

We were sorting for days, filling up a trailer, and bringing it back to our homes. There was so much crap we had to split it between my place and mom's. Near the end, we started saying hell with it. The storage unit was HOT out here in the Southeast summers, so an unconditioned metal box was like sorting boxes in an Amazon warehouse in hell. Not to mention how much the trailer was starting to cost, so we stopped going through it and just tossed everything in, unloading it in my spare room where we could sort through it without melting in the unbearable heat.

Gramps was in the Navy. I knew that because he bragged about it all the damn time. So coming across some medals or files from his time wasn't surprising. Seeing one labeled "Top Secret" was definitely a turn though, because as far as we knew he was just a torpedo technician on the submarines. Most of his "war stories" were about partying on various subs or aircraft carriers. We have a plaque and everything with his service record, commendations, and all kinds of crap. He served from 1955 until nearly 2005, and has all the awards to prove it.

So color me surprised when I found a box labeled "Operation Faultline 1954". A whole three years before his enlistment date. I called Mom to make sure I was right too before I even started going through the box, and she confirmed it was 1955, so I figured he had just gotten some old records or something. I wish I had left the lid on the box at this point. That must be how Pandora felt...

Inside were filings full of papers, typed-out records for whatever Operation Faultline was. They were all in fantastic condition at least, with no water damage or anything, which was a miracle considering how damp and hot it is in this godforsaken town. I started flicking through the pages, skimming as I went.

Location: Coggins, South Carolina. Mission Statement: To research and develop new means of aquatic and amphibious warfare by unconventional or natural means. Commanding officer: Daniel S Surms, Captain of USS Ghost Current.

I kept flipping through, looking for what the actual operation was, hoping to find some kind of TLDR at the bottom of the massive stacks of papers. Nothing in the main file but a load of military and bureaucrat jargon, which I've tried to read multiple times since, but it just hurts my head. Here are the bullet points for what I found though, just to make it easy.

The plan involved submarines with special prototype torpedoes. These were equipped with some sort of special payload that made a massive vacuum wherever it hit, essentially creating such a high impact against anything it hit that there was a big enough explosion to both drive away all the water yet suck all the air from the massive area it happens. That's as best as I can explain the science jargon behind it, to be honest. I'm a copy editor, science was never my thing, much less the deep ocean.

Anyway, they used these vacuum torpedoes to try and create natural ocean phenomena, a sort of environmental warfare at sea. Except it was done with the intent of creating potential tsunamis to terrorize enemy populations into surrendering. This was prompted as a response to the long-term devastation of a nuke, as opposed to a "natural disaster". Then it gave the United States an alibi to go in under the guise of "aid" and slowly insert themselves into the country. Sounds familiar, right?

The real discovery in there was a journal from Gramps himself. The damned thing was full of scribbles, writing in the margins and everything, wherever he could. Strange symbols took up some pages, while others were just full of what looked like another language. Transcribing his handwriting was a pain in the ass, but I think I finally got it all. Turns out, Gramps enlisted at eighteen, not at nineteen like he told us. Now, I honestly see why he doesn't want to remember that year, if he did at all. His transcriptions are below, though I've cut out some of the more... undecipherable ones that way it makes sense.

October 16, 1954

I'm shipping out for the first time! Can't believe it finally happened. Getting my orders and shipping out after boot camp seemed like it was going to take forever. Now I'm at Camp Picram! This place is small though, and that's really something with where I'm coming from. The little island here just has the Navy Base really, but there are a few stores and a little school just outside the main gates that keep things interesting. Not too many bars, though Anna told me I'm better off for that. I don't know why she's so nervous, not like I'm going to meet someone prettier than her out here.

I'm starting out as a torpedo technician's apprentice, and apparently it's one of the best jobs on the subs! All I have to do is make sure the torpedo tubes are clean and working, then load them in whenever we need to fire. Apparently after a few trips I can start taking over on the scope and aiming! I know dad wasn't really for me joining up after everything, but I think the submarines are going to be much safer now than they were ten years ago.

Alright, I've got to go to my first briefing in a few minutes, orientation stuff, all that. Fingers crossed we get some interesting orders soon!

October 26, 1954

Wow, wasn't expecting to get them that fast. I've been stuck doing a lot of grunt work around the base, but that's typical for new recruits from what we've been told. The guys in our unit are all nice guys. We're getting along fine at least. The Command are a little more on edge than the newest of us here, no idea why though. We've had some free time, and the beaches around here are pretty nice! Doesn't hurt that they're barely ten minute's walk from anywhere on the base, so we can get out there whenever we want to.

Anyway, new orders are that the sub is going to look out in the Atlantic near some faultline. Something about researching the natural terrain to detect earthquakes and tsunamis early? I don't know, not really the things I expected from signing up with the Navy. We're shipping out early tomorrow morning, supposed to be a ten-day trip. This'll be our first time really going down in a sub, so hopefully nobody gets some weird case of the crazies down there.

I don't think I'll get to do much, but it'll be nice to get a feel for the waters out there. It looks like a storm might be rolling in tonight, and the captain told us to make sure we have everything set before daybreak so we can get in and get out quickly. I'm turning in early!

October 30, 1954

It's been a long three days on the boat, and I'm just sitting down to sleep for the first time in at least two days. Things haven't gone well. We arrived at the fault line early this morning and started the survey nearly immediately. It's dark down here. Really dark, like nothing I've ever seen, and cloudy nights out in the rural south get damn dark. This was different though, like it was trying to get inside the sub with us, snuff out any light it could find in here. It's cold too, even with the close quarters and machinery of the sub.

Something happened when we started the survey, though. I was able to look from one of the ports and see the faultline, where it started at least. It was hard to make out, even with the bright light they were shining on it. That thing was bright too, like the beam from a lighthouse under the water. We noticed when it turned on that a lot of things suddenly darted away in the water. Guess the things down here ain't too fond of the light.

The fault was thin when it started out, but as we moved along it grew much, much wider. The light was shining deep down by now, but it still couldn't cut through the darkness deep in the line. Every now and then we caught a glimpse of some deep-sea fish or another, each one uglier than the last with bulging eyes and sharp teeth. Looked like nightmares in the light, but they never stayed long, retreating back to the shadows quickly like vampires. Around ten minutes in, we had to shut off our light because it started to overheat. Doesn't sound like something that could happen with as cold as it was, but that's why I just clean the torpedo tubes, I guess.

Think it was Nadler that first saw it out of his port. The light had been off for a few minutes and the darkness outside was trying to get in again. Then suddenly a dim light started shining through the port on his side. It started getting brighter and brighter, rising up toward the entire sub. None of us could tell what it was, but there was something like a sun rising up from the fault line. The shadows around it rose up, fleeing from the light and fish came swarming out of the cave down there in front.

Command wasn't saying a damned thing as the light rose up. Dorsey, one of the older guys on the ship, says it's not like them to be quiet about something like this, especially with the threat the Russians are posing right now. There's no way we can be sure that's not some weapon they planted there.

Our lead torpedo tech, Hanson, grabbed me then. He pulled me away from the ports and back over to the torpedo tube, telling me how we had to load one quick. I went toward the torpedo rack when he stopped me, opening a small compartment underneath us full of red torpedos. These didn't look like any I had seen before, with odd markings all over them. I didn't question it, loading it in with him and making all the preparations to fire. Command was screaming orders back at us through the tube, telling us to fire now, and finally Hanson hit the eject button after sealing the tube, sending a massive burst of smoke into our small compartment as it blasted out.

I ran out of the torpedo compartment just to find half the boys collapsed in the throughway. Most of them were knocked out cold, some twitching, some foaming at the mouth. I couldn't do anything but stumble through toward the bridge trying to find out what was going on. The one thing I did notice was that bright light coming through every port I passed. Then it veered off like it was going back down the faultline. All I saw as it swam by was a couple of tentacles trailing behind the light, covered in sharp spines or pins. They definitely didn't look friendly.

When I got to the bridge, Command seemed a little surprised to see me. They weren't too concerned about the bodies in the throughway, though. Said they just got a case of hypoxia from the quick rise to the surface we had to make. Everyone came back awake a few minutes later, but something just wasn't right about them.

After we got back to the base, they dismissed everyone to medical, with no word on why. We all went through some extensive stuff, but it was all... mental? They were constantly questioning our psychological state, asking us what we saw, are we sure of what we saw, things like that. I just had to tell them I didn't see anything, but the other guys were apparently scarred by whatever it was.

***

November 2, 1954

It's been a whirlwind couple of days in the barracks. Lots of people in and out with doctors and some head shrinkers coming in to talk to everyone. I can't get any damn answers from anyone about what went on. A fault line survey turning into a total meltdown for half a submarine just don't sound like something normal. I tried asking Dorsey about it when we finally got a few minutes alone; he thought it was something the Soviets might have come up with.

What that paranoid son of a bitch said shook me to my goddamn core. He thought everything was some new plan by the Reds to take us out, but whatever he saw outside that port was different. He said the light was just some kind of lure, like the bait we would use for a fish on a hook. Whatever was trying to lure us in wasn't of this world, according to him. Said it was like one of those pulp novel monsters that you see at drugstore counters, some real Jules Verne nightmare stuff. Apparently the thing came back up a little bit after I laid down in my bunk, the whole thing glowing this green-purple color. Dorsey said it was brighter than anything he had seen, right down here in all the dark.

When I asked him what it looked like, he said it reminded him of a squid he found off the coast of Japan a few years ago. The thing was bathing in radiation wash off from one of the bombs, and he said it was bigger than a steam engine with cars attached to it. This thing was even bigger apparently, because Dorsey told me it could have easily swallowed the ship if it wanted to. The most terrifying thing about it, he said, was that it was covered in teeth. The spines I thought I was seeing were just the tentacles of it, and the rest of it was covered in even larger, more vicious hooked points. Dorsey says the thing came up, one monstrous eye showing from the middle of a gaping maw, tentacles splayed out, ready to devour the sub before we got that torpedo loaded up. Dorsey was off the coast of Japan when they dropped the nukes... he doesn't shake easily. This thing must've been terrifying.

From what Dorsey told me, he saw something when he looked at it. Like a vision or some dream, I guess. He wouldn't really talk about the contents of it, but it got to him.

November 2, 1954

Dorsey started screaming in his sleep tonight. The barracks were mostly quiet, half the guys being kept in the psych ward. He was just kind of whimpering at first, no real words or anything. Then he starts screaming, talking about how we poked something. Said the thing was going to lay waste to all on the surface, that our minds and souls were forfeit for going down there... he wasn't making any damn sense. Sometime by the end of the ranting and talk of more bloodshed and hell, he started to get up and go through his trunk.

We were just transfixed by what he was doing. It was nothing for him to have some angry rant about one thing or another, whether it be the Reds or the commissary food. This was foaming at the mouth though, absolute madness. Nadler tried to give him a tap on the shoulder and bring him back, but Dorsey just shoved him off and kept going through his trunk. He finally found what he was looking for, too. An old pistol, dulled and scratched from time in war, was gripped in his hand now.

Dorse turned back to us, talking about how we were all damned now that we saw it. Said our souls belonged to that thing now, for a fate worse than hell itself. Then he looked right at me and said some words that will haunt me for the rest of my goddamn life.

"What's the point in living if I know what I'm in for after?"

The next thing that came out of his mouth was smoke after he put the gun in and pulled the trigger. First time I saw the insides of a person, splattered all over the bunker ceiling.

November 4, 1954

I found Nadler hanging from one of the showerheads in the bathroom today. He was gone before I got there. There wasn't any sign of his state, except for being a little more quiet than normal. Nadler left a message too though, scrawled on a little note he was clutching.

"We met God in a tin can. If you're smart, you'll follow me to hell."

November 10, 1954

The incident here never happened. That's the official report, anyway. The boys who were looking outside during the survey... they've all dropped like flies over the past week. There's nothing to say they were ever there, just a folded flag sent to the family and some words of a diving accident. Don't think they even got the bodies back, but not sure where they ended up. I've been told that I'm being released on a medical leave until February, and apparently that's my official enlistment now. Swear they've poked and prodded me to hell and back already, but apparently I haven't had any irregularities found like the others. From what upper command is telling me, I'll start out in February two ranks higher, so at least I get something out of all this. For now, I'm heading out tomorrow, going back home for a while before my time starts again. I'll probably never know what happened, but I'm going to do my best to forget about all this.

December 10, 1954

I started having dreams. Whatever the thing was down there, it's talking to me. I think that's it at least, I don't know anymore. The dreams are nothing but the black abyss, nothing around except that pale glowing light that starts coming up from the fault. I always wake up before it gets to me, but the voice that whispers at me says awful things. It tells me to kill and use the bodies. It wants me to make a shrine to it, to help it come here. It's... it's loud. I keep telling myself it's a dream. I'm going to go see the doctors when I get back in February.

That's... it. That's all there was in the journal other than the scribbles, which fill up most of the last half. I'm still not sure what the hell he saw down there, but after he went back, things must have been fine. Maybe he found some way to lock it all away somewhere, but part of me wonders about what the hell could have been down there. Gramps never said anything about stuff like this, and always told us the strangest thing he saw was a ghost ship drifting by empty one day. It's all just confusing.

After all that, hopefully, he's able to just rest in peace, somewhere with Grandma and their family. Hopefully not in whatever twisted hell this thing came from. I'm going to leave the journal be, though. I've watched enough horror movies to know that's a recipe for a bad time.

FLY ME TO THE MOON

Man has been on this Earth millions of years, exploring the planet, building civilizations, killing and creating in an endless cycle. Man first went into space starting almost eighty years ago. Think about it, we spend all this time getting around our own planet, arguing over the smallest bits of land, but when we finally set our mind to space travel, it only took us a few decades to get where we wanted to go.

I'm proud to say my grandmother was one of those that helped us to get there. She started out back in 1959, fresh out of college, as an intern for NASA. The space race was already going strong, the US vs. the Soviets, and she managed to get in right in the middle. Gram stayed there for forty more years, only retiring right before Y2K.

She's up there in years now, and I wanted to try to do something to preserve the memories she had of that time, so I began to collect her stories. We started out with the basics, talking about how she joined, what she did, the history surrounding everything when she was there... all the things you learn in a high school history class.

When we started discussing the missions she worked on, though, that's when I realized that there was a lot of history missing. Locked up, never to be heard or read by anyone, nor should it. There's a reason space exploration has slowed down. There are missions that were made off the books and off record, launched from secret blacksites around the world. Gram both saw and heard terrors beyond our comprehension from the dark void of space.

She shared these stories with me, these secrets kept from us by those in power. The human price of our curiosity is much higher than we're led to believe, and these people deserve to have their stories known.

I'm enclosing one of her stories here. She can get a bit long winded, as some do in their old age, so I've tried to edit down anything that isn't relevant. I'm still going through everything with her as well. With her age, she can't stay focused for very long, so we're doing these little interviews in hour sessions every day. I'll transcribe and upload what I can when I can.

What follows is the transcript of what Gram told me on April 4, 2020. Any interjections of my own will be formatted with brackets around them.

My name is Evalyn Lara Smart. I was a mission control contact with NASA from 1959 to 1999. I was the one that any astronauts or crew would speak to, the voice on the ground. I relayed this information back to whoever needed it in flight control, navigation, engineering and such.

I didn't set out to work there, it sort of just fell into my lap. I had worked as a switchboard operator, mostly taking emergency calls for the local departments. NASA was doing some recruiting and one of my supervisors recommended me. Then, before I knew it, there I was, sitting in the big mission control room, watching the big screen with the video feed, and talking to our very own spacemen.

[Here she goes into a tangent about how lovely Armstrong and Aldrin are, with many mentions about Christmas cards from the latter.]

So, one of the first missions I was there for was the first picture of Earth from orbit. Obviously being in communication I wasn't really necessary, but we all crowded into the control room to see the picture as soon as it was transmitted. Granted, it was the late fifties, so we were waiting for quite a while.

We expected cheers when it came through finally. It started that way, at least, then everything quickly died down. There was the Earth, the huge curve with a beautiful crown of light from the sun shining around it. We captured something else too, though. Something that I fear I'll see again one day.

Behind the Earth, off in the distance, was something... giant. It wasn't completely clear, but what you could make out was a clearly defined torso, arms outstretched with wicked spines jutting from the outside. Large red eyes blazed against the dark void behind the figure, with a gaping maw underneath opened in a terrifying roar.

The scale of this thing was huge. No way it couldn't be seen from a normal telescope here on Earth. We aimed our most powerful scope at the coordinates we estimated it to be at and swept the sky, but couldn't see it anywhere. Took another picture from the satellite and it was gone. As if it had never been there.

To this day, we don't know what the hell it was. We check for it in every photo we take, every sweep of the sky, and it's only shown up two more times since then. Once in 1979, and once in 1999. I don't know many people in the agency now, so god knows if it's been there again. Every time it showed up, though, it appeared larger.

[Here she goes on about a few other notable advances in tech. Most irrelevant to what we are discussing now.]

What a lot of people don't realize is that there were manned space flights before the ones in the history books. Sure, there's always been the theories about "lost cosmonauts" and such from the Soviets, and there are definitely true cases of that, but we had our share as well.

There was an initial manned space flight in 1960, the *Daedalus*.

[She noticed the look of shock on my face, apparently, and laughed}

Never read about that one, eh? It was kept tightly under wraps. We didn't want anyone to know about it until we had them back on the ground successfully, otherwise it may kill morale around the office. No, we kept a small crew, launched the rocket off from an isolated area of Alaska. We did a lot of launches from there, kept the Reds on their toes back in the day.

Anyway, this was a three man crew. There was Bill Zask, James Hanlon, and Terry Duncan. Those three were a tight crew. They were supposed to go up, orbit for twelve hours, then come back down. We would pass it off as a comet if anyone saw, but never got that chance.

Things went south fast. They took off, all was fine until they hit the upper atmosphere. They tried to ease back on the jets, make sure they made it into orbit and didn't overshoot. Everything went to hell. Jets wouldn't cut off. We don't know what caused the malfunction. I heard them shouting... trying to fix the issue. It didn't happen. They flew straight through, getting just enough adjustment from the orbital pull to be shot off course and toward the direction of the sun.

[She lets out a sigh here, shaking her head.]

Jets continued firing, taking them even further out. We maintained radio contact with them for twenty hours after take-off. I spoke with them as fuel ran out; they began drifting into the void, no hope of turning. Never to feel solid ground again.

To this day, I don't know if it was something they really saw or the insanity getting to them as they died and faced their mortality. James was the first to begin raving. Telling us about the bodies floating by the cockpit windows. I tried to clarify what he meant, assuming celestial bodies. I'll never forget the response from Bill.

"No, Evalyn," he said to me, "Human bodies. Dozens of them."

They described the field of bodies. Male and female, old and young. All naked as the day they were born. Bill swore that one smiled at him as he went by. We didn't have live feed cameras at the time, unfortunately, so we weren't able to confirm. The way they described it, though... I have no doubt they were seeing all of this.

A lot of the transmissions got lost in static. Limits of the tech at the time. The last broadcast we received was Bill. He was raving, still talking about the bodies. Said they were talking to him now. Telling him he could live forever with them. He said he was going to open the emergency hatch. Maybe it was my emotions getting the better of me. Right before he opened it and the static took over, I swear there was another voice.

[She drifts off and stares out of the window next to her. The sun went down an hour ago. Stars were plainly visible, shining in the inky darkness. I asked what the voice said.]

It's ingrained in my head. I can hear it clear as that moment sixty years ago.

"Come. Be with us. Become as stars and drift immortal."

[Gram is tired, says she's going to bed. End transcription.]

———

Gram is in one hell of a mood today. Not sure if she's just feeling better than usual or something has got her riled up. Either way, she's letting her feelings be known. That's just a forewarning before we get into this transcription. There are things about her in here that I personally NEVER wanted to hear.

No, really. She can tell me how she saw eldritch beings in the vastness of space and none of that is as terrifying as her talking about hooking up with astronauts in the training areas. Ugh. Here's the transcription. I'm going to go chug bleach.

[Conversation from April 5, 2020. Again, this is being told by Gram and translated by me. My own interjections are in these brackets.]

Ah, you want to hear more? Alright, guess it's time to turn this bullshit off. Live through the damn missile crisis and I'm going to get taken out because nobody is competent enough to stay in their damn houses.

[Gram has been cursing like a sailor all day. She only does this when she's either very happy or very anxious.]

So... let's see. I told you we had some crews up there already, yeah? Just couldn't get any successful returns down. Damn Reds beat us to that. Joke was on them though, they just tossed Gagarin up there in a metal tube and waited for him to come back down on his own. We actually had our own man pilot themself back down to earth. How's that for you? Russians don't have shit on American determination.

So we did a few other missions once we finally got the hang of putting people up there and bringing them back down. It was all smooth sailing for the most part. So now what did we decide to do? Put a man on the goddamn moon.

[She gets up and goes to the kitchen, returning with a bottle of red wine and a comically large glass. I mention to her that it's only around two in the afternoon.]

I worked with astronauts, darling. Days don't matter when you're orbiting the planet. Anyway, it was '62 that we crashed a vessel on the far side of the moon. That was something of a test run I suppose, seeing just how bad we could crash and burn something before we tried it again with people inside.

We had the Ranger 4 vessel that we sent up there. Had it do a fly by of the moon for a bit and take some photos before dive bombing it to the surface and taking some pictures for us there. We never released those to the public. Scared the hell out of all of us in the command center when they transmitted back. Keep in mind all the pictures we had at the time were black and white still, no color photography on that scale yet.

So Ranger 4 lands there and immediately begins snapping pictures. All of us are standing around, expecting to see just a barren expanse of grey rock, nothing all too special. Lo-and-behold, the first picture comes back and there's someone just... *standing* there. Right in front of the crashed capsule. We couldn't tell gender or race or anything. They were in a spacesuit that looked remarkably like the ones we were developing.

So naturally we think, *Oh no. They beat us to the moon*, because who else could it be at this point? The Russians were the only other country keeping any kind of pace with us. Then we realized it couldn't be them. They would have already been rubbing it in our faces if they had landed a man on the moon. There's no fucking way this is from anyone on our planet. That's when the rest of the pictures started coming in.

The suit kept getting closer and closer to the capsule. Maintaining the same stance the whole time. It just kind of floated over to it. Then you could see into the visor on the helmet. Where there should have been someone's face visible, there was just... fire. Pure, bright flame. Then the pictures stopped. Nothing else came from Ranger 4.

[She finishes off her first glass of wine. Or half-gallon, it's hard to tell from the size of the glass. She immediately empties the rest of the bottle into it.]

I'll give the higher-ups at NASA credit, though. Crazy bastards didn't let seeing a flaming cosmonaut stop them from going ahead with their plans. We plugged away at it, sending up more and more missions to orbit the Earth, do fly-bys of the moon, Mars, Jupiter... anything we could get near. We saw a few oddities here and there as we went, but things stayed mostly silent for those few years. Maybe we just didn't notice it because we were so focused on the mission at hand.

Then it finally happened in '69, as you well know. We got to the moon, beat the Russians there after all. There was that big televised bit with Neil and Buzz taking the steps onto the surface and everything. I really hated those suits they had them in. Didn't get to accentuate Buzz's best features for sure. That man had the best ass in this entire galaxy...

[This was one of five tangents about Buzz Aldrin's physical features throughout the day. I've edited these out for the sake of mine and your sanity.]

You ever consider that we landed someone on the moon and sent up missions to land again and again for the next three years, then just quit cold turkey and never went back? Why do you think that is? Huh? Hey, I thought you wanted to hear all this!

[At this point in time she threw the remote for the television at me. I had retreated to my mental safe space during the Buzz Aldrin diatribe.]

Well, we DID go back! A few times. This wasn't for the scientific research we did the last three years. No, this was for anthropological purposes. We found things on the moon. We weren't the first beings there.

No, we started finding small signs with the Apollo 14 mission. There were some little remnants of previous visitors. The first thing they found were some symbols carved into crater walls. Nothing that we could translate, of course. Nobody knew what the hell they meant. But we knew they weren't naturally occurring, that much was obvious.

So they took pictures of all the ones they found. Pretty sure they're still working on it to this day. They'll probably crack the Zodiac cipher before that damned thing.

Apollo 17 was when they knew they needed to carry this one on privately. That's the "last" manned moon mission that happened back in '72. For all the world knows, we ain't been back since. That's the way they want to keep it.

Apollo 17 found way more than anyone previously had. They found full on structures. Altars of worship is what it looked like. I can't even describe the images transmitted back. The way these things were built... it wasn't natural. There's no way that structures built that way should be allowed to stand. It was like the ghost of Lovecraft possessed Escher and made him design some fucked up church.

We advised them not to go inside. We would send another mission up there with some better training and equipment to document all of this. That's where Apollo 18-22 came in. Before they left, though they photographed the structure from every angle. We didn't notice until the end that it appeared absolutely identical no matter what angle it was viewed from. One hundred percent symmetry. Everything aligned perfectly, no matter how insane it was built up.

[Gram finishes the second glass of wine. Leaning back in her chair.]

Well, I believe that's enough wine for one hour. Time for a good nap. All that talk of Buzz got me thinking about the old days...

[I turned off the recorder and ran from the room. I can still hear Gram cackling from downstairs.]

[April 6, 2020. I'm going stir crazy. Gram seems to get stronger every day somehow. It's like she's stealing my youth and thriving in isolation. This may end up being a record of me going insane with her stories mixed in.]

Let's go sit out on the porch. It's a nice day out. I'm tired of being cooped up in here.

[I concede that I could use some fresh air, but make her promise not to go near the neighbors or anybody walking by on the street. She gives me an entirely too sarcastic scout salute and swears she won't.]

Alright, that's better. Feel my battery recharging already. Now... ah. The Moon Church was what I was telling you about yesterday, right? That was some crazy shit.

So, Apollo 17 found this crazy structure that was just perfectly built. Strangest architecture I've ever seen. Made no goddamn sense to anyone how it remained standing after all this time. So we trained some other crews to go up after and look into it further. Specifically, we got a few people trained that had degrees in anthropology and ancient cultures. Maybe we could find some links here between this and things that had been found on Earth.

Well naturally, nothing is ever that easy. They head up there in 1973, land smack next to the structure found by the previous mission, and get to it. By this point technology has thankfully improved so we have cameras in their helmets that allow us to see everything they see. They were in color too! Thank god.

[I asked her how they had this kind of tech in '73 when a lot of things were still incredibly basic with video, especially transmitted over that vast of a distance.]

Pffft. You really think the stuff you saw from that time was the most advanced technology being used by the government? Don't underestimate the amount of money the American government will throw at something if they feel it's a threat. The cameras and equipment we had on those missions were on par with that little video camera your momma gave me for Christmas a few years back.

[She's talking about the GoPro she got four years ago. That records in 4k. What the fuck. Now she's laughing at me again.]

Like I said. Don't underestimate government spending. So anyway, Apollo 18 was a three man crew. Jason Voss, Ben Codd, and Arthur Wayne. Wasn't too happy about Arthur going up there. We had spent a few months together while he was training down at Cape Canaveral. God, if he could do half the things he could do in our gravity up there…If only I could edit my memory the same way I do this transcription.]

So, they got to work. Jason stayed in orbit around the moon, making sure everything on the main ship was fine. Arthur and Ben went down to the surface and set up base camp. There was the structure, and not even one hundred feet away was their little landing pod setup with everything in it. They were equipped for three days on the moon.

First day goes off fine, just walking around the thing, taking measurements and samples. They determine that most of the structure is made from an unknown element. To this day, I don't think they've found out what it is.

So, end of day one and they go back to their basecamp. Now, we have a couple of cameras set up in the pod so we can see everything going on, just in case there's any issues technically or god-forbid something happens between them. Arthur and Ben are both fast asleep, we've got the feed playing in command just to monitor and keep an eye on everything, and suddenly it glitches. Not a drawn out one though. Just a quick scramble, then it's back. Arthur and Ben are still there asleep. Now there's a figure standing there in the airlock, though.

Like nothing I've ever seen. Long limbs, big hands that almost look like bulldozers, and just a rounded off nub right at the shoulders. I hit the intercom speaker for the capsule as fast as I could move. Screaming at them to wake up. Poor Ben fell straight out of his bunk and onto Arthur underneath him, belly to belly. Now that's something I normally would have paid to see, but right now my heart was racing for the wrong reasons.

So they both scramble up and look towards the airlock. That damn thing is still just standing there, I think it was looking at them. Arthur shouts at it, asking what the hell it wants. There's this… low garble of noise that happens. Nothing discernible. It could have been interference for all we know. But by god I saw Ben's face drain of all color when it happened. Arthur went a bit slack, looking from Ben to the creature. Then, as fast as it showed up, it was gone. Poof, right into... well, guess you can't say thin air being where it was.

Ben sat down on Arthur's bunk and just cried. It took him a good hour to actually calm down. In the meantime, we had no idea what was happening. Finally he chilled out enough for us to ask him what had happened. He said that thing had looked at him, no eyes or anything but he *knew* it was looking at him. It said, "She was never meant to live."

Now this shook all of us. Almost a month before the mission, Ben and his wife suffered a miscarriage. She had been six months along; they were expecting a little baby girl. Then one day the baby was just gone, no heartbeat, no activity. They didn't know what had happened. It tore Ben and his wife apart, though. They had a huge fight a week before liftoff because she didn't want him to go. Didn't want to lose another person she loved. I can't imagine what he felt when he heard that damned thing talk.

They cut the mission short after that. Everyone was afraid of what may happen to Ben's mental state if anything else happened. They packed up quick and got the hell out of there. Ben drank himself stupid afterwards, ended up driving his car off the interstate going 150 at around three in the morning. They barely got anything to bury.

{Gram wipes a stray tear from her eye. A man is jogging down the street with his dog, coming closer to our house. Gram calls out a greeting to him. He walks up and begins talking, much to my displeasure. Gram is speaking animatedly and leans down to pet the dog. I remind her we're supposed to be distancing just to be safe.]

Sorry, Jerry, my grandson here is a hardass. I'll see you some other time.

Anyway, that was the end of Apollo 18. Not a whole lot found out, but we were ready to try again. I was just grateful that Arthur made it back in one piece. We were actually engaged you know. Way back in the day before he went back up on the 19 mission in '74.

[I was a bit surprised at this. As far as I was told, Gram had never been married, and my grandfather had been killed in a car accident not long after she found out she was pregnant with my mother.]

We spent a lot of time together during that time. It was lovely. I miss that man...o, Arthur and Jason volunteered to go back on the 19 mission. I think Arthur was determined to get into that structure and see exactly what was going on with it. They had a new recruit along with them as well. Paul Orson. He was a former Green Beret during the Vietnam war. Tough son of a bitch, and not one for conversation. They didn't know what they would find though, so they wanted someone with combat training to go up.

Everything goes as normal, it's old hat at this point. They land in the same spot for base camp, Arthur and Paul this time. They got there on day one and set everything up, then decided to just rest up for a few hours and go straight in.

Well, they didn't realize that they needed to find a way in first. Apparently in all this time researching the structure, everyone just *assumed* there would be a door somewhere. No such luck. Every wall on the outside was smooth, no cracks or seams signaling a door. They searched every damn inch of that thing, nothing to be found.

Lo and behold, I'm watching in on Arthur's camera while he's walking around the structure. Even in low gravity he had two left feet, he tripped and fell straight through the wall. We thought we had lost him for a minute. It looked like the camera had hit something and shorted out. Then he asked us if we were seeing it too.

The interior of the structure was larger than the exterior. Way more room to move about. Lights hung in the air like stars, bathing everything around him in a soft glow. It was like its own miniature galaxy contained in that one building. Probably one of the most beautiful things I've ever seen.

Arthur backed out then, wanting to make sure he could travel freely in and out of the structure before he got trapped there, and it seemed to work fine. It was like there was a portal, a thin veil where it looked like a wall but wasn't. He grabbed Paul, and showed him what he had found. Don't think he was too impressed, more like he was ready to shoot it if he could have found a gun.

Exploring it further, they found a small spiral slope, almost like a ramp that went downward from the main chamber. They followed it for probably an hour before it got anywhere, seeing more of those strange symbols all over the walls on the way down. When they got to the bottom... it was like some kind of church. No idea what they worshiped or who, but there was an altar right there against the far wall. A statue rose up in a recess behind it.

Looked to me like an elongated pyramid of sorts. Not really sure how to describe the geometry of it. There were angles that merged with smaller angles, curves where lines were... it was like my brain was trying to comprehend it through the camera feed, but just jumbled everything instead. That was about the time we noticed the spots on the altar.

We're not a hundred percent sure to this day what it was, but we had a good enough guess. It was dried, had obviously been there for quite a long time. But it still had that rusty red color that only comes from dried blood. It was splashed all over the place up there, like someone had slit the jugular and waved all about up there. Had to have been gallons spilled.

That was enough for the two men for that day. They headed back up to base camp to make record of what they found and go back to sleep. They were out for maybe two or three hours when it happened again.

The camera glitched just like last time, and that thing appeared. It wasn't in the airlock this time, though. It appeared right next to their damn bunks. We tried warning them, but it didn't seem to work. It's like our speakers were jammed.

We were only able to watch in terror. That thing leaned over Paul and said something to him in that garbled noise we heard last time. God knows what it was. Then it was gone again. Nothing there. Paul got up and started putting on his suit to go outside then. I kept hitting the button, trying to ask what the hell he was doing, got no response. Our line into the main capsule was dead.

When he had the whole suit on, I tried the line going directly to his helmet. I said, "Paul, what the hell did that thing say to you?" You know what he told me?

[I shook my head in response.]

He looked straight up into the capsule camera before stepping out, and said, "Finishing what they began."

I still get chills thinking about that. It was one of the coldest things I've ever heard. By that time, Arthur had woken up and was getting his suit on as fast as he could. God, I begged him not to go after Paul. Not to go into that damned church. Whatever was done in there before was bad, and there wasn't going to be anything good coming of it now.

He was too good of a man though. He got everything on and chased Paul in there. No idea how he had moved so fast, but Paul was waiting down there for him already. Standing right on the altar and holding an old combat knife. Arthur shouted at him, asking what the hell he thought he was doing. He didn't say a damned word. Just started lunging towards Arthur, brandishing that knife.

I... I watched it. All of it. Each of their helmet cameras was on a different side of the big command screen. Our coordinator was shouting at me to tell them to stop, to get their shit together. It wouldn't have done anything. That wasn't Paul in that suit anymore. There was a blind rage in his eyes. His breathing in the mic was like an animal that had been cornered. No, he wanted to kill, and he didn't care who saw.

They went back and forth for a while, throwing each other all around that unholy place. Finally, Arthur managed to wrestle the knife away from Paul. He stood up, holding it out in front of him...

there were tears in his voice when he was talking. Telling Paul to stay away. Telling him they could go back home and have a drink. Act like all of this never happened. It didn't matter. Paul rushed and Arthur had no choice. He ducked down and thrust the knife upward. The camera in Paul's suit was splattered with red as he depressurized in seconds.

Arthur screamed, looking at that Altar and throwing the knife at it. He just lay there for a while, sobbing and shouting curses. He was alone up there.

[Gram's voice cracked. I've tried to transcribe the next part as best as I can, but some parts were difficult to make out.]

Arthur started pulling Paul's body back up towards the exit with him. Even if he had tried to kill him, he wasn't just gonna leave him up there, all alone on a rock. He got to the top and tried to go through the wall back outside, but it was suddenly solid. No give. He tried the other walls, trying to make sure that he wasn't using the wrong one in his emotional state. Nothing. Still no way out.

He collapsed against the wall, taking in deep, shallow breaths. His oxygen tank only had about ten minutes left by his count. The suits weren't designed for long outings back then. I hit the button to talk to him and tried to soothe him. He was almost hysterical, but I like to think hearing me helped him go quietly.

I still remember seeing his face in that helmet camera. My last words to him. The little smile that he got right before he passed. He got to know that even though he was dying up here, on a mission completely off the books, there would be part of him still living on right here on earth.

{Gram wiped tears away from her eyes. She had been openly sobbing, obviously reliving something painful. I put my hand out for her to take.]

The last three missions they sent up there served two purposes. They were recovery missions, to get those bodies back home and give them a proper burial, and demolition missions.

They couldn't get back through the wall into the chamber the normal way, so they tried drilling through. There was no chamber, though. Just solid rock no matter how far they drilled into it. So, they gave up after that. The next two missions brought explosives and detonated them around the structure, destroying it,

We haven't gone back to the moon since then. Not after that loss. Even if we had, I wouldn't have worked the mission. I would have absolutely refused. I told them I wasn't taking on any more crewed landing missions after that. They would have to find another communications head.

[She stared at me for a moment before looking back out toward the sky. The moon was already hanging there, right at the cusp of night. She let out a long sigh.]

Some nights I look out at the moon and like to think he's still out there watching over me. Watching over us. He would be so proud that I'm finally telling someone this. He had always talked about having a family and grandchildren one day... I think he's up there right now, giving that sly grin he always had. I'm sure he's proud of you wherever he is.

[Gram looked for a moment more as I sat there, stunned. Then she got up, gave me a hug, and went back inside to get ready for bed.]

―――――

[April 7, 2020 I'm going to try to give Gram some space today. She still seems a bit out of it after last night.]

[She stayed up to watch the Pink Moon. Said she felt better after seeing it, like Arthur was at peace up there.]

―――――

[April 8, 2020. She's back to her normal self.]

Well, look who's finally up. Thought I was going to have to draw a pentagram on the floor and summon you down here. Grab me that loaf of bread off the table. I've never wanted a grilled cheese this bad before in my life.

Alright now... let's see. Did I tell you about Skylab yet? God, that was a clusterfuck if I ever saw one. They want you to think it just decayed out of orbit, but they knew what they were doing. They made sure that son of a bitch went down in flames.

[She settles in with her sandwich and another glass of wine. I don't know where they come from. I only saw one bottle on the counter when I got here, and I don't recall getting any with the grocery delivery. I swear, she's some sort of witch.]

So, we had about four crews up there that did different experiments and such. We had your normal run-of-the-mill stuff, working on plants and small animals, zero gravity, blah blah blah. Then the final crew came in. I about marched my ass down to the science department and smacked the shit out of every one of them when I saw what they brought with them up there.

It was a goddamn block. Not just a block, though, it was a piece of debris from the temple on the moon. They were still trying to figure out what the hell it was made out of after all this fucking time.

So they're up there poking and prodding at it, trying to heat it and see how it reacts. These idiots don't have a damn clue what they're doing. They leave it in the lab one day after they're done and next thing you know it starts growing right in front of us.

It's just... expanding. Growing outward and inward, taking over the entire compartment in Skylab. We don't understand how it's been in storage for so long and it just now starts to do this. Maybe it was the proximity to the moon or something. Maybe whatever they were doing to it. I don't know. That thing took over half of the station by the time twenty-four hours had passed though.

[Gram gesticulates wildly, stretching her arms out to show some measure of what had happened.]

So this thing is turning the station into a new version of the moon temple. There's protrusions coming from it, odd angles sloping off here and there. It looks demented. They thankfully hightailed it out of there on the main shuttle right after it happened. The structure just kept taking more and more of it as it went.

The cameras inside were still giving off a feed. That's the weird part. No matter how much this thing took over and reshaped all the metal and tubing of the station, the cameras kept going. We saw the small galaxy form right there in the lab. The crew quarters ebbed and changed, stretching until they resembled a hall of worship. That damned altar appeared at the end. The very same one.

That was what sealed the deal for the superior officers. Skylab was obviously a lost cause. We didn't know how long this thing would keep growing up there, or where it would latch onto next. So they started working on sending a probe up there carrying a payload. They were going to knock it straight out of orbit, either let it drift off into deep space or burn in the atmosphere.

The whole time they were doing this we were watching the cameras. I saw things on there, things that weren't meant for the human eye to see. On occasion the feed would blink, and the altar hall would be filled with a writhing mass, creatures that looked like that same one that appeared on the moon. They would be feeling, swirling around one another in a throng. It was some worship ritual or something; I don't know. Just as soon as it started, it would blink right back out.

There were other creatures. Masses of darkness, tendrils of light stretching from them. They didn't seem right for the space they were in, like they were somehow larger than the station, yet microscopic. They devoured one another with no care. It was its own contained environment up there.

Finally, the payload was read and sent up. We watched the feed as it hit, blowing a hole in the lab before knocking it into a decaying orbit. The worship started again, more frenzied this time. They were excited to be going to earth.

A crew was dispatched to clean up any wreckage that could be found. Not entirely sure what they did with it, but I hope it's buried as far as it can be.

[She finishes the glass of wine she had, getting up and hobbling towards the sink. She started the water and began to wash dishes.]

From then on I think we made it a point to make sure all the testing and such was done in a more controlled environment. They started sending out more probes too. Voyager was launched a few years later. We wanted to see what was beyond our little space in the galaxy.

There's a lot. That's for sure. I remember when they told us Voyager had reached the edge of our solar system. We couldn't believe something had gotten that far. We looked in at some of the pictures it had taken along the way. There were the usual things that inspired awe, the stars, planets up-close, far-off comets and asteroids. Then there was the follower.

[She shuts off the sink and comes to sit back down.]

Creepy little shit, that thing was. Looked like a human male, honestly. Kind of tall, scrawny. He was naked head to toe, not wearing a goddamn thing.

[She notices my look.]

Before you ask, no it didn't have a dick.

It just followed the Voyager like a lost little puppy for a while. Poking and prodding at it occasionally. We got plenty of close-up pictures of it, saw right into its eyes. The close ups were what made us realise it didn't have eyes like a human. Instead it had stars. They burned hot, almost causing a flair on the pictures. There was one where it opened its mouth and you could see a void like a black hole, singularity and all.

[She shakes her head, letting out a little shudder.]

The weirdest thing was the message it transmitted. Perfect English. Sent it through the Voyager's onboard microphone as a microwave signal. When it came through and translated it said, "So nice to meet you. I'm a bit early, but I'll be seeing your planet soon enough."

That wasn't even the scariest thing Voyager picked up though. Right before I retired in '99 it started sending back a message. Took forever to decode it because everything was so scrambled. After all that time it was still a mess, some language we didn't understand and a cypher to go along with it. It was like someone had done a rush job translating.

[What did it say?]

"Turn back before it notices you too."

[Gram said she wants to go get some air. I notice she's taking more time than usual to move, like it's hurting her. I ask if she's okay.]

These old bones are better than you'll ever be. Now, I'm going for a walk.

[Evening of April 9, 2020. Gram asked to sit on the porch and watch the moon tonight. Says this is the last of her stories.]

Can't believe I've been retired for twenty years now. Seems crazy at this point, leaving the job, helping raise you kids. It was worth it, though. You turned out okay.

[She gives a little chuckle here.]

So, there's two more things that happened right before I quit. One is a direct result of the other. Care to hear?

[I nodded.]

So in '97 we put the very first rover up on Mars. We started it looking to see if it could support life up there, you know, trying to expand out beyond our own planet. Hell, it's already too crowded here. Has been since man first walked. Best thing about all this social distancing is I have an excuse to tell people to fuck off.

Pathfinder was something though. Ugly little contraption. You wouldn't think it could get ten feet, much less across a barren planet full of dust and rocks. But damn, that little thing moved. It was zipping here and there across the land taking pictures and videos, scooping up samples and analysing them right then and there. Wonder of science.

So we're looking at all these pictures being sent back, amazed at everything we're seeing. There's huge sand dunes, cliffs, this place is like a giant desert but it's *beautiful*. That was when the first storm moved in.

Storms up there aren't like ours. There's no rain. Just wind and lightning. The wind stirs up the sand and makes it hard to see, blocks out most of the light. So Pathfinder is up there, sand and dust swirling around, then in a flash of lightning, you see this towering figure. It was thin, incredibly tall. Everything about it was disproportionate, though. It wasn't until the next flash of lightning that we connected it.

It was another of those damned things from the moon. The ones that appeared when Skylab turned. This one was so much bigger though, at least ten times the size of the first one we saw.

When this one spoke, we all heard it. It wasn't some garbled mess of noise this time, it was plain as day. After it happened, we all realized that we hadn't heard it out loud though, but in our own minds, each one hearing the same thing.

"The temple will live on. We ruled and shall rule again. Worshiping amongst the stars."

Then it was gone along with the storm. Never saw one as large as that again, haven't seen any of them since then actually. Pathfinder didn't have any other encounters up there the entire time, and as far as I've heard from the folks that are still working, they haven't found anything else out of the ordinary.

NASA made it a point to contact the other countries and tell them about the temple at that point. Naturally the Russians already knew about it, the bastards. Turned out they had gone up to the moon at some point and found the ruins of the temple up there, took some of it back with them and ended up having it lose all kinds of control back in '86.

Lotta lives got lost up there because they didn't know what they were fucking around with. They were experimenting with it in some underground lab when it went out of control. But of course what's their first reaction when a fucking space temple and those damned things show up in their backyard? They nuke the thing straight to hell, killing a ton of their own citizens and covering up as some reactor meltdown. The footage they showed us... I'll never forget it.

These bastards didn't even nuke it right away, that's why there was so much fallout. They let it go on for at least a week, absorbing everything and recording what happened. There were people inside that altar room when their worship session broke out. Those poor souls deserved so much more mercy than anyone could give them.

After that, we all agreed that our first priority was protecting the earth from whatever this was, not allowing any of that back down here. That was the time they started on the space station. Now I don't know much of what they've been up to recently with it since it was just being launched when I retired. They built it to keep a better eye on things out there in orbit though, where they could conduct experiments and run some countermeasures right there, without anyone here on Earth being any wiser. Smart move, I think.

I know now long before I left they had a satellite that found that chain of bodies again. The same one that took the first manned crew up there. We could hear the whispers being transmitted back. I still wake up some nights hearing those whispers.

[What did they say?]

"Come to us. Be sacrifices. Float eternal as a living altar to them."

[Them?]

Beats the hell out of me. Maybe it was that big thing they saw on the photos. Maybe that's what the temple was built to worship. Or whatever we were warned about by the Follower. There're so many things we still don't know about what's out there. Probably things we never will know. It's all just lost in the vastness of space, never meant to be understood.

We're still here though. That's something, so they've been keeping us safe until now. Maybe it's something else though, watching over us.

[The moon was out in full on the horizon now, shining bright as it rose further. Gram got up and walked out into the moonlight, looking upward.]

I know you're there, Arthur. I know you're watching over all of us. You stayed up there because you were a stubborn old bastard, thinking you had to do everything to keep people from seeing what you saw. I felt you the other night, though. That full moon, you were there.

We're going to dance in the moonlight together again, real soon. I love you.

[Gram tells me she's going to stay out here for a while. I'm going to go up and start transcribing all of this, maybe get some actual relaxation in. I'm tired of being stuck in this damn house. Gram was dancing around in the moonlight as I walked back inside, humming *Fly Me to the Moon* to herself as she did.]

[April 10, 2020. Gram passed away early this morning. I had walked into the kitchen for a drink and noticed the front door was still cracked open. This wasn't normal for two in the morning, so I walked out to check. Gram was sitting in her rocking chair on the porch, drenched in bright moonlight. She had a smile on her face. She died peacefully in her sleep, carried off into the moonlight by the one she loved.]

TECHNICALLY, HAUNTED

I'm about to break so many NDAs just posting here. There's something really fucky going on though, and people are dead, so something needs to happen. I'm a freelance video editor, and a few weeks ago I got a call about an indie production working on one of those Big Brother-style game shows. This time, the twist was that the guests were going to be in a haunted house, unbeknownst to them.

Look, I'm not here to debate the morality or ethics of that. The producers said nobody would be in danger and they'd be the ones pulling the strings as "ghosts". Yeah, don't think they knew what they were getting into. Whatever, I needed the money and took the job. Now, I don't know if I'll even make it through the next week.

The house in question was massive, with room enough for everyone to maintain their space. Eight main rooms, a huge kitchen, a separate dining room, a separate den and foyer, along with a pool/hot tub combo out back. Honestly, would be a dope house to live in. Except for the ritual suicides and subsequent mass murders that happened in the seventies. That kind of throws off the vibe, no matter how low the real estate price.

From the research I did before taking the job, this house was home to some major tech mogul back in the 90s. Was going to compete with Gates and Jobs, and had all kinds of genius going for him. Then one day he just... broke? Said he found the truth of the world and was going to break us all out of the "manufactured reality we live in". Dude wrote a TON of bullshit about finding some 'precursor' to humanity. From everything he said, it just sounded like he was a few years early to the Matrix. Either way, he took it the Jonestown route and offed his thirty or so followers in a ritual, setting them up in a damn firing limbo line, with each one of them shooting another in the head to dwindle their numbers. Dark shit, and apparently the mogul, Shane Pike, was never seen again. Nobody knows if he got taken in or maybe legitimately ascended, but odds are he's dead.

Everything started simple enough. The contestants, six of them, were in one haunted house. I and the producers, Saul and Shana, would alternate shifts in a nearby trailer, watching a live feed from inside the house at all times. From there, we would mark moments in the tape, saving them to compile into the show after it was done. Not the strangest gig I've taken to pay the rent.

The first few days were pretty normal, to be honest. Everyone settled in—Frank, Indy, Carol, Megan, Pete, and Jacob. All are in their late twenties to mid-thirties and, of course, attractive to ensure drama pops off. Don't fix what ain't broken, as they say. So far, they were all amicable, not really getting on each other's nerves yet. That was until the third night when everything went weird.

It was maybe eleven at night, pitch dark outside with no moonlight to spare, and almost everyone in the house was asleep. Except Pete, who was making his way into the kitchen for something to eat. I was on watch, with the huge camera display up in front of me and at least thirty different angles to see every bit of their lives. Think they only stopped short of putting cameras in the bathrooms because of privacy concerns.

Pete made it down to the kitchen okay, rummaging around cabinets for a minute before finally getting to the fridge. The camera I was watching from faced the refrigerator directly from above, so I could only see him from behind when he opened it. Static started humming over the audio. He could hear it too, turning away from the fridge and shouting at something nearby. The static grew louder, a constant hum in the audio feed as if it was about to completely cut out. He reached into the fridge after deciding whatever was there wasn't worth worrying about, and that's when it went wrong.

The camera glitched for a moment, a figure popping up right next to Pete. Almost as tall as him, but contorted in odd ways. Too many edges and angles to be a real person, but it looked like there were parts of them stretching outward. The static roared to thunder, and the figure disappeared. If Pete noticed it, he didn't even get a chance to make a sound. The camera glitched again before something dragged him away, straight through the door back into the hallway, before he could scream. As quickly as it happened, it was over. The kitchen was still, with the door swinging slowly shut on shelves of food inside.

I almost immediately lost my shit, switching between every camera I could to see if he just ran somewhere else or I was hallucinating. Nope. Pete was nowhere, not a trace of him in the whole house. Poof, gone. It was like he went through a whole other doorway because he never even appeared on the hallway camera, just a black square of darkness in the doorway. Naturally, I called Saul because one of our damn contestants disappeared from thin air, and he was over in a few minutes.

This motherfucker told me he would handle it, I just needed sleep. I know what I saw, Saul, and it wasn't because I was tired. Nevertheless, he kicked me for the night, telling me to get some rest. Didn't have much choice then, so I went back to the hotel.

When I came back in the morning, Saul told me he had found Pete. Though he would no longer be taking part in the contest, citing what Saul said as a "family emergency". In hindsight, yeah, it sounds fishy. At the time, I wasn't going to argue though. They told me there was network interest for the show, so that might mean I could have a steady gig, and I wasn't about to throw that away over a glitched camera.

He announced to the rest of the house and had them do their journals for the day with feelings on them. All the basic "oh, hope he's okay" stuff, y'know. Things got weirder that night though, and I don't think they believed it for long.

Everyone gathered for dinner that night, sitting together in the dining room. Drinks were being poured, and everyone was talking, laughing, shooting the shit about life outside the house. Indy was the first to mention strange happenings.

"Hey, so I was in the bathroom last night and the lights suddenly flickered really bad. Was one of you playing a prank on me?" she asked the entire table. Nobody came forward, everyone just looked at each other unsure.

"I mean I'm not mad. It's just when the lights flickered, I got one of those weird horror movie experiences. It looked like someone was just... standing beside me. There was a big burst of static too. I got goosebumps."

Everyone else still maintained their innocence. Telling her that there wasn't anything to worry about. From the dining room camera I could see the entire table, and into the kitchen through the doorway. If I hadn't been paying attention already, I would've noticed someone walking through the door into the room.

Just a note—for being a relatively low-budget seeming production, Saul and Shana had sprung for the good cameras, and I mean GOOD. These things were giving 8k resolution, and the monitors were able to match it. That's the part that made me concerned about what happened next.

The figure walking in was like god used the least amount of polygons available, only a basic demo of a person. Even worse, there weren't any actual features on the face, just a smiling, ear-to-ear grin with wide eyes that looked as if it was pressed on flat. I felt my skin grow cold as it stood in the doorway, staying there for almost fifteen seconds, surveying the room. I almost fell out of the chair when it turned to me, face suddenly extending on its neck toward the camera.

Apparently, the others in the house took notice of it too, because everyone jumped up screaming. My screen glitched out again, the horrible face briefly popping up in front of me, not just obscuring everything else in the camera but almost popping through my screen. Everyone in the dining room was freaking out, all standing as Carol ran out of the room screaming. Indy was pale, literally having just seen a ghost, and Frank looked ready to fight. Meanwhile, I'm shaking trying to figure out what the hell I just saw. It took me a moment to realize the audio feed was coming in again, with Frank shouting for answers to whoever was listening.

All the noise must have woken Shana in the next room. She came out, asking what was the matter and what the loud noise was. If she understood anything I was babbling about, more power to her, but eventually she said she would just go speak to the guests herself, assuring me it was one of the scares they had set up. All part of the act, supposedly.

I don't buy it. It's been a few days since without much incident, but I think things are only going to get worse. I've seen a few weird things here and there. Glitched pixels moving in some of the cameras, and occasional static when there shouldn't be any interference. Yesterday, one of the couches scooted across the floor around midnight. If these were scares set up by producers, they didn't bother making me aware.

I'll keep a running update if anything happens. Right now, I'm choosing to believe it's just their setup, hopefully all fake. Something's gnawing at me though, telling me that there's something else behind how casual they are about this. There's no way something popping out of my screen was just some kind of glitch.

Nope. Nope nope nope. This place is fucked. And I mean capital F *fucked*. My career is probably done if I make it out of here.

Jacob died today. For sure died, I saw it happen. He had been staying in his room since the dining room incident, almost catatonic after seeing it. Can't say I blamed him, considering the damned thing almost got to me too over the monitor. The others were trying to check on him, but he didn't really want anything to do with the rest. At some point, he turned on the TV, though Saul and Shana only allowed a couple of streaming services for entertainment.

Look, I'm not one to judge someone's taste in movies or anything, and I don't want to speak ill of the dead. That said, the Spawn movie from the nineties was... a hell of a choice. Maybe it was a comfort thing, who knows?

He didn't make it far before the television started glitching out, screen pixelating. I was watching the other camera at the moment, but it caught my eye when the pixilation started because it was extending out of the TV. Spawn was still playing, yet this thing was somehow moving through the actual space in front of the television.

There wasn't even a way to tell what the hell it was. Just pixilation in the air, constantly changing colors like a digital stream. I was fixated, wanting to shout and wake him up but frozen in my seat, blood running cold. It felt like this thing was aware of me, like I was being watched as some kind of... dare? I couldn't shake the chill that was settling over me, making me shake from the cold.

It kept extending from the television, stopping right before the bed as Jacob stared in total horror. He must have been as frozen as I was, sitting with his mouth open but no scream coming out. Crawling backward, pressing himself into the wall wasn't enough to save him. The pixels stopped for a moment before leaping forward immediately toward him. I saw his face open in shock as it pierced his chest, lifting him against the wall as it rose up. He grabbed at it, only clawing at the glimmering air in front of him.

The tendril suddenly retreated back into the television, snapping Jacob back with it. I saw his body fold in half backward as it hit the edge of the television, the tendril still pulling on him. Over the mics I could hear his spine snapping, probably ending any pain he might have felt if he was still alive. As the tendril moved back from the television, yanking him back one more time to make sure everything came through. Indy must have heard the bump, because she ran in out of breath from the next room over.

What she found was an empty room, shitty movie still playing on the television, with no trace that anyone was there otherwise. The sheets were bunched up like they had been left behind that morning in a rush, but otherwise, everything was in place. Indy stood in front of the television, back to it, looking at the bed where Jacob once was. I was breathless, unsure of what to do while watching things go down. Neither Saul nor Shana were here right now, either, so there was nobody in the room with me to tell to go help. I was afraid that if I looked away from the camera, something else would happen.

Whatever happened didn't wait until I looked away though. Indy was grabbed by the neck and yanked backwards through the television in a somehow less violent matter than Jacob. She was gone in seconds, nothing to mark she was there. Three contestants were now gone, with no clue where the fuck they may have gone.

I called Saul, freaking out, and of course, it went to his damn voicemail. Okay, try Shana next... nothing. Fucking voicemail again, except this time I got an "inbox full" message with it. I looked up from my phone, trying to see if anything had changed on the screen. Another figure was standing in the room now. Not one I recognized though, someone dressed a few decades out of style, tall, with messy brown hair falling over thick glasses.

He turned to me, lifting a finger to his lips in a hush sign, looking directly through the camera at me. Pixilation hit again, and he disappeared, totally gone with nothing left. Shana finally called me back then, asking what was so frantic that I called both of them (super bitchy in hindsight). Then she told me that I'm freaking out over nothing AGAIN, emphasizing that they're in control of everything and will handle any issues that happen. She reminded me that they have pre-planned scares that will mess with the guests, but that's not reassuring AT ALL. When I tried pressing her to give me a list of scares so I could at least be prepared, she said she didn't want me spoiling it for any of the contestants left.

This has to be a prank on me, right? One of those hidden camera reality shows, but on some meta-level where I'm the joke? I don't like it, even if it's not some cruel joke. There's no way the sound I heard his back make was fake.

I finally made the decision. Not going to lie, I was kind of expecting the outcome, but it is what it is, I guess. I called the police and told them I had just witnessed a possible murder, and they were on their way. Took probably two hours for them to get there, even then. Gotta love the police system in America,

When they finally got there, Saul had arrived around the same time. He intercepted them before I even realized they were there, pulling up to the main house and waiting at the doorway like a goddamn realtor ready to make the sale. He assured the cops that there was nothing wrong, showed them the filming permits, and laughed it off, saying that maybe they would make it on television. That seemed to get one of them pretty excited, saying his wife would be so jealous to hear. Then they got back in the squad car and left. Not a thing was done, nobody in the house was even aware of what had happened.

Saul came up to the editing trailer after they left, a look of disappointment on his face like I was a kid caught sneaking out. This jackass gave me a legitimate "I'm not mad, just disappointed" speech and told me I could go for the day, he would take over. I want to leave. I want to get the hell out of this place. I don't like anything that's going on. There's this constant feeling of cold on my skin that won't go away, like I've got permanent goosebumps. Hair standing on end as if I was in the middle of a storm of static. Nothing made it go away.

I can't leave though. I can't let the three left in there meet the same fate. I'm going to do something about it, but I'll have to wait until Saul and Shana are gone to do anything. If I get out of this I'll update, wish me luck.

Fuck that house. Fuck Saul and Shana. Fuck this job, I'm going back to a damn call center. I have no more fucks to give about editing.

I formed a plan last night laying in my hotel room. Honestly was just waiting to hear that Saul and Shana cancelled my stay since it was on their dime. Thankfully things seemed to go on just like normal. Guess they needed me more than they wanted me gone. Shana switched out when I got there, just giving me a glare when I came in before she left. Guess she had heard what happened. Whatever, it made things easier for me since she left so quickly.

Unfortunately, that's where the easy parts would stop. I was planning to wait for a few minutes and watch cameras, just to make sure neither of them were coming back. Maybe I was trying to steel my nerves too, keeping a watchful eye over the remaining three guests while contemplating my next move. They obviously were on edge at this point, even just from their body language. Must have figured out something fucky was going on at this point.

At one point, Frank walked outside, producing a cig from his pocket and lighting up by the pool. It was only a moment before the entire pool began shimmering like moonlight hitting it in waves. A dark figure began rising out of the water. Frank didn't notice right away, only turning after whatever the figure was had risen above the surface in the middle of the pool.

I was out of the trailer and on the ground before I realized I had moved. All I could think was that he wouldn't be there by the time I got to the door, but I still had to try, right? The dark figure that was rising from the pool looked formless, soaked as if wearing long robes, water sliding from it. The air around it was pixelating, distorting itself on the screen. I feared what I would find when I got there.

Nobody opened the door as I furiously knocked, so I took it into my own hands, running around the back toward the pool area. The small fence had a rusted latch, thankfully, or running into it full force probably would have hurt a lot more. Though I wasn't feeling much pain as I took in the sight before me.

The entire pool was bubbling, the water putting off massive amounts of steam as it boiled. Frank's back was still to it, so I'm assuming he hadn't noticed yet. It took only seconds for everything to go straight to hell. The figure rising from the pool snapped a tendril forward, almost making the burning water come alive. It must have still been incredibly hot, because Frank screamed out in pain as it wrapped around his torso. He was jerked back so hard the force of it made something snap inside him. Barely a scream came out as his flesh was boiled, sloughing from his limbs in the pixelating water.

"NO!" I screamed before I realized, angry at myself that I was too slow to save him. That meant Meagan and Carol were the only ones left, and I had no idea where they were. That was the least of my worries though, because the pool was still boiling, water starting to splash out from the ferocity of the frothing, steaming Frank stew. His body was bloated and red now, his blood mixing into the water as it boiled. In the middle of the pool, above him, the form began pulsating, taking shape into the same terror that had taken the others.

The Glitch began moving toward me, gliding over the surface of the water as it kept absorbing stray parts of Frank's flesh, now pixelating in the air as it floated toward the terror. It was becoming more clear with every bit that attached, taking a more humanlike shape. The smiling, painted on face stared at me as it moved forward, hunger in the static eyes.

It was only by dumb luck that I fell backwards out of the gate, scrambling back out of the gate. I rushed as fast as I could back around to the front of the house, still determined to get the women out alive if I could. Instead of waiting for someone to open the door though, I picked up one of the decorative stones lining the garden, hurling it with all my might through one of the large windows out front.

"The hell?" A voice from inside, Meagan's I think, shouted faintly as the glass shattered into dangerous blades. Even the sting of glass cutting my arms and legs as I climbed through faded into the background, my heart beating with adrenaline. Both women were standing in the living room area, staring at me as I fell to the ground on the other side. Carol was holding a lamp for self-defense. "Who the hell are you?"

I couldn't really blame them for being scared. I know I looked like a fucking madman breaking into this house. Maybe they thought it was a part of the show, likely they had no idea at this point that this wasn't really a show.

"You need to leave. Now," I managed to gasp out, blood running down my arm in warm trails thanks to the glass. "Frank is gone. It's on its way. Please."

It was too late. I could see the Glitch moving in from behind them, passing right through the doorway like it wasn't there, leaving scorch marks around it like an electrical fire. Meagan went stiff, falling over like she was hit by a taser. Before she could even hit the ground, the Glitch pulled her in, absorbing her without a sound. It turned to Carol, frozen until the last moment when she jumped away from it, running for the door.

She burst through, myself following close to escape from the damned thing. I didn't make it three steps off the porch before I felt cold steel pressing against my forehead, hard.

Saul stood in front of me, a pistol in hand aimed at my head. Nearby, Carol was in the same situation, held up by Shana. She was crying, hands over her head, begging Shana for her life.

"I told you not to interfere. All you had to do was watch the footage," Saul said, putting his finger to the trigger. "You were supposed to help us show the world."

"You're killing people, man. What the hell is this place? What are you?" I was shaking. I've never been in a situation like this, staring death down the barrel. I see why people piss themselves in fear now, because it almost happened.

"We're being good disciples," he said simply, motioning with the gun for us to go back inside. "Go to the pool. We'll hand you over ourselves."

"I can't wait to see him again," Shana said, glee in her voice. She kicked Carol forward, making her fall on the porch. Despite that, she still scrambled up, working her way toward the back door. The Glitch was nowhere to be seen, with only the burn marks on the door to show it was ever there.

When we finally got out to the pool, Frank's cooked body was floating on the surface, eyes melting and flesh exposed on his face. It looked like other parts of his body still under the water were just bone at this point, muscle barely hanging on. The water began boiling again, bubbles building from the bottom in anticipation. I noticed the temperature and jet control for the hot tub nearby, flickering with the number display constantly changing, finally zeroing out with an error. I had an idea, I just wasn't sure if it would work.

Saul and Shana came in behind us, dropping their guns down to their sides as we stood behind the rolling water. Saul was maybe five feet from me, close to the temp control. I could see the figure forming in the middle of the pool again, rising from under the water.

"I'm sorry it took so long, father," Shana said, looking at the silhouette. "We have the last of them, and an extra just in case. They have to let you go now."

The figure from the pool began to arise, another face forming in it. Though I couldn't quite tell, it looked like the same figure that made the shush sign to me yesterday, but it was... emerging from the Glitch as it moved closer? The water was boiling even hotter now, steam rising fast from the surface. I readied myself.

"Oh my faithful," the figure said, gliding forward as the Glitch still enveloped him. "Thank you for returning."

Saul and Shana were smiling, waiting for him to reach the solid ground and anoint them. It was quite the shock they got when instead the Glitch stabbed two tendrils out, the boiling water quickly piercing them through the stomach, scalding them from the inside out. Their mouths were open in horror as his face came closer, flashing and pixelating between human and the low-res, drawn on texture from the Glitch.

"I didn't ask you to, though," the figure said, malice now dripping from his voice as it distorted with static. "I quite like it on the other side. It's quiet, solitary. I would rather not leave."

They began to break down, Saul and Shana decaying into red pixels in the air that flew toward the Glitch. I took my chance while they were otherwise distracted, making a dive for Saul's gun that was now on the ground. The Glitch only looked at me, the textured face showing an eerie smile.

"You don't have to be violent. That won't work on me anyway now," he said, still looking at the gun in my hand. I aimed it at the wall, right in the direction of the control monitor. He must have recognized what I was doing. "Oh, go ahead. Like I said, I don't really want to leave."

It whipped Saul and Shana back into the Glitch, tendrils retracting quickly to absorb them into the digitized, glitching body.

I pulled the trigger, hitting the monitor right on the screen, making a small electrical fire start. As power faded from the box, the Glitch began breaking down, water slowing as the temperature cooled. He was just smiling as his face disappeared in a storm of pixels, digitizing into thin air.

Carol was still sobbing on the ground as I threw the gun away, causing it to land in the pool. I made my way over, offering a hand to help her up. The fire was starting to grow nearby, spreading along the wall.

As both of us walked from the house, still shaking from the ordeal, flames began to lick inside, from the living area to the other rooms, enveloping everything in moments. We left into the night, letting the funeral pyre burn itself into cinders as firetruck lights lit up the distance.

WAVES

Have you ever just sat on a beach watching the waves crashing into the shore and retreating back out to sea? Have you noticed driftwood or shells being dragged back out, not knowing where they would end up next?

Every morning I sit here, looking out into the ocean where the grey sky meets the dark water on the horizon. I wait. Wait to see one of *them* wash in with the tide, drifting up onto the hard packed sand. As soon as I see them, I run from my position, grabbing them and dragging their limp bodies further up the beach, laying them to rest in the soft sand near the brush-filled dunes.

That's when I set to work. It's a ritual I've performed since I was a child, being trained by my father, just like his father did for him. I look down at the naked body, always different. Sometimes a man, sometimes a woman, ranging from a younger adult to decrepit and old. Some have been thin, some obese. Once the drifter was missing a leg, making the ritual difficult to perform in its entirety. I make do, though.

I lay them on their backs, feet facing land, and head to the water. Their arms stretched out to their sides in a crucifix position. I know I have to work quickly, before they wake up. I've never had the misfortune of seeing it before, but have been told the stories of what happens if they wake before the ritual is complete. The entire island could be erased in the blink of an eye. Generations of work, my bloodline, all for naught.

I'm getting distracted, sorry. The ritual. While in the crucifix position, I start the runes. Beginning with each hand and foot, I carve the same sequence going inward towards the body, from the tips of the fingers and toes, moving counter-clockwise from the left hand to the feet, and finishing with the right hand. The work is methodical. My knife moves with a determined precision, honed with twenty years of practice. Their blood flows blue, staining the sands with an almost neon hue. A scent of ammonia lingered with it.

When every limb has been carved, I start at the top of the head, moving from the small bump in the middle of their forehead down toward the chest. They bleed much more when I get to the neck, as one of the runes must cut right across the jugular. Their blood sprays, leaving a shower on the surrounding sand. Some days it mixes with the drizzle of rain, creating a bluish mist that floats across the beach.

Finally, the runes are finished. The ritual is almost complete. I lay my knife down and wipe my hand across the drifter's throat, making sure I have enough blood to finish. I swipe their blood across my own forehead, leaving a horizontal line above my eyes, then drawing a vertical line under each of my eyes. This is my warpaint. I alone stand against these terrors, protecting my island community, and by extension, the world.

The preparations are done. I pick up the knife once more and walk to meet the crashing waves. The final step. My hand dips under the saltwater, opening with my palm up. The waves crash in, and as soon as they begin to be pulled back to the sea, I swipe the knife across, letting my own blood flow freely and mix with the water. This is the final offering, the plea to whatever gods rule over the sea, to end this monstrosity and keep us safe.

The saltwater stings as I bring my hand back up, the cold air adding to the pain. My feet slide across the sand as I walk back to the drifter. Lifting the knife, still dripping with the mix of my blood and saltwater, I plunge it into the middle of the drifter's chest, into the diaphragm.

The same reaction every time. Their eyes snap open. A final, desperate gasp for air. All in vain. I've severed the muscle that allows them to draw breath. They slowly drown as whatever blood is left in them fills their lungs, screaming curses in a language I don't understand.

When the ritual is done and the last spasms go through their bodies, I grab the can of gasoline and the herbs I keep in a small shack on the beach. I douse the body, setting it alight and throwing the herbs on top. Like sage for cleansing spirits, the bundle of lavender and catnip smolders, sending wisps of their scent through the air. With this, the drifter is cleansed and the island safe once more.

I head back to the village, taking the beaten path carved into the brush by the generations before me. I exchange nice pleasantries with others as I pass by. They thank me for what I do, protecting us from the drifters. I simply nod, telling them it's my duty, nothing more.

I make my way to the village square, heading into the courthouse at the other end. Briggs, our mayor, is waiting for my daily report. He looks up from the papers he's signing as I walk into the room.

"Raleigh, how are you today? Any happenings at the shore?" He shuffles the papers aside and leans back in his seat, motioning to the chair across from him. I sit down in the stiff leather chair, hearing it squeak under me.

"There was one. Older, male. They're coming more often these days. This is the third this week. When I started twenty years ago, we got one every two weeks or so. Should we be worried, sir?"

His brow furrowed with worry. He was an older man, at least sixty. He had lived on the mainland for a while before coming back to the island in his younger years, world-weary and in disbelief at what we had to worry about compared to the outside world. They knew nothing of the drifters. The dangers they posed to our world. The heretic god they served.

"We'll certainly need to keep an eye on it. The records show that more show up preceding times of trouble. The earliest we have on record preceded the black plague. They were at an average of two drifters per day, with the highest number being five washing up at once. Your post was manned by five watchers around the clock, making sure none went uncleansed. We must be vigilant, make sure this doesn't become a problem like then."

"Do you think there could be something terrible on the horizon?" I asked. I was the only one trained in the ritual. My father had me to help when he was my age, and his father and brothers before him, but I was alone. I had taken no wife, had no children, and my only brother was killed as a child. If they began washing up more often, I was the only defense.

"As of yet, there's no way to tell. We simply must pay attention. Find someone from the village that shows promise, take them to be trained. You may need help," he answered, waving me off. I got up to walk out. "Raleigh?"

I turned back, giving him a questioning look. He dug around in his desk drawer before withdrawing a long, thin blade in a black scabbard. He pulled the blade out of the sheath by a few inches, showing me a startlingly pristine edge with the runes I use inscribed on it. He sheathed it again and handed it over to me.

"This has been handed down from elder to elder. If the time comes when there are too many, use this. It allows the ritual to be bypassed."

I bowed and thanked him as I took the saber. In all my research and learning about my position, I had never heard of this. We had always been told the ritual was the only way. I headed out and back to my house, lost in thought as I walked. I was shaken from my daydreaming by screaming coming from down the path, the direction of the shore.

"Raleigh! Raleigh!" Vale, one of the village teenagers. She was shouting for me in a panicked voice, fear rising to overtake any other emotion. "Quick! You have to go to the shore!"

"What's going on?" I stopped her as she ran up, panting for breath. She leaned over and grabbed her knees, gasping.

"Another one.... a drifter... some of the kids were playing in the water and it washed up," she wheezed.

"Shit." I didn't even wait for her to finish. When she said "drifter" I took off, sprinting with all the energy I had. They never washed up past noon, rarely ever after daybreak, even. Two in one day... this is bad. If one wakes up while I'm not there... ruin would follow.

Thankfully, it wasn't far to the shore. As I passed over the dunes, I saw the children gathered around it. The drifter this time appeared to be a woman, old and covered in wrinkles. One of the children had a stick of driftwood they were using to poke at it, nudging it as the waves lapped around.

"Stop!" I shouted, waving my arms as the children continued poking. They looked toward me, a quizzical glint in their eyes. "Get the fuck away from it!"

It happened in slow motion. The drifter's eyes opened. Their unearthly green hue, like emeralds reflecting a blue sea, shined through the haze. I saw the sharp teeth bare themselves and the hands reach for the nearest child. Long claws tore skin and red blood mixed with ocean spray. I heard the boy scream in pain before turning to a low gurgle as blood filled his throat instead.

I wasn't thinking. Instinct took over, and I drew the blade I had just been given. The runes reflected the grey sky, the sharp edge of the blade shining like the sea. I jumped at the drifter and plunged the blade between its neck and shoulder, stabbing downward through the chest and into the gut. It let out a high screech and the wind around picked up, intense howling echoing the drifter's cry. The ocean churned in response, sea foam churning into madness where calm, small waves were before.

"Fucking die!" I screamed. I plunged my hand down into the wound, covering it in blood and painting my face with it. I withdrew the sword, quickly slicing my palm and dipping it into an incoming wave. The drifter screamed again. Clouds moved in, erasing any light that was left. The weather turned from a grey morning to a small hurricane in moments. I knew this had to end quickly.

In one deft movement I stabbed upward, bringing the blade out of the water and impaling the creature. Right on target. The screams died out along with the wind. Peace had returned to the shoreline.

I sat there for a moment collecting myself before turning to look at the gore mixed with ocean. The poor boy, his throat torn out, had passed. I took him in my arms and carried him up to dry sand before going back and gathering the drifter's body. I covered the boy with my coat, and the creature with gasoline. I wanted it to feel the flames of hell.

I sat and watched it burn for a while. Long after the local doctor had come and taken the boy, his mother screaming in grief as she watched. I couldn't come up with words to say I was sorry. I was supposed to protect these people. I was the one that should be dead.

When the last ashes had fizzled out, I still remained. Thinking to myself what could be done to prevent this from happening again.

I didn't know that it would only get worse from here.

<hr>

An account on the discovery of the first drifter

There were two more this morning.

I was waiting, watching the sea thrash and roll. I'm not sure when I drifted off. The same nightmare that kept me up the night before covered me again, leaving me in fits.

I saw the boy's corpse laying in the waves. Blood being pulled out with the sea foam. Suddenly the clouds started rolling in, wind whipping up sand and spray. I saw lightning flash down the shoreline and felt the thunder boom in my chest immediately after. Something was coming.

The waves grew taller with each one that crashed to shore. When I looked closer, I saw that it wasn't just water hitting the shore.

Drifters. Hundreds of them. All tangled into each other in the waves, piling on top of each other as they hit the shore. Levees made of bodies started to block the waves. Suddenly the sky opened above me. The wind stopped. The ocean calmed. The drifters lay in their piles, sleeping like the dead.

The eye of the storm. Just as soon as it started, it was over. A million eyes snapped open at once. Their screams layered each other, creating an unholy chorus as they awoke and began flooding inland.

Right before the flood, I caught a glimpse of the horizon. Grey clouds mired above rolling waves. Through the rain and wind I could see something moving against the sky, wading through the depths of the water towards my home. I had seen pictures of skyscrapers, and this dwarfed them. Just as it began to become clear through the sheets of rain, a bolt of lightning struck in front of it.

I woke with a start, jumping from the sand and looking in the direction it had been. The flood was gone, the day was grey but still. Just a dream. I shook the sleep from my eyes and resumed my vigil.

I spotted one washing in with the waves. Male, middle-aged, other than the bump in the middle of their forehead and the long, claw-like nails, he could have passed for a normal islander. I set to work and was almost done with the carving when I heard a voice from behind me.

"There's another one."

I looked up, startled. Nobody else came out here this early. After what happened, I didn't think anyone would ever come here again. I was surprised even more to see that it was Vale, now nodding towards the shore a ways to my left. I followed her gaze and saw another motionless form crumpled there, sea foam washing over.

"Damn it all," I muttered. Time to kill two birds with one stone. I left the one I was working on and walked over to the new arrival. Before grabbing this one, I dunked my hand into the water and sliced my palm, completing this part of the ritual ahead of time. As I began to drag the body back towards the first drifter, Vale ran up and grabbed the other arm, helping me along.

"It wasn't your fault, you know," she said, grunting with exertion. "I was nearby when they found it... I should have told them to get away before I came to get you. I didn't even think they would do something like that."

"Don't blame yourself," I replied, letting go of the new drifter and kneeling down next to the first. I took out my knife and plunged it into the diaphragm. The piercing scream began, then died out quickly. The new drifter didn't stir.

"If they're showing up more often you're going to need help," she said again, still watching as I doused the first one and struck a match. "Teach me. I can handle it."

I didn't answer her, but threw the match down and started carving the new drifter. Small sizzles could be heard as ocean spray and light rain hit the burning body. I could still feel Vale's eyes on me, intently watching my hands work the knife through skin, carving my legacy in a living canvas.

When the runes were done, I beckoned for her to follow me to the water. She stood beside me as waves lapped over our feet. I looked out at the grey sky and rolling sea, remembering the moment my father brought me out here. How he had carved the runes, then walked me out to the water.

"Have you ever lost someone, Vale?" I asked her. She seemed taken aback by the question at first, and looked down at the water as she pondered it.

"You knew my mother," she said. "You know I lost her."

"You didn't know your mother. She died giving birth to you. Have you ever lost anyone you truly knew and loved?" I shot back.

"Then... no. I guess I haven't."

I sighed and unholstered my knife, turning toward her.

"If you take this on, you will lose someone you love. Maybe more than one. That's what we give up in order to protect the island. Are you prepared to take that on?"

She seemed scared. I couldn't really blame her. She saw the aftermath of what happened yesterday. She knew what we would be dealing with. But underneath the fear there was a desperation. Desperation to prove her strength and protect others.

"I am," she finally answered after staring out at the forming waves. "What do I have to do?"

"You're not of my bloodline, but there are certain cases where others can be allowed in to take over." I looked down at my hand, the cut already clotted with blood. I swept the knife across to reopen it. "Come. We have to go further out."

When we were waist deep in the water, I handed her the knife.

"Cut your palm and hold it open," I said. She winced as the sharp edge of steel sliced her hand. The blood flowed quickly, dripping into the water and leaving a red cloud. I held my hand above hers, making a fist and squeezing so a trickle of blood fell onto her cut. I then opened my own palm, placing it flat on hers so our cuts aligned, and took her hand under the water. She drew a deep breath in through her teeth as the saltwater hit open flesh, but composed herself quickly.

"I, Raleigh Carrous, do hereby pass my bloodline on to Vale Jensen. Having no living children, and having taken no wife, I realize that any day my bloodline may die and our cleansing end. Vale has offered herself as a tribute to the ocean, pledging to protect the island and all inhabiting it from the drifters and the heretical gods they serve. Do you accept this duty, Vale?"

"Yes," she replied. I motioned for her to walk further into the water, letting go of her hand. She looked at me, asking, "How far?"

"Until the sea takes you," I replied. She nodded, walking further. At about ten meters out she was completely engulfed, going under the water. She came up moments later, walking back to my position. Her usually wild, curly hair was now limp and soaked around her shoulders. She shined with a new purpose as she rejoined me.

"You are aware that with this acceptance you may never leave the island, being the first and last defense against the unknown. You know that the ocean requires a heavy toll for your service and the power bestowed upon you. Do you still accept?" I hoped she would say no but knew in my heart she couldn't. It was the same feeling I had, thinking back to when I took the oath, my father standing in my place. Once you had the notion to take on this duty, it never left you.

"Yes," she said again.

"Vale Jensen, by my power and authority, being the last remaining of my bloodline, I surrender you to the sea. Today you are born anew in the salt and brine of the ocean." I withdrew my hand from the water, turning my fingers down so the mix of saltwater and blood coated my finger tips.

I drew the rune of rebirth on her face, a clockwise spiral ending in a smaller spiral spinning counterclockwise from the center. The ever flowing dichotomy of life and the sea.

"I swear to serve with my life," she replied, giving a small bow.

"We'll start your training tomorrow." I told her. "For now, I will finish this ritual. You will walk back to the village and stand in the square until I return. Tell anyone that asks you are now my apprentice."

"Yes, sir," she said, walking back up the beach.

I sighed as she left, taking myself back up to where the newest drifter lay on the sand. I kneeled next to it, hefting my knife once more. I placed it above the diaphragm, one hand holding it steady while the other was poised above it, ready to thrust downward. I bowed my head, closing my eyes and whispering a prayer.

"Protect her. Let me be the father to her I could never be to my own daughter," I muttered. My hand raised up, tensing at the expectation of pain when it hit the knife handle. I was more surprised to feel the hand on my wrist as it moved downward. My eyes snapped open to see the drifter grabbing on, holding my hand back.

"Our numbers are infinite," it said. "We serve, and we will be rewarded. We will devour you. Drown you in the blood of your loved ones. We are vast as the ocean and relentless as the waves. We. Will. Break. You."

The pure hatred in its eyes terrified me. I had never seen anything like it, the pure, dripping spite. It bore through my skin and into my soul. It despised me, and that cold, unfeeling stare almost seemed to freeze the entire world. I forced myself to move as it opened its mouth wide to scream, making the wind pick up and clouds go dim.

My other hand plunged the knife in. Its screams turned to wet gurgles as it drowned, choking on blood. I fell back in the sand, shaking. After what seemed like eternity, I pulled the knife from its chest and got the gas can and herbs, beginning the final step of cleansing. I didn't stay to make sure the fire was put out, but instead rushed back up the path to the village, stopping at the first person I saw.

"'Ello, Raleigh. Anything I can do for you?" he said. I didn't remember his name, but recognized him from the butcher shop in town.

"I need you to go to the shore and keep watch. If any wash up, come get me. I'll be speaking to Briggs in his office." He looked at me quizzically, not quite understanding why I would want an untrained person watching the shore. I ended up losing my temper, "JUST FUCKING GO!"

He tore off up the path, leaving a dust cloud behind him. I rushed into the square, grabbing Vale who was standing in the middle, chatting with some of the village women who were congratulating her. We barged into the office, to Briggs' surprise.

"Raleigh. You didn't tell me you had chosen an apprentice already. I should have had final appro-" I cut him off before he finished.

"What the FUCK is happening, Briggs?" I shouted, causing both him and Vale to wince in return. "One of those damned things GRABBED me and FUCKING SPOKE! They've *never* spoken before."

His eyes grew wide. I could see Vale bring a hand to her mouth next to me. Briggs sat back in his chair, reaching into a drawer and pulling out a tall bottle filled with dark amber. He produced three glasses from the same drawer and started pouring.

"I'm sorry for overstepping your authority," he said, raising the glass to his lips and sloshing half of it down his shirt from shaking hands. "I had hoped this wouldn't happen while I was in charge. Guess I hoped for too much."

He drained his glass, then got up and walked over to a portrait on the wall. Pulling the portrait up and setting it down on the floor, he revealed a safe behind it. He opened it and pulled out a large, leather-bound book, yellowed with age. The next item he revealed was an old flintlock pistol.

"Everything you'll need to know is in there," he said, motioning to the book. "I'm sorry, but this... it's just too much."

"Too much?" I asked him, getting to my feet. "I don't know what the hell is going on, Briggs. Don't tell me how it's 'too much'."

"Did I ever tell you about my travels as a youth?" Briggs spoke quietly, not making eye contact. "I spent a lot of time on ships, going from port to port and trading goods. Saw a lot in those days. The beauty of nature out on the high seas, and the terror of it... I know you're aware of what it's like to lose someone you love, Raleigh. I lost the woman I loved. Desperately grabbing for her, hanging over the side of our boat as she was dragged under. It's things like that you never forget."

He raised the gun to his temple and cocked the hammer. I barely had time to grab Vale and avert her eyes when he pulled the trigger. Warm blood and sharp skull fragments sprayed over us.

———

The past twenty-four hours have been a blur. I only remember walking Vale out into the square, both of us spattered with blood and grey matter. Everyone looking at us, some screaming, some crying. I sat Vale down on a bench and motioned for a nearby woman to come over.

"Take care of her. If she's not in shock yet, she will be soon," I said, then turned to walk back into the building. "Also, call for the doctor. I'll need his help moving Briggs."

The smell had already gotten bad inside. Copper. Sharp. It took me by surprise after dealing with the ammonia-tinged blood of the drifters for so long. I looked down at Briggs' body, small wisps of steam rising from the open wound as cold air drafted in.

"Cowardly fuckin' bastard," I muttered to his body. For probably the first time since my father had brought me out to the beach, I was scared. I had seen the soul drain from Briggs' face when I told him about the drifter speaking. He knew things I never did, things that he didn't want to face. But what?

The book was still lying on the desk where he had left it, now covered in a messy layer of gore. I grabbed a nearby cloth and wiped it clean, trying my best to get all the pieces of brain and skull off. Runes were emblazoned on the cover. Some of them I had never seen before.

I opened the book and began reading. The pages were old and yellowed, with spots here and there from where ink had been spilled and, what I think, was blood. There were illustrations of drifters, making detailed notes of their anatomy and physiological traits. The next page showed the rune configurations, as well as the carving for the ritual. I had just begun to flip through to another when there was a knock on the door.

"Raleigh... what the hell happened here?" Gareth, our local doctor, was standing in the doorway, a handkerchief held over his face. He gazed around the room in horror before settling on Briggs' body. "Oh... god. Briggs..."

"You know anything about all this?" I asked him, drawing his eyes to the book. He shook his head, looking instead at the flintlock pistol still clutched in Briggs' hand.

"So he did this to himself?"

"Yeah. Told him about the drifter that just spoke while I was doing the ritual. He handed me this book, then blew his goddamn brains out. I haven't seen anyone that terrified since, well..."

"Your brother," Gareth finished my thought. "Go, Raleigh. I'll take care of this. I know this brings back painful memories for you."

He moved from the doorway, revealing that Vale was standing behind him, still with a look of shock on her face. I snatched the book off the desk and walked briskly out, grabbing her arm and turning her from the grisly scene. There were tear tracks through the blood on her face.

We walked in silence towards her home. When we finally reached it, I sent her inside to clean up and sat on the porch to look further into the book. The first half seemed to be all things I already knew, about the ritual, the drifters' anatomy, a cypher of the runes... then something different caught my eye.

It was another illustration, but this one of a human. Multiple drawings of the same person, but with subtle changes between each one. Initially, it was a lengthening of nails and teeth, small gills growing in near the nape of the neck... then the eyes turning. I don't know what they used to capture the color of the eyes in the illustration, but it was hauntingly lifelike.

The next page held notes and more illustrations. Large ships at sea during a storm, being rocked by the waves. A figure standing in the water, towering above them. Then the ships being torn asunder by the wind and surf.

One survivor of cargo ship Fate's Rest, a man by the name of William Stetler, noted that before the ship sank, he witnessed a looming giant on the horizon.

I remembered my dream. The giant looming behind the waves of drifters, a general commanding his army.

Stetler swears he saw this figure smash the ships with its own hands, causing all onboard to fall into the water. Here he says they were set upon by people that looked just like them, save for a small bump in their foreheads and elongated claws and teeth. Stetler says these figures would drag the surviving crew and passengers under the water, never to resurface.

The book went on to explain how Stetler had survived. He was knocked out by a plank of wood hitting him in the water, and managed to wash up on the island, much like the drifters do. When the watchman on the shore at the time found him he was almost cleansed with the ritual, only saved because his blood was red instead of blue. Safe to say this was a surprise for the watchman.

Stetler joined the watch through marriage eventually, choosing to stay on the island instead of going back to his home on the mainland. He is responsible for one of the greatest breakthrough in our understanding of the drifters.

Ten years after the accident and Stetler was on duty keeping watch one morning. When a drifter washed in, he moved to retrieve it as he normally would, but was frozen with fear upon looking at the face.

Vale walked back outside, looking at me with concern as she wrung water from her hair.

"What are we going to do?" she asked, sitting down next to me. I didn't answer, still reading and re-reading the same sentence.

Stetler recognized his brother, Jacob Stetler, who he had last seen dragged under the surface ten years previous. He hadn't aged, and the only difference was the small bump on his head.

"Vale," I said, looking at her. "There are things I'm still learning, along with you. Things that may cause me to falter in the coming days and weeks. I need you to promise me that if I hesitate, you will step in and finish the job."

"I promise," Vale said, still looking concerned. "What's going to happen, Raleigh?"

Just then, someone came running up the path, shouting my name. I recognized the same man I had stationed at the shoreline, out of breath and wild-eyed.

"Please! Please come quick! It's going into the village!" He stopped in front of the house, panting and shaking.

"Calm down, what the hell do you mean?" I asked, jumping from my chair. "And how did you know I was here?"

"Doc Gareth told me you were taking Vale home. I saw... well, I saw Briggs." He almost looked like he was going to vomit when he said it, thinking of the mess in Briggs' office. "A drifter washed up on shore. I saw it and started coming to get you but then it, well, it spoke to me. It asked where you were, Raleigh!"

"Fucking hell," I said, beginning to gather my things and start back toward the village. He stopped me again before I could walk off.

"No, Raleigh. This one... it ain't like the others," he said, waving his hands frantically in front of him. "It's him, Raleigh. I don't know how, but it's *him*!"

"Who, goddammit? Who is it?" Vale was shouting at him now, trying to make sense of this whole situation.

"River..." the man whispered, looking down at the ground. I stopped dead in my tracks. I couldn't move. There was no way it could be him. He was gone, dead, his body was never found. This guy just didn't remember what he looked like. He was confused.

"Who the hell is River?" Vale asked, getting impatient at the lack of answers.

I turned to look at her, grabbing the rune inscribed blade from my bag in the process. I handed it over to her.

"You don't know the ritual yet, and I may not be able to see this one through," I said.

"Will anyone please tell me what's going on? I can't help when I'm in the fucking dark here." Vale was practically screaming now, tearing at her hair. "Who in the *fuck* is River and why are you so worried about him?"

I felt tears forming in my eyes as I looked at her. Hot bile burned in my throat and I almost choked on the words as they came up.

"River was my brother."

Silence smothered us as we walked back to the village square. I was beyond lost. It hit me when I read the book that something like this could be possible, but I didn't think it would happen this soon. Vale was certainly worried, shooting me looks of concern between looking down at the blade I had given her. Finally, she spoke.

"What did you mean that he was your brother? What happened?"

I knew that she needed to know. Knew that she was only asking so she could be prepared. I resented it all the same. I had grieved River since the day I lost him, and it was only compounded by losing dad days later. Did my dad know about this? Is that why... why he did what he did?

"Makes sense you don't remember it. You would have been very young," I finally replied, the words sounding as if they were coming from somewhere far away. "River was out with dad and I one day keeping watch. He was playing in the water while dad and I were patrolling... he was there one second and gone the next. I don't know if it was a riptide or something else... he was just gone."

"So you never found his body?" Vale whispered. I could feel the chill in her voice. She realized where this was going.

"That was twelve years ago, Vale. He was six years old. We never found him." There was a noticeable shakiness in my voice as I started to say what I feared. "Dad... dad blamed himself. Or maybe he knew the truth. Either way... he killed himself that night. Walked right out to the beach, stood in the waves and slashed his own throat."

"Dear god." Vale let out a small gasp.

"I found him the next morning. Tide was going out when he did it, so he didn't wash away. He was just laying there in a tide pool of his own blood. I-" My voice cracked, remembering that day. I could still feel the cold rain stinging as it hit my skin. The wind scraping my face. Sitting in the pool of his blood and shaking him, hoping he would wake up. "I just sat there until I saw a drifter wash up. Then I had a duty. Something I was the only one fit for. Only I could do until now."

The village square was in sight now. I could see a crowd of people gathered around, all holding on to each other and staring at something in the middle. I stopped in the path, causing Vale to almost run into me. She hefted the blade in its sheath and looked at me expectantly as I turned to her.

"Remember what I told you."

"Step in if you falter." She nodded to me as she said it. If she was scared, she wasn't going to show it. Her grey eyes like the steel of the blade. She was well suited for this.

"If I make any sign of weakness, of not being able to do this, kill it," I said, reaffirming. "I can't promise emotion won't get the better of me. If I move to stop you, cut me down."

"Raleigh!" She looked shocked at this, but the resolve returned moments later. "... okay."

We walked the remaining hundred yards or so into the square, the crowd parting as we came. As the last of them moved, I could see what they had been staring at.

A boy, no older than the day he had disappeared, standing in the middle of the square. He had the signature bump of the drifters, and pointed fingernails and teeth. Nothing had changed. He still had the short cropped haircut that Dad had given him just days before he disappeared, and I could see the small slits in his neck where gills had taken shape. He gave me a sharp smile as I approached.

"You grew up," he said. His voice was more guttural than I remembered. The innocence of a child's voice was gone, replaced by menace and bloodlust. "I've missed you, big brother."

"River," I replied simply. I could feel hot tears stinging my eyes. I knew he was dangerous. He could rip me to pieces in seconds if I let my guard down. It didn't change the fact that he was my brother once. He still looked like that six-year-old boy that disappeared in the waves.

"You don't seem as happy as I thought you would. I was hoping for more of a reunion," he replied. He looked around at the crowd that was still looking on, staring at him in horror. "What? I feel like you're all scared of me."

"What happened to you, River?" I managed to choke out. I was showing weakness. No doubt he would try to take advantage of this.

"The ocean takes us all, eventually," he replied. "Some of us earlier than others. You and Dad didn't keep your eyes on me, and now here I am. I've come back for you, though. I wanted to show you all the wonderful things I've learned. All the amazing sights and feelings. They've taught me a lot in these few years I've been gone."

"Who?" I asked.

"The others like me, of course. There are quite a few of us, as I'm sure you've noticed in the past few days. We've been busy. Recruiting, creating, swelling our ranks. We bring more to him, and he makes them like us. I'm sure I can put in a good word for you all."

"River. This isn't you." I was talking more to myself at this point than him. I didn't want to believe this was what my brother had become. Didn't want to believe he could be this monster.

"YOU WOULDN'T KNOW WHO I AM!" he roared, causing dark clouds to roll in and the wind to rise. I looked around, motioning everyone to stand back. I noticed then that Vale was no longer beside me.

"Please, brother. Let's not do this. Come back to us. You don't have to be this way," I said to him, trying to look around for Vale without him noticing. I finally spotted her in the crowd of people, slowly moving her way through the masses, trying to flank River. I had to keep him distracted.

"There's no going back now. This island won't exist for much longer. All will be swallowed by the ocean soon enough. You'll all join us, or drown. Some of you have a choice. Some don't." He took a step forward, opening his arms toward me. "I wanted to bring you with me, Raleigh. To extend an offer. I can bring you with me, and you can be made new. Quick. Painless."

"I want to help you," I continued.

Vale was almost behind him. Just another minute and she would be in place.

"Oh, but I want to help *you*." River sneered back at me. Vale looked at me and nodded. *Now.*

I lunged forward at the same moment she did. Her with the blade drawn, me with my knife. All I could see before striking was River's twisted smile.

Vale struck just right, stabbing right into his spine. My knife found its mark in his throat, cutting any sound from him short. He managed to get two good swipes of his claws in, one striking Vale across the face and leaving four long, jagged ravines of open flesh from her left eye down to her chin. The other hand managed to catch me in the stomach, knocking the wind from me and gouging into my flesh. I felt his hand tighten into a fist, closing around whatever internal organs he could.

"Get some fucking rope!" I shouted at the onlookers. Two of them ran toward the nearest building and found a halfway weaved fishing net that had been left there in the excitement of the day, throwing it to Vale and I. We quickly wrapped it around River, making sure he was bound right before cutting a strip of fabric from my sleeve and stuffing it in his mouth.

"There. No storms if he can't scream," I said, sitting back on the ground and clutching my stomach. I looked down to assess the damage and could see heavy bleeding, as well as some of my insides where they shouldn't be. "Gareth! Where's Gareth? Fuck!"

Vale ran to my side, taking off her coat and applying pressure to my stomach. Her eye was swollen shut at this point. She would be lucky to see out of it again.

"Vale. Help him. Please." I was gasping at this point. The adrenaline was wearing off and the pain taking over. The last thing I saw before passing out was Vale, tears mixing with the blood on her face, and River smiling at me on the ground.

I'm awake again. It's been two days since we subdued River. Gareth patched me up best he could, but the diagnosis is grim. River managed to do some damage while he was in there.

Vale told me she has him locked away in Briggs' office. Said he's fucking tied up in there, smiling at anyone who comes by. Half her face is covered in bandages. Gareth said her eye should heal, but she'll never regain one hundred percent of her sight.

"I've been researching the book," she tells me. Says she's learned the runes and memorized the ritual. She said there's also some talk of an older ritual. One talked about from long ago by long gone ancestors. Something that may be able to stop all of this once and for all.

"That... god, I guess you could call it," Vale says, "The giant that creates them? There's the thought here and there by whoever put this together. They translated from some ancient notes left behind by the first inhabitants of our island. Whoever wrote this thinks that if two sacrifices are made then he can be weakened and bound undersea."

She went on explaining this further, but I was drifting in and out from pain. Eventually, Gareth came back in and gave me a new dose of medicine. It didn't do much for the pain, but it sedated me.

I'm in and out now. Vale is working on figuring out this ritual. If she can crack it, we may just have a way to end all of this. I just hope I'll live to see it.

———

Hell came to our island. Death came to our island.

It was beginning to get dark outside. I was still recovering, hoping for the medicine that Gareth had given me to kick in soon so I didn't have to feel this throbbing pain nearly as much. I flipped through the book as I waited, the lamp beside me causing the pages to almost glow yellow.

There were notes scribbled in the margins wherever they would fit, all in different handwriting. I had to wonder if these were written by cleansers before me. How old was this book? What happened to all of these people, if they had these notes and theories about the end, but still couldn't bring it about? Was there something we weren't seeing in all of this?

I flipped the page again and noticed there were no notes scribbled for the first time in at least a hundred pages. Instead, there was just one stanza of a poem, like a prophecy being laid out before me, written in beautiful script.

When waves ride high and oceans flood
Rain and wind howl, filled with blood
Into the sea brothers of red and blue Ending waters wrath, be-
ginning days anew

"Holy shit," I said under my breath. This was it. This was the answer. This was how to stop everything. "Raleigh! Raleigh wake up!"

He stirred from the bed against the opposite wall, still in a drugged stupor. Gareth had said his condition wasn't promising. When River plunged his hand in, he had severed quite a few of his intestines, causing massive internal bleeding. Gareth did as much as he could, but he wasn't outfitted for major surgery on this level. Raleigh turned to me, eyes barely open.

"Josephine?" he mumbled, looking at me in surprise. "Are you here to take me away? You've grown so much..."

"No, Raleigh. It's me, Vale," I said. Gareth had told me he may hallucinate due to the medicine. "I've found it, Raleigh."

"I'm not ready, Josephine," he muttered back. Tears stung my eyes seeing this man broken. He had protected our island for so long. Brought me under his wing without a question. I cried a little more as tears tracked their way across my still open wounds.

There came a soft knock at the door as Gareth walked in, holding another vial of medicine and an armful of clean bandages. He looked at me as Raleigh muttered for Josephine once more.

"Poor man... he hasn't spoken about her in years," Gareth said.

"Who was Josephine?" I asked him. He let out a sigh and sat next to the bed, beginning to dress Raleigh's wounds again.

"The only person he ever loved," Gareth replied. "Josephine was his daughter."

"Where is she now?"

"Whatever heaven you believe. She only lived for an hour after birth. Passed away not long after her mother," he answered. "Think that's why he took to you so well. You reminded him of what he lost."

I couldn't hold it back any longer. Tears began to flow freely, stinging my wound even worse than before. I had no family. My mother died during childbirth. My father killed not long after my conception. The village raised me, and Raleigh had always been there, offering advice or helping where he could. Now here he was, dying just a few feet away.

Gareth finished wrapping the new bandages and stood up, handing me the vial.

"Give this to him when he wakes up, it'll help with the pain." He patted me on the shoulder as he began to walk out the door. Raleigh stirred.

"Gareth?" he muttered. "Gareth, I need to go."

He turned back around, looking to Raleigh.

"Rest, old friend. We'll be safe until you're ready," he said.

As he opened the door to step outside, a scream pierced the air. Rising wind followed it within seconds.

"Help! Help me, please!" came a voice from somewhere outside. It began to scream again but was cut off in a moment.

"Drag them to the waves!" Came another voice, this one guttural, like the sound of rocks scraping against the ocean floor. "Bring them to Panthalasin, so he may shape them in his image!"

"Fucking hell," Gareth said, stepping back inside and slamming the door. "There's a horde of them out there."

More screams cut through the air, causing the wind to strengthen once more. I could hear rain begin to pound on the roof of the small hut. The walls creaked as they were moved.

Raleigh stirred yet again, suddenly more alert.

"What's happening? Where's the blade?" He began to sit up, then screamed out in pain, falling back on the bed. "Gareth, I have to get out there."

"Afraid I can't do that, brother," Gareth told him, pacing the room in thought. "They've never come this far inland. Other than River, of course. I don't like this. They'll find us soon enough."

As if on cue, the door was kicked open. A towering drifter barged his way in, claws tearing at the doorframe. It screamed at the sight of them, bringing more heavy rain onto the hut.

"Back away, Gareth," I whispered, moving my hand down to the blade still sheathed at my side.

He dove aside, leaving a straight path. I had to make sure I was on target, even with my crippled eyesight. I drew the blade slowly, leaning forward and focusing on the diaphragm area. Just like Raleigh had shown me that day on the beach.

It ran forward, rushing at me with arms held wide, claws brandished. I lunged forward, stabbing up toward it.

I missed.

It screamed in pain as the blade struck in the middle of the ribcage, above the diaphragm. I heard the bone crack as it was cleaved in two. The drifter fell on top of me, teeth gnashing as it tried to recover.

I moved my other hand to the hilt of the blade, grasping it and starting to saw downward. The drifter threw its head forward, attempting to bite down on my neck as I moved to the side under it, furiously working the blade lower. I heard the final gasp as I hit my target.

The drifter collapsed, twitching. Gareth ran forward to help roll it off of me as I pulled the blade free, splattering blue blood on the walls.

"Vale, are you okay?" Raleigh asked, sitting up slowly this time so as not to hurt himself. He still winced in pain.

"Raleigh, thank god," I said, moving over to him. "Look, I found how we can stop this. We have to get River."

I grabbed the book from the table nearby, flipping to the poem. I shoved it toward Raleigh to read.

"*Brothers of red and blue...* that can't mean us, can it?" he asked, looking up at me.

"I think so," I said. I could see the fear in his face. He was putting all of this together, the same puzzle I had pieced together just hours ago.

The wind was constant now, a continuous roar, a monster tearing the island apart. A board was torn from the roof, leaving an opening for rain to begin pouring through.

"Help me up, Gareth," Raleigh said, swinging his legs over the side of the bed. "We need to go get my brother."

I hefted the blade, getting ready to make our run across the square. Gareth stood, holding Raleigh up on his shoulders. We exchanged a small nod before running out of the hut and into the chaos.

The square was bathed in red. Drifters were dragging bodies out of homes, taking no care if they cut them open or not. Anyone that resisted was torn open, treated as a game by the attacking monsters. I could see one in the distance grabbing a woman away from her screaming wife, slashing her throat so blood covered the woman she loved. It let out a demented laugh before lunging at the other woman.

We made our way through, dodging what we could and trying to cut through what we couldn't. We finally reached the door of Briggs' office, busting it in and charging through.

River sat there in the center of the room, staring toward us. A smile playing behind the gag over his mouth.

"Grab and run," I said, looking towards Gareth and Raleigh. I took hold of the chair River was in and began dragging it out into the storm.

We tried to go around the perimeter of the square and toward the path to the beach so as not to be seen. A drifter chased someone out into our path, stopping as it saw us. I charged forward, stabbing it through the eye this time. It fell to the ground shrieking, causing the storm to strengthen.

When we finally made it to the path, I saw that we didn't have far to go. The amount of drifters congregating in the island and the chaos they were bringing had caused a storm surge, bringing waves crashing just a few hundred yards away. The dunes were gone, now the island just consisted of the square and surrounding area.

"Oh, it's time, brother!" River shouted over the chaos. I looked back to see he had chewed through the gag, allowing him to talk once more. "There is our god, waiting just as promised!"

I looked in the distance to see an inky silhouette on the horizon, moving ever closer to our position. With every stride it sent a towering wave toward us, taking more of the land for its own.

Drifters were frothing in the waves, moving closer to the square. There had to be hundreds, all crashing on top of each other as they scrambled to be first to the feeding. They stopped as they saw us.

"Set me down," Raleigh said. Gareth gave him a look to confirm what he was asking, then a small nod before setting him to his feet. Raleigh came over to me then, putting his hands on my shoulders.

"Whatever happens, I want you to know how proud I am," he said. He deftly slipped the blade away from me, hiding it in his coat pocket. "Well, brother. Does your offer still stand? Will you take me to the sea?"

"I thought you would never ask." River smiled, showing his sharp teeth. Raleigh walked over to him, holding his knife to the rope ensnaring him.

"I will let you free, but you must promise me you will not harm them." Raleigh was wheezing with the effort of standing on his own. River simply nodded in return. With a quick flick of the knife, his restraints fell around him.

They walked together toward the water, River shouting to the other drifters in victory. When they were waist deep, he turned to Raleigh.

"Behold, Panthalasin." He motioned to the Giant figure, features still obscured by the wind and rain that seemed to emanate from it. "The Great Sea, Ruler of All Beneath the Waves. I bring you a sacrifice: the last of the cleansing line."

He turned to face Raleigh, looking at him as he did the same.

"I've waited so long, Raleigh." He thrust his hand forward, impaling Raleigh through the heart.

He let out a gasp, leaning forward on his brother. River took him in a great hug, bringing him close. Raleigh wrapped his arms around him in return.

"I, as well," I heard him say. He flipped the blade from his pocket and held it to River's back, hugging him tight with one arm before thrusting towards himself.

River let out a noise of surprise as he and Raleigh were joined by the blade. The drifters standing around began to scream and writhe, causing the wind to rise with them. Suddenly, they stopped.

Gareth grabbed my arm and pulled me back away from the water as we watched. The two brothers, their blood mixing on the blade and running into the water, seemed to melt away into a pool of red and blue. It only took moments for them to disappear completely, the color in the water branching out further toward the crowd of drifters.

When they were touched by the blood, the drifters turned to water. With each new mass, a rising wave was formed, holding its place as a wall of water at the shoreline. I could almost make out the two brothers in the middle of it, still locked in their death embrace, translucent in their new state of being. When all the drifters had been reached, it was a towering tsunami standing at the ready.

Panthalasin stood in the distance, the storm still swirling around him. He hefted his first, crashing it down into the water and sending his own wave forward. The great tsunami rushed to meet it, absorbing it as they collided. It picked up speed as it moved ever closer to the sea god, rolling with fury.

There was a loud crash as it smashed into the Giant, knocking him from his feet. I saw it try to get back up and regain its footing, but as it did tendrils of water shot forward from the surface, ensnaring him at every possible point. Finally, two tendrils, one red and one blue, shot forward to wrap around the ancient neck of the sea, pulling it first to its knees, then under the surface forever.

We've started taking count and burying our dead now. The island is destroyed, houses gone completely. It appeared as though we had suffered a direct hit from a hurricane.

I was walking along the beach earlier when I spotted something shining in a tide pool. As I ran forward to look, I was able to make out the hilt of the time blade. The blade itself was broken, nothing but jagged splinters after a few inches, but I kept it anyway.

It's to remember the father I only had for a short time. The man who gave his life for us, as long as he lived. I know when the waves crash in, it's him telling me that he's still there, keeping the evil at bay in death as he did in life.

Thank you, Raleigh.

MOVIE NIGHT

I wasn't upset when I got the call last week. Honestly, I was kind of expecting it. Surprised it hadn't happened earlier, really. The old man had been fighting off heart trouble for years and it finally got the best of him. The hospital he passed away at called me in to confirm who he was, and the funeral arrangements had already been taken care of in his will. Now all there was to do was pack up his house.

I know, I know, it seems kind of cold for me to talk about him like this. He was my father, after all. Truth is he wasn't much of a father other than in name. He was constantly pouring himself into his work, almost never home. When he was, he was distant or asleep, usually passing out on the couch by noon on his days off. He didn't talk about his work much, said it was classified. I just know he worked in some lab studying quantum something or other.

I didn't hold any of that against him at first. Not until I was fourteen, when I got home from school and found my mother collapsed in the kitchen. I had tried shaking her, doing chest compressions, anything that may bring her back but... she was cold to the tough already when I found her. Her eyes had the white film over them that death brings, and she was stiff, not easily moved. I called dad three times with no answer before I finally gave up and called 911 to report what happened.

When they got her in for autopsy, it was discovered she had an aneurysm. Completely random, no way to predict or stop it. A nurse consoled me at the hospital as they wheeled her body into the morgue. They tried to call dad too, but had as much luck as me. He finally showed up two days later, looking like he had been through a bender that would make Charlie Sheen jealous. He mumbled something about being sorry and sleepwalked through the funeral. After that, it was business as usual, with me fending for myself while he worked.

Naturally I got away from there as soon as possible. Went off to a good college, got a scholarship and full ride through, and am currently finishing up my doctorate degree. Things have been stressful (it's a doctorate, I don't know what I expected) but I'm managing. I made the arrangements with my professors to take a couple of weeks off class while I closed everything out back home, and here we are now.

Stepping back into my childhood home was surprising, really. The place looked immaculate, just a small layer of dust on everything. It almost looked like he hadn't come back home since I left eight years ago. Hell, he probably hadn't. Probably just stayed at the lab and crashed on a bench or something when he was tired. At least this would make packing up and cleaning easy.

I got to work, clearing out the kitchen first, then slowly making my way further into the house. His bedroom was the last to go, and I took a deep breath as I entered. There was not a single thing out of place. The same bed, dresser, and lamp that he's had since I was born, still in the same place after all these years. The only thing that was strange was the box sitting on his bed. I noticed there was writing on the top as I moved toward it, making it out to say "For Mark" as I drew closer.

So this bastard couldn't call or write for eight years after I left home, but he could leave a box sitting here, completely sealed before he goes through heart failure? I felt a small tinge of rage build up in my chest, hot fire pushing up through my throat. God, the last thing I needed was for my stress ulcers to start up during all this. I grabbed the box cutter from the kitchen table and sat down on the bed. The box was heavy, packed full, but perfectly stacked to fill out every inch of space. What the hell could he have left after all this time?

Upon opening the flaps of cardboard I saw stacks upon stacks of old VHS tapes. Each one was meticulously labeled with a name, date, and five-digit number underneath that. On the top of all of it was a letter from dad.

Mark,

I just want to tell you how sorry I am. There's no excuse I can make. Nothing I can say that will take back how awful I've been, but I want you to know I truly am sorry.

I was so absorbed in my work that until your mother died I didn't even think of being part of this family. Once she was gone, it just hurt too much to be here. So, I lost myself even further in my work, trying to make sense of everything that had happened and what had yet to happen. I wanted to tell your mother how sorry I was as well...here are things I've never been able to tell you. My work, most of my life, has been kept secret from those I love most. You see Mark, I work for something called the Collective. We monitor events out of the ordinary and try to keep them from happening again. What this mostly includes is keeping an eye on parallel universes, making sure the walls between our world and theirs stay intact. I thought I was pouring myself into my work to protect you from these things, Mark. There are creatures beyond our imagination that have come to our world from others, things only some of us can see without help.

This is my research. Sure, it isn't quite everything, but it's what I could manage to get out of the lab. For the past thirty years I've been monitoring other worlds for apocalyptic events, hoping to study what happens there in order to help prevent such an event here. Each of these tapes contains an emergency broadcast or some other bulletin from a now-extinct universe, as well as a detailed report on what happened.

There's a lot of technical speak for how we got these, but I'll leave that for another time or letter.

With all that said, please, continue my work. Help to ensure the survival of our world. I won't make you do this, but I ask with everything left in me. I leave this box of tapes, some horrifying, some tragic, and ask that you look through them. See if you can find patterns I haven't. When you've decided you want to do this and research more, find the Collective. Speak with the Cognizants there. They'll be waiting for you.

I love you, son. I'm so sorry.
Dad

———

I couldn't believe any of this. Had he been struggling with dementia before he died? Was he schizophrenic? God, I couldn't believe I was actually about to watch one of the tapes. I dug out our old VCR from storage and plugged it up to the TV, grabbing the first tape off the top of the stack. Inside the sleeve with the tape was an envelope containing a few slips of paper. I put the video in, sat down on the floor, and started looking over the report.

———

12/17/1975
    SPIDER BABY
    EARTH 02-258
    Broadcast intercepted by Cognizant enhanced airwaves during late-night movie hour on local broadcast television. Cognizant on duty was Ralph, who said that during inter-dimensional surveillance he noticed a bright flash around 10:17 PM, after which phenomena began.

Cognizant reported that multitudes of people began materializing in streets. Subjects appear human, but do not speak or communicate in any human manner. Cognizant reports that subjects' looks ranged from preteen children to senior citizens of both genders. Subjects began by approaching people on the street. When approached, they will stand in front of native humans and study them, before multi-jointed appendages jut from the backs of subjects, impaling the humans in question.

Once they have impaled the humans they then begin to absorb them, slowly, while the victim is still alive. Cognizant quickly linked with Collective of the victim world, warning them of situation. Emergency broadcast was sent out not long after.

Cognizant continued recon, noting that once the streets were cleared, the subjects began knocking on doors and feeding on anyone that opened their door. This continued for hours after. Cognizant eventually had to be forcefully removed from recon due to mental toll of seeing unprecedented death.

Second Cognizant, Agatha, then took over. Noticed that as the creatures absorbed more humans, the variety of people they appeared as grew. Made sure to note one house in particular where a toddler aged girl knocked on the door, then proceeded to grow multiple limbs much like those of an arachnid and absorb a family of four on its own.

As subjects absorbed more and more victims, they began to grow and merge into a seeming collective. Cognizant noted that creatures operated on a hivemind with one singular goal of feeding and merging.

Cognizant continued to watch events unfold, switching out in shifts for five days until the subjects had fed enough. Once this was done all subjects vanished, appearing at a point above central America, and merging into one over the course of five hours. Once they had merged, the subject showed its true form. Cognizant described it as still humanoid, though with armor plating like that of an arthropod, with human limbs and six more segmented limbs rising from the spinal area. Creature is reported to have large mandibles, as well as four red eyes.

Creature pierced the earth below it with all six segmented limbs, each one landing in a different area of North and South America. From here the creature nested for four more days, curling the main body into a tight ball while the segmented limbs held it up. Humanity of this respective earth attempted to fight back, but nothing was able to break the plating. Midway through the four-day rest it was determined the creature was feeding on the energy of the earth. Fault lines began to appear from the spot each limb landed and move out from there. Cognizant reported the patterns of spiderwebs made by the lines.

At the end of the four days the earth was in serious drought, with ocean levels dropping by nearly four hundred feet. Finally, the planet shattered in on itself, leaving segments of broken earth swirling in the atmosphere where a whole planet once stood. Cognizants Agatha and Ralph are currently on leave and on suicide watch due to high mental strain. Will update as more info becomes available.

UPDATE: 1/8/1976

Ralph found dead in dormitory this morning. Bashed his head against the dorm wall until unconscious. Brain trauma was too much for revival.

Agatha has covered her dormitory walls in paintings of large arachnids. There is a black widow spider nested in the corner of her room. Upon janitor attempting to remove the spider, Agatha attacked him, claiming he would anger the Arachnid God.

Jesus Christ.

I couldn't believe what I had just seen or read. I knew the movie. It was Spider Baby, an old b-horror from the sixties. But halfway through the film this emergency alert broadcast came up, telling everyone to stay indoors and not answer any knocks on their door.

Maybe dad wasn't crazy. Maybe he's just fucking with me from the afterlife and he edited these himself. Maybe I'm the crazy one and I worked myself into a fucking breakdown this semester.

I'm going to transfer the warning part of the video over to digital and try to upload it. Maybe that will help me make sense of all this. I don't know if I want to watch any more of these tapes, but I feel like I have to. There's got to be some kind of thread linking everything. There must be some way to stop these events from happening here.

———————————

I transferred the video. Here it is. I'm going to try to go through the rest of the tapes in the next few months but... I think I'll need to take it slow. My head is spinning as is. Take care everyone, and I'll keep you updated.

I'm going to be honest right off the bat with everyone. I didn't want to make this update. I don't want to keep this up. I want to destroy these goddamn tapes and lobotomize myself. I want to forget any of this ever happened. I want to forget I ever had a father.

I've gone through a few more of the tapes as well as the case files contained with them. Some were uneventful, just a news broadcast or late-night film with a stock Emergency Broadcast System message. One warned of an impending meteor strike, then went to static. One just cut off in the middle of an old cartoon, no message or anything. Turns out that one was a universe where a black hole suddenly formed somewhere between Mercury and Venus, collapsing the entire solar system in fractions of a second. No pain, no mess, just something to nothing.

All of this though... it's taking a toll. Looking into all this death and destruction, all these untold horrors that lurk out there in the world. There has to be something out there to counter balance this. For every world that ends violently there has to be some world where they've found the cure for cancer or ended world hunger, right? God, I hope so. Otherwise, what I have here is a box full of nihilism and analog tape.

I've been doing a little more research into what dad said in his letter as well. These... Cognizants? That's what they keep getting referred to as, anyway. They can apparently see into other dimensions and see inter-dimensional beings in our own world. Apparently on occasion the walls between realities will tear and things will slip through. In most of the reports I've seen, they're referred to as Aberrations. Dad had a couple of files in here about a near apocalyptic event months ago caused by some tearing into our world.

I'm going to transcribe a couple more of the case files now. I tried my best to get the tapes transferred over to digital, but some of them were so old they didn't make it. The ones I did get were attached to old movie reruns on late night TV again. Night of the Living Dead and Carnival of Souls. At least the other realities still have good movies, I guess.

10/18/1977

CASE: NIGHT OF THE LIVING DEAD
EARTH 24-601

Cognizant on duty today is Agatha, for the most part recovered from her trauma earlier this year. Still protects whatever spiders she can find, but has managed to let us take the Brown Recluses to a "safe area". She does not realize this entails Robin throwing them in the incinerator.

Tuned universal surveillance over to Earth 24-601 where Agatha said tensions between the United States and communist Russia were highly elevated. Also mentioned that Vietnam was still ongoing as well, with much higher casualties to American troops as well as deployment of a new Uranium based biological weapon, codenamed Agent Green.

The American military, desiring to bring a swift and decisive end to the Vietnam conflict as well as intimidate potential enemies, decided to drop a hydrogen bomb on Ho Chi Minh city. The devastation of the blast is immeasurable, leveling the entire city as well as most of the surrounding countryside. An unintended effect soon follows, however, that will bring about the end.

The nuclear capability of the hydrogen bomb reacts with compounds in Agent Green that have been sprayed throughout the Vietnamese jungle. This causes any deceased that were not immediately evaporated by the blast to begin to mutate, rising from the dead into a reanimated state. Mutations typically consisted of grotesque boils growing on exposed patches of skin, extra teeth growing on arms, legs, and in a few observed cases, stomachs of deceased. Subjects typically wandered aimlessly once reanimated, roaming the countryside and ruins of the city until they came in contact with anyone still living. Upon seeing a living being they would grow into a frenzy with the singular goal of attacking and capturing the live victim, upon which they would pull them in close, lacerating skin with the exposed teeth then popping the boils, allowing the pus to seep into the victim.

This, in turn infected the living victim, who would first die a slow, painful death much like that observed in victims of radiation poisoning after the bombings of Hiroshima and Nagasaki. They would begin the mutations while still living, often screaming in pain while doing so. Typical time to expire was one week after initial infection.

The infection spread slowly through Vietnam, mostly among remnants of guerrilla fighters at first, then eventually through to

US troops that were still stationed along the beaches and in the jungles. Military leadership initially did not take reports of infection seriously, leading to higher rates of infection in the early days of outbreak.

Infection spread to neighboring countries after approximately two weeks, with infected individuals seemingly acting as a hive mind after gathering enough numbers. They would swarm cities in what appeared to be coordinated waves, attacking and infecting large groups of people, then retreating before mounting another attack hours later. This ensured that the living were slowly picked off, with the infection spreading exponentially as more and more joined the subject's ranks.

Overseas transmission was accomplished by infected walking into the ocean. They did not appear to require respiration of any kind, thus they were able to walk across the ocean floor and, although at a slow rate, eventually move into other countries across bodies of water. Once on land, they would then seek out the nearest living being and begin the cycle.

Humanity attempted multiple methods of killing the subjects, though none were shown to work. While gunshots to the head appeared to stop them temporarily, the subject's bodies seemed to allow mutations which moved smaller, more rudimentary brains to other parts of the body, thus allowing basic survival and motor functions even with separation of the head. The only method found for complete and total destruction of the subject was burning to ash.

The subject arrived in mainland America within three weeks of the first infection in Vietnam. Any word of the disease had been suppressed initially, with American troops and citizens being told that the infected were victims of a "Communist Biological Weapon". This facade was kept up in order for America to appear blameless in their use of biological and nuclear warfare, whereas meanwhile most other countries across mainland Europe and Asia were also dealing with their own outbreaks of infection.

Subject spread across most of the earth in a matter of weeks, attacking and infecting anyone unfortunate enough to cross paths with carriers of the pathogen. Infected numbers grew exponentially in the first few days, soon outnumbering humans ten to one. The infected then began coordinated attacks on any surviving communities, systematically rooting out and turning any humans found. In a desperate final bid at eradicating the disease, the American military conducted bombing raids. Nuclear arms were dropped on hordes of infected as they traveled in packs.

These attacks decimated a large amount of the infected population, but had unintended effects on those not destroyed by the initial blasts. The radiation only strengthened the creatures, turning them into walking nuclear reactors. This in turn scorched any ground they came across, leaving fallout and infection in their wake. This also ensured that any human within range of subjects became infected simply through proximity.

Agatha notes that two months after infection approximately ten thousand healthy humans are left on earth. Most have been forced to adapt a nomadic lifestyle, constantly staying on the move to avoid roving groups of the infected. Cognizant will continue to monitor and update on situation.

UPDATE: 3/20/1978

Agatha reports ~300 survivors remain, most having lost any hope to continue. Radiation has spread into most of the world's water supply, and storm systems spread nuclear fallout across the earth. Agatha reports that the remaining humans are divided across the planet, with most believing they are the last remaining alive. Infected are still hunting, using their hive mind to develop a network across the world to find survivors.

UPDATE: 4/7/1978

Agatha reports that the final human has been killed, opting to die by gunshot to the head instead of from the encroaching infected. Will continue to monitor dimension for any sign of anomaly and potential Aberrations, as well as research for any potential countermeasures in the event of Aberration.

I still can't believe any of this. It's so insane. How could dad see all of this, deal with all of this, and not go insane? No wonder he rarely came home. Facing these horrors had to change him.

Until now, I've just been taking tapes off the top of the stack in the box and going on by one. I've gone through three layers of what I estimate to be about ten layers. This is the point when I found something new. There was a large envelope, almost filled to bursting with papers. I opened it and slid the pile out onto the floor. On top was another letter from dad.

Mark,

I know what you've seen so far has been a lot to take in. These tapes, the case files, everything that's been in this box... I know I didn't sleep for weeks after being taken into the Collective. I never knew there could be such terrors. Now, I'm honestly just happy to die and not have to worry about any of this. If there's a heaven or hell, it can't be as bad as the things I've seen.

What's enclosed in this envelope is two-fold: there is a brief history of the Collective. This entails the founding, how long we've known about the parallel worlds, Cognizants, and a brief history of who's who in the organization. You'll probably be surprised by the amount of famous historical figures that were more special than they let on.

The second part is an archive of high-casualty Aberrations that have crossed into our world. Many events throughout history were given a natural explanation because the real reasons were far too much for ordinary humans to handle. There are things you'll learn here that will scare you, and honestly they should. Our world is not safe. No world is.

Here is where I leave you. Again, I'm so sorry. Even now, as I write out this letter, I'm tempted to take it all and burn it. Part of me wants you to continue living in ignorance, not knowing the horrors that lurk out in the world. The father in me wants to protect you. The scientist in me though, knows that this research needs to continue. Someone has to do it, and I trust it more to someone that I know is smart enough to see the connections I could not.

I love you,
Dad

There was a case file along with an old newspaper clipping kept in a plastic sleeve. The paper was yellowed, and the print on it faded to nearly nothing. I could see the edges disintegrating in the plastic. The headline read GREAT FIRE DEVASTATES CHICAGO.

There was a case file attached.

The Great Chicago Fire

Cognizant Martin Ford and his partner were in the city of Chicago on their annual rounds when an Aberration appeared in the city. Ford describes the being as being humanoid, but made of pure flame, burning white hot. Ford said he attempted to make contact with the creature, asking it of its intentions on our world, and where it came from. The creature reportedly appeared uncaring of Ford's presence, instead looking around before finally touching the nearest building, setting it ablaze.

Ford began to attempt to chase the Aberration, trying to force it back through the dimensional tear it came from. The creature did not acknowledge, instead continuing to move along the city street, setting buildings afire as it went. Ford, thinking resourcefully, began to find whatever water he could around their immediate vicinity, dousing the Aberration and beginning to force it towards Lake Michigan.

Although they were moving the creature quickly toward the water, the fire continued to spread wherever they went. Teams of local firefighters scrambled immediately to fight the blaze. Finally, after a long struggle, the creature was cornered at the end of the port on Lake Michigan. In a heroic sacrifice, Ford's partner, Ezra Jennings, threw himself at the creature using Ford as his sight guide. Upon grabbing the Aberration, he threw both it and himself into the lake, immediately killing the creature. Ford dove in after him, noting the near boiling temperature of the water as he dragged Jenning's body back to shore. Jennings burns were beyond repair, and he expired seven hours after the Aberration was destroyed.

Let it be known that Ezra Jennings is receiving the highest commendations the Collective can give, as well as a hefty retirement sum being paid to his widow and family for future generations. He will also be memorialized in Collective HQ and archives as one of our most honored members.

I want to throw up. It was one thing seeing these things that destroyed other worlds and realities. The fact that they could just stumble into our reality, though... it terrifies me. This is why dad gave me these files. There are things to watch out for, things that nobody else can see. Hell, I can't even see them.

I'm combing through whatever files I can. I may transcribe some if I think it's important. Some may deserve to stay as they are, though. These things shouldn't be known. I'm torn if I should keep sharing these things. I don't want other people to know about these horrors. I've barely slept in days, thinking that at any moment some cosmic terror could break through and destroy us, rending our minds into fragments. There would be nothing we could do.

I need to think on this. There's a lot left to go through, but I may just stop here. I may do what dad couldn't and burn it. Maybe check myself in somewhere or have a drink or twenty until I can forget. I keep hoping I'll wake up, find out dad was really just your normal everyday absentee father. Maybe mom will still be alive, and I've dreamed the past decade of trauma. If I'm lucky, I'm actually dying, and this is all just the last delusions as my brain fires off every synapse until I die.

Here we are though. I'm alive. You're alive. Who knows how long we'll stay that way.

This will be my last update, at least for a while. I'm giving up on the tapes. The death and destruction... it's just too much. After this is uploaded, I'm going to set off and try to find the Collective. I've found something. A pattern. I'm afraid something big is about to happen. Something awful.

I've gone through more videos. Some worse than others. There were more that were the typical apocalypse stuff that everyone expects. Earth's sun goes supernova, biological and germ warfare kills the world. One was gone in an instant due to an accident at the Large Hadron Collider. The damn thing went off and took half the earth with it, splitting the globe right down the middle and transporting one half just over two miles away from where it started. Naturally this was enough to cause instant death to the entire world due to gravitational shift.

This last one though... I think it's literally Hell. Hell coming to earth and tearing our world apart for its own needs. I can only hope that it stays in that dimension, and we don't have a hell of our own.

So. Here's the case file with it. I managed to get the video transferred over as well, though with a few minor hiccups that came along with it. The tape wasn't in great shape, so this one is a bit more shaky than normal. After you read it, say a prayer. Our world will need it.

———

CASE: CARNIVAL OF SOULS
10/02/1987
EARTH DESIGNATION 00-666

Cognizant on duty today is Sun. Tuned to late night broadcast of Carnival of Souls on local public access channel for earth of U-666. Dimensional analysis and energy reports suggest a major cataclysmic event soon to take place.

Current state of this earth is much like our own, with the exception that disco never happened and heavy metal came to be much sooner. As such, this earth has been experiencing their own version of the Satanic Panic since approximately 1977. In response to this, there has been a much greater focus on purging the nation of anything deemed evil. Book burnings and film burnings are rampant, with those caught possessing anything deemed unholy are punished with torture and lengthy prison sentences. As such, a radical cult of satanism has sprung up in protest,

According to Sun, said cult was conducting an open protest at Capitol Hill in which a pentagram was drawn on the outside courtyard. Worshipers then gathered around the symbol, chanting in what appeared to be Latin. Two minutes into the chant, they were attacked by riot police wielding shields and batons, who immediately began brutalizing the group. At least three protestors were killed and several wounded.

Sun reports that the blood spilled during the encounter was absorbed by the pentagram, seemingly fueling a glowing light which began to emanate from the symbol. Cracks began to spread outward from it, eventually growing into fissures which opened underneath the groups of protestors and counter-protestors caught nearby. These fissures reportedly sprang open very suddenly, not allowing anyone to escape. Fire was said to flow from the cracks as more and more humans were taken.

The fissures closed after ten minutes, leaving nearly no trace of being there. Violence began to resume amongst the gathered humans, with people from both sides attacking anyone and everyone within reach. Sun noted that the first ones to begin attacking were those that had been injured in the initial chaos, and those that were injured by them in the ensuing brawl then began to attack others after freezing and convulsing for a moment.

The brawl continued moving outward from there, with more and more humans becoming violent as they expanded to the outskirts of the city. By that evening, most of the DC area was in a full-blown riot. Sun noted that some who were attacked and hurt were not being overtaken as others have, depending on the severity of their injuries. Those attacking seemed to be focused on simply drawing blood, and anyone hurt beyond superficial wounds, such as with broken bones or gaping wounds, were simply left to bleed out or killed outright. Cases were noted of some of these victims being crucified on light poles or dismembered and arranged in occult patterns by the attacking group.

As the sun set over DC, the attackers began to bloom outward to the surrounding areas, aiming to move into surrounding cities. Smaller groups were left behind to roam the streets and weed out what humans were left in the capital. These roving gangs seemed more intent on terrorizing and slaughtering the survivors than turning them to their cause, frequently standing outside and taunting them before dragging them from their homes and brutally murdering anyone found.

Sun was relieved of duty by trainee Cognizant Alexander the next morning due to shock. Sun had been monitoring the outer cities around the capitol as the subjects spread, and when decided to check back on DC after a few hours. It should be noted here that Sun is currently six months pregnant with her first child. Upon looking back, she was greeted by the sight of multiple dead in the streets, homes painted red with blood, and any children and infants that had been found cut open and thrown over power lines between homes.

Alexander resumed surveillance, noting that subjects had moved into the tri-state area and were commandeering cars, planes, and other vehicles in order to go further. The subjects referred to humanity as "filth", frequently claiming to be from Hell, and referring to one another as "Fallen". These descriptions coincide with the Biblical description of demonic entities.

After the second day, they had successfully taken the Eastern seaboard and begun moving west across the United States. Some began commandeering aircraft and boats to move into other countries, while others crossed the Canadian border and began work there. Fallen that were moving west were noted to begin losing interest and appearing to become bored with how the operation was going. As such, they began disguising themselves as authority figures and other people in power in order to fool victims before killing them.

It should be noted that across the world, more humans were becoming possessed at random, seemingly tied to wounds on the skin and blood being spilled. Though unconfirmed, there is belief that some world leaders were taken before anyone else in their country, as a mass operation to let blood from citizens and perform acts of aggression against other countries, attempting to start war.

Some possessed were noted to eat parts of victims if they were deemed beyond saving. They did not seem to do this for any nourishment, but simply for pleasure and to "defile". Multiple Fallen were noted as recognizing each other in their human hosts and speaking of how there were trillions of others still waiting to get a human host.

ONE WEEK FROM INITIAL RIOT:

Most countries are in complete disarray. There are less than ten million living humans on earth scattered across most countries.

At some point a beast rises from the Atlantic Ocean, fitting the Biblical description of having seven heads. The creature glowed with an unholy black flame wafting from it, filling any immediate area with the smell of rot and sulfur. The Beast stood tall, with its upper extremities almost reaching the lower atmospheric clouds. The Beast was welcomed to shore near the Middle East by a tall, thin human who at first glance appeared as an attractive woman or man, depending on the viewer, but upon a longer look became a rotting corpse.

Once they were united, the Harlot climbed to the top of the Beast, proceeding to perform various sexual acts for the Beast to see as it spewed fire and brimstone, covering the Earth and cheering demons. The world became a hellscape of fire and death, with possessed humans shedding their skin and revealing the true form of the demons. Reptilian creatures with cloven hooves, large, twisted horns, and flames bursting forth from every orifice. Earth 00-666 was deemed as a loss nine days after initial breach, with any humans left alive at the time being captured and tortured until death.

UPDATE 10/10/1987

Sun has suffered a miscarriage.

UPDATE 10/15/1987

Alexander has requested a leave of absence in order to attend seminary with the Catholic Church.

No. That's it. I'm done with these fucking tapes. Done with these transcripts. Done with anything dad left here. There's been a pattern showing in each world. One has ended each year without fail. Who's to say that ours won't be next?

I need to find them. This Collective. They have to have a map or something showing where these universes were in relation to ours. If I'm right, then we're due for an apocalyptic event soon, assuming it hasn't already started. I dumped everything out of the box finally. There was a paper on the bottom with an address. Somewhere in south Georgia, looks like the middle of fucking nowhere. I'm heading out tomorrow. Until then, I'm leaving the papers and tapes here. Once I've spoken to them, I'm going to attempt to find some more information and hopefully find a way to prevent whatever fucked up thing may happen to our world.

Eventually, I'll try to scan everything in and upload it. These things have to be known. People need to see what's really happening in our world and be better equipped to fight it. I'll set up a site to dump all the info on when I finally can.

In the meantime, I need to rest and make some final preparations. I don't know if this is what dad had in mind; me telling the world about the Collective and the terrors that lurk beyond our own world, but I hope he's proud. He may not have been there for me or mom, but at least he was trying to save and protect us in his own weird way. I'm going to finish this. For him.

Love you, dad.

WHEN THE LIGHT LEAVES US

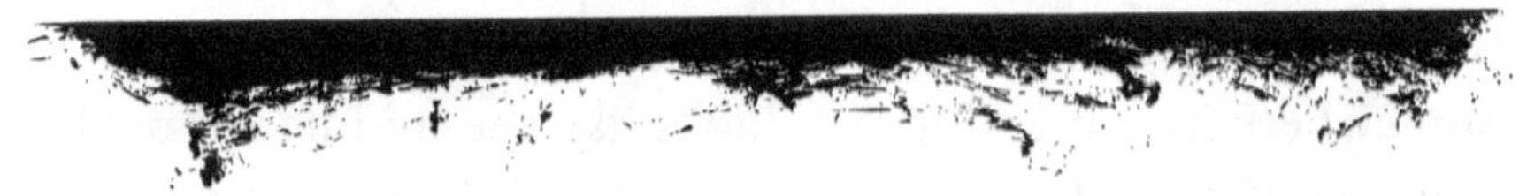

Gunpowder was all I could smell, with smoke drifting across the battlefield creating a solid haze that was impenetrable by human eyes. I could only pray that no bullets or cannonballs would hit me, much less the bayonet of another soldier. Everything was chaos, dead soldiers of both blue and grey littering the vast fields of Gettysburg. I believe that's what brought on the end.

My regiment had been called up to Gettysburg a week ago, told of an impending battle with the Confederates that could be the last. We had to make this count and stop this bloody war once and for all with a final sacrifice. Freedom is what we were there to fight for. Freedom for every man from being a slave to another man. We won that, but found ourselves free in a world where every moment is survival.

I don't know how long it's been since that initial cannon fire. A trumpet that broke the most deafening silence I've ever heard, signaling the start of this massacre. That single trumpet call seems now like the trumpet of heaven, sounding out to all that Revelations has begun. I pray that the lord raptures us soon if that is the case. All hell broke loose as we charged in, firing guns and stabbing with bayonets at our enemies. The Confederate soldiers we once called brothers now fighting viciously against us. A soldier beside me let out a war cry as we charged in, though he was cut off quickly by a cannonball. His voice trailed off as the top half of his head was sheared off, scattering brain matter over the rest of us. Only his lower jaw and beard remained, still open in a primal, silent war cry.

I can only assume some god was watching over me, as I was one of the few to survive the initial volley. My brothers fell around me, struck by cannons and rifle fire. Bodies were already thick on the front lines, starting to form a natural barricade as more fell on those already there.

While my rifle ran out of ammunition before long, there was plenty to pick up from the dead. Many of us began to throw our guns aside once they were out of bullets, instead looting our fallen for their lead.

Darkness fell suddenly, surrounding all of us in the pitch black. No moon above, no sun, no stars. Just an empty, dark void open above us. The only light came from still sporadic fire, quick flashes before the darkness smothered us once more. Unable to see, most stopped, unsure of what to do in the situation. I believed it to be an eclipse at first, but what came after was much worse.

Fiery blue lit up the sky, accelerating from every direction. As they began falling to earth, the horrors began. Lit by the blue flames above, all of us could see as both armies were swarmed. Men became beasts before my eyes, contorting as they were set upon by other horrors. They appeared from nowhere, as if summoned from the depths of hell. Towering, human-like figures with leathery skin, sheets of flayed flesh hanging from them in cloaks roamed the battlefield, picking up soldiers and ripping their skin off, leaving them flayed, lying in the blood of their brethren.

Falling blue flames were still pounding the earth around us, more terrors emerging from the cocoons of flame as they settled. Creatures slithered along the ground, bodies like water rolling over the battlefield. As they rolled, more bodies were picked up, increasing their size as they captured more. The bodies inside melted as they rolled, fading into a deep red that glowed in the flames. Hell was here, and we brought it.

I can only assume this was our punishment for spilling so much blood. God finally decided to let the heavens fall and the earth open, granting us judgment for our sins. By now, fires were raging throughout the field, scared soldiers screaming as the terrors took them down. The blood was running thick, with puddles under my feet as I desperately tried to escape.

A cavalry soldier rode by, convulsing atop his horse as his face contorted, blood spraying as his eyes burst open. He bent down, biting into the horse's neck with sharpened teeth, causing the poor creature to shriek in agony. The soldier ripped another huge chunk from the horse's neck, causing it to fall over on him. As he was crushed under the dying creature he writhed and screamed, inhuman notes coming from his vocal cords. A cavalry saber fell a few feet from them, sticking upright in the mud. My gun empty once more, I picked it up by the handle as I ran by, just in time to quickly slash away the soldier's head as it lunged at me, stretching grotesquely from the crushed body to reach me. As the saber slashed a gash in its long neck, the creature screamed at me again, almost knocking me back to the ground. I felt dizzy, confused even.

No, I had to keep running. There was no other choice than to run or die, possibly becoming one of these terrors. Some soldiers were still alive, trying to fight back against these punishments sent by God. Though it was only getting them killed. A great beast, like a fierce wolf-ish creature larger than even the elephants I had seen in drawings from across the seas, jumped through the air, landing on a group of soldiers. Fire radiated from the burning fur on it, making it appear like a terrifying hellhound. As the soldiers were devoured, their screams only added to the chaos, inciting more terror to the discordant battle.

I pulled out the pistol from my waistband, wielding both it and the cavalry saber while trying to get my bearings. I couldn't see where the battle lines were, but there was a faint tree line not too far away. There was where I would make my escape to, hopefully finding safety in the forest. A small, pale white figure ran at me, making a leap with sharp teeth as it screamed. It looked like a small child, but with pale, damp skin that was almost waterlogged. I discharged my revolver; the bullet going straight through its middle, bursting gore from the other side. It fell to the ground, twitching as I continued to run.

When I broke the tree line I thought about hiding, but my legs had other ideas. Run, run, run was all I could do, taking myself as far as possible from this hell. Before long, the flickering light of flames faded behind me, leaving me in complete darkness once more. The forest was still, not a soul stirring through the leaves. My feet finally collapsed beneath me as I tripped over a root, twisting my ankle on the way down. Now that my own footsteps weren't crashing down around me, I could hear something crunching over leaves and branches behind me. Closing in fast.

A faint light began to flicker through the dense branches, casting eerie shadows on the pitch black. It appeared to be a torch, surprisingly not setting the entire forest on fire during the dry season. At this point, perishing in a fire would almost be a mercy. As the flame grew closer, I still couldn't see who or what might have been behind it, but I gripped my pistol and aimed it at right at the base of the torch, hoping I could hit whatever it was in the center.

"I'm friendly. Please don't shoot," a gruff voice said from the trees. "Sorry, wasn't trying to scare you."

A young man stepped through the trees, the distinctive dark blue of his uniform contrasting with the shadows. I put my gun down, seeing that he was another Union soldier, and pushed myself up on my hands, wincing while my ankle throbbed. As he came closer, I was finally able to get a good look at the soldier approaching.

Sweat was shining off his dark skin, a look of wild fear in his eyes that were still twitching to look around.

"Any of those things follow you?" I asked.

"Don't believe so. Think they don't like the fire much," he replied.

I started gathering sticks and brush from around the ground, piling them in the center of the small clearing we were in. If fire kept them away, we would go ahead and make sure it was available. He moved over closer, helping to gather fallen branches along his way to strengthen the pile. When there was finally a decent amount, he set the torch to it, bringing a small campfire to life.

As the flames grew, more of the forest around us came into sight. This man sat across from me at the fire, a small pile of wood and sticks beside him to throw on the flames when needed. Now that there was light I could pull my boot off, getting a good look at my ankle. Swollen, and it was definitely going to hurt for a couple of days, but I could still move.

"What's your name?" I asked, watching the young soldier pull a rifle from over his shoulder and start cleaning it.

"Vincent Strand," he replied, "Yours?"

"Robert," I grunted. Exhaustion was starting to set in, since I was finally in a place of relative safety. The day's battle was only the start of weariness, with survival now the only thing on my mind.

"General Lee?" he asked, squinting through the darkness at me, hand on his gun. Don't know why, but it was the first time I've laughed in weeks, probably.

"If any bastard deserved what happened out there, he would be the one." I chuckled, pulling the canteen from my bag. "Where you from?"

"Philadelphia," he said, unpacking his own canteen now. An inhuman screech ripped through the air, making both of us jump while reaching for weapons. It faded away as quickly as it came, as if flying overhead. As we sat back down, keeping a firm grip on our guns and blades, he asked the mutual question, "What happened there?"

"Hell finally got tired of waiting," I retorted, watching as his eyes grew wide. The darkness wasn't letting up, with not a star in sight in the sky. No moon, and judging by what time things started this morning, it should still be around noon. Not that the sun was anywhere to show it. Just a dark, abyssal void above us, making it even more evident how along we really are. "Can only assume this is what we get for so much blood spilled."

His only response was to stare off into the sky. Another scream ripped the air, this time a human one, recognizably. It sounded like a woman. Whatever caused her to scream quickly ensured she stopped, as it was cut off after just seconds. Vincent started praying, muttering under his breath pleas to God to protect his family back in Pittsburgh. At least the kid still had something to hold on to, considering everything else looked like the worst case possible.

My body ached, the toll of today's battle finally settling in. My ankle was probably the worst injury, but there was a saber cut on my shoulder that I didn't notice until now. Must have been the rush of survival numbing it.

"Get some sleep, kid," I told Vincent, throwing more wood on the fire before settling back against a tree. "I'll keep watching for a while. We'll trade off at sun up then figure out where to go."

"Do you think the sun will come up?" he asked, still fervently bowed with his hands up in prayer. All I could do was shake my head and shrug.

"Don't rightly know. Whatever happens, we'll figure out a plan to get you back to Philadelphia."

His eyes had a look of hope for the first time since I met him. Though he wasn't quite in the belief that I was going to help just yet.

"Thank you, sir," he said, bowing his head in a rush.

"Call me Robert," I said again, motioning for him to knock it off. He eventually settled in against the tree, dozing off into a restless sleep.

My efforts to stay awake and keep an eye out were in vain as the day caught up to my body. Before I realized it, I was dozing off myself.

I was snapped awake by the sound of trees falling nearby, something heavy scraping itself closer along the ground.

"Vincent, wake up," I said, loud enough to rouse him from his sleep. "Something's coming, we have to go."

He stirred quickly, jumping up and grabbing his bag. I quickly grabbed a long branch from the ground, hoping it would be enough to support my injury. Vincent quickly found another stick, still covered in tree sap, and lit it from the still-smoldering fire.

It was almost useless. Darkness was still dominating the sky, making sure we were practically running blind through the forest. My ankle hurt like hell, making me slower, but the fear in my veins overpowered it. Whatever was moving towards us, it was massive, and likely wasn't friendly.

Vincent helped me through the last bit of the trees, seeing that my leg was definitely not going to hold up. We came out near a dirt road, worn from years of foot and wagon traffic, and ran into a rain-filled ditch beside it, jumping in the water and extinguishing the makeshift torch to hide.

It crashed out, taking trees with it. In the darkness, I could see just the faint outline of a massive creature, one long body with pasty white flesh covering it. If I didn't know any better, it looked bloated from drowning, all color drained from the entire thing. It opened a huge mouth, many tongues emerging to lick the air, trying to find what it was chasing. We both submerged ourselves as far as we could in the water, desperately trying to hide.

A torch appeared from down the worn road, illuminating the pathway ahead. The creature sensed it, tasting the scent of the flame as it drew closer. Whoever was holding it didn't realize what they were walking into. Vincent began to rise up, ready to shout at them. I had to put a hand on his shoulder, gripping hard and giving him a quiet signal. We couldn't give ourselves away.

"Hello?" A voice called from under the flame, moving closer. "Please, do you know what happened?"

The creature moved exceptionally fast for its size, at least twelve feet in height with a long stocky build. Before we could process, it had slithered to the torch bearer, giving them barely time to scream before swallowing them whole. Vincent let go a short gasp into the water beside me, immediately closing his mouth to save air. Satisfied, the monster walked back into the tree line with a grumble, knocking over more trees as it went.

Vincent and I waited until the thuds of the forest fainted before emerging from the water.

"That... that was a demon," he said, looking at me in fear.

All I could do was nod, the wind chilling me in my soaked clothes.

"We gotta move forward, though. Follow the road until we find out where we are." I was already moving forward, desperately trying to keep my composure as the crushing weight of reality was starting to set in. As we walked along the road, not a word was spoken, only silence as we both stayed on high alert.

No sign of light peeked over the horizon. I don't know where we were, or even what time it could be without the sun to guide me. My eyes were much more adjusted now to the darkness, at least, allowing me to get a slightly better view of the world around me. Once I really was able to pay attention, I could notice stars shining faintly in the sky again. They weren't constellations I recognized though, not even the North Star could be found despite my desperate searching. I couldn't notice at first, but the stars were pulsating, light growing and fading as if the cosmos were breathing.

"Sir, look," Vincent said, putting a hand on my shoulder and shaking me from thought. "There's a light ahead."

He was right, through the distance there was the faint flicker of fire, with smoke rising up toward the stars from a chimney. There wouldn't be a fire going after this long if the place was abandoned, but there was no guarantee those inside were going to take kindly to two Union soldiers coming to their door. Damned if they would even recognize us in this ragged state, but we held hope while approaching that they wouldn't turn us away. A discordant screech rang out from in the distance, something making known that it was on the hunt. Despite the pain in my ankle, I sped up, desperately seeking shelter in the light.

We approached the door cautiously, with a hand on our weapons just in case. Vincent kept a revolver drawn, hand steadier for aiming than mine were, though my saber was ready to cut anyone or anything that threatened us. I don't know why I had a sense of responsibility for this kid, but I knew he still had life burning in him that I couldn't let go out.

Two raps of my knuckles on the door and a voice came from inside, "Get away."

"We just want to know where we are, please. We were chased and got lost," Vincent said, trying to keep his voice low enough to not attract attention but loud enough for the man inside to hear. The gruff voice came back again, inquisitive.

"Where are you going?" It asked, with the sound of a bolt being drawn from behind the door. "You're outside Lancaster."

"Dammit," I swore under my breath. We were closer than I expected, and surprisingly went the wrong way, but the idea of going through the city in this mess had me cautious. I replied to the man as the door opened a crack, the muzzle of a rifle poking out at us. Both Vincent and I raised our weapons as well, concerned for our own lives. I tried talking to him before things went even more downhill, "We were at Gettysburg. Had to run when everything went to hell."

"Hmph. You traitors?" he asked now, opening the door a little more to look at us. His eye caught Vincent, sizing him up. "This one yours?"

"No sir, we're both Union," I offered, "I'd show you my papers, but I don't think they're in good shape for reading. And no, I ain't nobody's owner."

"Good. Come on in," the man said, opening the door a bit more so we could walk in. "Christ, what happened to you boys?"

Vincent and I looked at each other, the light of the roaring fireplace letting us see each other clearly for the first time. He was covered head to toe in mud and blood, dirt all over his face.

"It's been quite the day. I think it's been a day at least, not really sure without the sun to say," Vincent replied, walking in toward the fire to warm his chilled bones. The man walked back to a chair, a small wooden table with a knife out, whetstone nearby. He must have been preparing for whatever horrors he had heard outside.

"We were at the battle. Don't know how long it went, but then... well, you see what happened. It's everywhere," I said, moving toward the fire as well. The cold fabric on my skin started taking in warmth like a greedy child hogging candies, slowly bringing my body back from the edge of freezing cold.

"Guessing we didn't win," he asked, looking at me with worry. I could only shake my head and shrug in reply. He sighed, sitting back in his chair. "I knew we were insulting god with all this killing."

"What have you seen?" Vincent asked him, peeling off his coat and laying it over the hearth to dry. "I mean, the creatures."

The old man looked surprised then, looking at both of us in turn. "Y'all saw them? I've only heard the cries, but I didn't know what it was. Demons, I assumed."

"Not far off," I snorted, looking into the embers in the hearth. Everything I had heard of hell was fire and brimstone. If this was hell, it was a cold, dark one. I think I may prefer the fires at this point. "They came out of nowhere. Everything went dark, then the chaos started. It didn't matter which side you were on. Those things have a war on humanity. They're probably going to win, too."

Vincent and the old man just looked at me, concern on their faces.

"Well, guess all we can do is fight," the old man said. "Name's Peter, by the way. Nice to meet you."

"Robert," I said, nodding toward him. Vincent gave his name, doing the same, "Thank you for letting us in."

"Shit, the least I can do after y'all put your lives on the line for us. Can't say I don't blame those Confederate sons of bitches for bringing this on us, though."

Vincent and I could only stare in silence at the flames, lost in our own heads. I'm sure he was worried about his family in Philadelphia, but all I could think about was how we were supposed to survive this new world of horrors.

"We can't stay long, Vincent," I said, bringing myself back. If his family was alone in the city, time was of the essence. "Peter, have you heard anything from the city?"

"If you're heading to Philadelphia, no, nothing from there so far. Though it's a bit soon for anyone to be passing through from there. You're about two miles out from Lancaster heading east. Pass through the city and stay on the main road, suppose you'll hit Philadelphia in... maybe a day if you go fast?"

"Alright. Appreciate it," I said, standing up and beckoning for Vincent to follow. "We don't want to make your family wait."

"Yeah. Yeah, you're right," he said, taking his coat back from the hearth. "Thank you very much, Peter."

"Y'all don't have to go back out there. You can rest if you need to," he said, looking at us with concern. I know we were ragged, but from his look, you would think we were walking corpses.

"I'm trying to find my family," Vincent replied, "My mom and little sister are in Philadelphia, so we're trying to get there fast."

Peter's eyes softened, holding a hand out to both of us to shake, "Good luck then, and godspeed. I'll pray for your safety, if there's anyone listening to prayers still."

"We're grateful, thank you," I said, hefting my saber and stepping back out. On the way, Peter passed me a tinder box, a block of flint, and a rod of steel to create sparks.

"Keep some light on you, just in case," he mentioned.

We said our goodbyes quickly, getting back on the road and continuing on our path toward Lancaster. The sky was glowing orange around it, but whether it was due to gaslight or flames, I couldn't tell. Vincent still had the look of worry on his face, unsure of what we would find in Philadelphia if we even managed to make it to Lancaster.

"I know they're probably dead," he whispered quietly, choking back tears. The call of a creature sounded in the distance, multiple frequencies crying out in discordant symphonies. Another answered it, as if speaking to each other. Vincent continued without paying mind, "They've probably been killed. Mama's been sick for a while. Eliza can't do anything for her but try to keep her comfortable. I don't know that Eliza can even survive on her own with everything that's happened."

"Your sister?" I asked, looking in his direction. The stars were still pulsating slowly above my head, the universe breathing deep as if savoring the terror of the earth. There wasn't any sign of the sun, still, as much as I was praying it would show itself. "Don't think about the situation, just focus on finding them."

"She's only fifteen. I know she won't be able to do anything if one of those demon's attacks," he said, still choked up.

"And it ain't gonna do you any good wondering if they're dead or not. If that happens, we'll deal with it when we get there," I answered.

Lancaster was coming into view, the flickering glow brighter now. It became increasingly obvious that we weren't going to make it through the city. Flames were waving from the rooftops, screams of humans and demons coming from the streets.

"Jesus Christ, save us," Vincent whispered under his breath. Over the flames, a figure flew, leathery wings beating against the rising inferno. Most of the body was human, but that same pale color of the forest creature. Hands and feet were adorned with sharp, pointed talons at least a foot long, making me shudder at the thought of it hunting. From this distance it looked like it was savoring its work, taking in the screams of the dying. It flew in circles, surveying the scene. We watched for a moment, terrified by the sight, until we saw it dive down into the inferno, coming back up with a body cloaked in flames. It flew up high, wings rising with loud flaps, before holding the figure up with one hand, using the other to plunge through its chest as the flames made them scream. Their voice sputtered out as the demon withdrew its hand, before a geyser of blood poured from the wound, with the demon taking immense pleasure in the scarlet shower. It let out a screech of joy, throwing the body to the ground before circling again, searching for another meal.

"Let's go. Nothing we can do," I said, grabbing his shoulder to lead him away. We needed to go around the city now, which means it's going to take longer and lose us time.

"We're not even going to try and help?" he asked, resisting my grip. "There are people dying in there!"

"And you think you won't be one of them?" I asked coldly, staring him down with the inquisition. His eyes burned before averting, mumbling an apology. Taking my hand off his shoulder, I sighed and started walking, Vincent following close behind. "I know, it seems awful and callous. But we need to find your family and time is our greatest enemy right now."

"You're right..." he said, following in a stupor. After seeing that, I couldn't really blame him for losing hope in finding them. The world was darker now, literally and figuratively, and it looked like survival wouldn't be much longer for humanity.

Trying to ignore the screams of those dying in Lancaster was the worst thing about going around the city. Even though we were still relatively far away, cries of horror and death echoed through the dark skies, reminding us of the new world where humans were purged. In a way, nothing had changed from the war.

I was focused on the path ahead, keeping an eye out for anything that could be waiting for us when a voice cut the darkness.

"Help." The voice of a small child. "Please, I don't. know where I am."

We stopped, silent in the dark, not knowing where the voice was coming from or who it could be. It chimed in again. This time I was able to pinpoint it as being in front of us, a little off to the left of the road.

"Hello?" The voice called again, "Are you human?"

The small figure emerged from the side of the road, walking toward us. They couldn't have been taller than four feet, maybe. Just a kid, left all alone out here.

"We're human," Vincent replied, making sure it could hear us. I shot him a glance in the darkness, wondering if he was trying to get us killed. The child moved closer, coming into view better as it did. I realized very quickly we weren't prepared to be out here, even if we were in fighting shape.

"I'm so hungry," the small figure said, finally stepping close enough to catch a glimpse of the mottled, pale skin. I pulled out the flint, holding it ready against the steel of my saber as I drew it. As it got closer, tendrils of shadow began to grow from behind it, inching closer toward us. Vincent realized as well, putting a hand on the pistol at his hip. I hope he's quick on the draw...

It whipped one of the tendrils toward me, grabbing onto my ankle which was already hurt. I felt the hot sting of something cutting through my skin, pain coursing through my veins.

"Run," I said, barely giving a shout to not attract more of them. Running the flint against the saber blade, sparks begin to fly and illuminate the area. The demon child fell back, tendril releasing my ankle, shielding dark, hollow eyes from the glow of the light. Vincent began to move as I used the opportunity, slashing at the blinded creature. Before it could react, the saber cut right through its neck, separating its head from its shoulders. I didn't stop to make sure the damned thing was really dead, running full burst on my hurt ankle as fast as it would let me. A discordant scream echoed behind me, the creature still managing to cry even without a head.

We ran, until the city was out of sight, until our breathing grew ragged and our feet collapsed beneath us. The demon didn't follow, whether it could, I don't know. The screaming head kept going behind us until it was out of earshot, with both of us feeling relief that its cries weren't echoing in our heads anymore. I felt dizzy, sick, almost like I was going to vomit. Collapsing to my knees, I gripped the ground in front of me to desperately steady myself.

"The cosmos would welcome you," a voice said, not audibly in my ear but inside my mind, "We can help the pain. We can give you everything beyond your wildest fantasies."

Images flashed through my mind. A woman with a baby. Wait... she was... familiar? The wife I lost years ago, holding our baby that was never destined to see the light of day. He had a full head of hair and eyes in a smile when he looked at his mother. I felt my heart leap as they both looked at me, great smiles growing on their faces.

"Let us soothe you," my wife said. God, I could still remember holding her hand as she passed, disease taking her only a month before our child was due. We were over the moon, excited to usher in our small, burgeoning family. The sickness came fast, taking her health in only weeks. She grew weak, and gaunt, as her muscles broke down and her mind faded. Before she passed I was holding her hand, each of us with a hand on her belly to feel our child's excitement. There was no movement. A week later, she passed, whether from disease or heartbreak, I don't know.

"Robert... Robert!" Vincent shook me from the vision, tears stinging my eyes. I was on the ground, curled into a fetal position, looking up at the stars. They were brighter now, pulsing faster, trying to coax me to them.

"No. No, they can't come back," I muttered to myself, dragging to my feet. "Sorry, ran out of breath."

"Are you sure? We can stop and rest for a while," he responded, concern in his voice.

"Need to get to your family," I grunted, picking up my pace again, heading down the dirt road worn over decades. "Ain't losing yours like I lost mine."

I could tell he had questions, but at the moment I didn't have the heart to answer any of them. We kept moving in silence, my ankle throbbing with every step. As we walked, I searched the ground around the road, hoping for a good branch or anything that could take some of the weight off, but the entire path was bare.

"You didn't hear that, did you?" I finally asked, taking him by surprise. All he did was shake his head and shrug, barely visible in the dark. Another screech echoed over the land, moving through trees ahead of the path.

"Hear what? A creature?" he replied with his own inquiry.

"No, no. Probably just tired, imagining things," I reassured him. If only I could do the same thing for myself. The voice echoed in my head still, a chorus of voices, all screaming in unison like one massive legion. I don't know what it wanted from me, but I wasn't accepting whatever offer it gave. I made a promise to Vincent. I plan to keep it.

We walked on, silence filling the darkness between us, while keeping an eye on the road ahead. Every so often we would stop for a moment, sit down, and take stock of where we were, what might be ahead, and generally just trying to rest and numb the pain. Nothing was working though, and I was feeling more feverish.

"Where are we going when we get there?" I asked, realizing I didn't know what to prepare for when we reached the city. Going deep into the heart would be dangerous, judging by what we saw back at Lancaster, and there was no guarantee we could even make it through to them alive ourselves, if they were still surviving.

"Don't have to go far. We live on the outskirts of the city, on the Western side, so we should be able to get there easy." He was running a finger along his revolver, nervously keeping it in his hand in case something came along. "Hopefully that means they'll be safe."

"Sure they are," I said, trying to reassure him. It didn't do much good, but he looked thankful, at least.

The hours finally passed as we slowly reached the city, seeing a sign that said 'Philadelphia Ahead' in big white letters.

"Almost there, Vincent. Your family is waiting," I said, still trying to keep a steady pace toward the city. Glowing lights were illuminating the night, showing the city around. Sporadic fires were burning, sending up funeral pyres to let people know where not to tread. Vincent looked even more worried seeing the flames taking the city, and I can't say I blamed him. "Which way do we go?"

As we reached the city limits, he beckoned me down a side street. He looked back at me, gaslights illuminating his scared face, still caked with blood from the battle. His eyes were hollow, terror setting in as he saw his hometown being devoured by hell in front of him.

We wound through the streets, occasionally hiding as some demon made its way by. They were even more gruesome lit by the fires and streetlights, a clear view of the humanoid ones' features finally defined for the first time. Hollow, sunken eyes with no discernible pupils, just darkened pits. Fangs grew from their mouths, over the lips to ensure they could tear meat no matter how tough. Many crawled on all fours, but some walked bipedal, hunched over as if they were always ready to lunge forward. We were able to hide in alleyways, but eventually, the streets grew too crowded, with homes sitting wall to wall.

"In here," Vincent said, stealing over to a small shack in the middle of another row of houses. He knocked on the door briefly, calling out in a soft voice, "Eliza?"

"V... Vincent?" A girl's voice from the other side. The door flew open, a young girl standing in the doorway with tears in her eyes. "Oh my god, you're back."

"Where's Mama?" he asked, looking behind her into the small shack. I could see it was only one room, a small bed in the corner.

A white sheet pulled up over something lying in it. Vincent must have seen her at the same time, running past Eliza and kneeling at the bedside. "Mama? Mama! Eliza, what happened? Why is she covered?!"

"I'm sorry Vincent… yesterday… she just… I don't know, she stopped breathing, and I was too afraid to go out to find the doctor. There have been these things walking the streets and people screaming and all I can smell is smoke…" She was getting frantic before Vincent stood, grabbing her and hugging her close while shushing her.

"It's okay. It's okay. We're going to get out of the city and find somewhere safe, okay?" he said, pulling her toward the door. "Don't worry about grabbing anything, we don't have any time."

"But what about Mama?" she asked back, tears choking her voice.

"There's no time, Eliza!" he said, yanking her toward the door again. Her sobbing grew louder, a screech from outside echoing it. "Shit. Shit, they heard you."

As we exited the shack, leaving the siblings' lives behind, one of the demons, walking on two feet, towering over the gaslights in the street, was walking towards us.

A sudden pain entered my head again, making me fall to the ground as my vision flashed. I was blinded, the voices coming back again like a chorus of hell.

"Join us in the stars, Robert." My wife's face again. Our baby held to her chest, hand reaching up for her.

"Rachel…" I said, reaching out for her as well. Suddenly I was being smacked in the face, jolted to our hellish reality once more. I still had something to do before I could join them, if that's even what was going to happen. I don't care, I could die as long as these kids get somewhere safe.

"Robert! We have to go!" Vincent was still smacking me, trying to get my attention. "There are two of them walking from down the road. We can slip out through a side alley, but we have to go NOW!"

I stood, shaking, to my feet, taking stock of my surroundings. The first demon was still lumbering toward us, dark eyes filled with longing and hunger. Another was lagging behind it by a few feet, walking on all fours with the same hungry look. I knew what I had to do.

"You two run," I said, looking at him while sheathing my saber and drawing the rifle from my back. I know I only have a couple of shots left in it from the ammo I scavenged yesterday, but an idea hit me that might work. "I'm hurt. It'll slow you down. Take her and run back to Peter's shack if you can. He might help you out."

"I can't leave you after all this. You're the only reason I'm alive, dammit!" he yelled back, raising his voice and fighting tears. I smiled at him, hefting the rifle to my shoulder.

"So stay alive, go live some for me. Make sure she's safe, maybe y'all can find some peace in this goddamn nightmare," I said, turning and taking aim with the rifle now. I timed my shot, waiting for the first demon to walk by the next lamp-post, still burning with whatever lamp oil or gas was still in there. Breathing out, pulling the trigger, the shot popped off and immediately shattered the glass of the nearest lamp. The oil splattered, catching fire from the barely burning wick and spilling onto the demon. I looked at Vincent again, nodding to him to run. He gave me one more look, nodding his head in thanks, before ushering Eliza away down a side street. Seeing them disappear around a corner, I turned back to the demons advancing toward me, "Time to raise hell."

The first one was still burning, shrieking into the night as the orange tongues of flame licked up and down its mottled body. Putting the rifle to my shoulder again, aiming, I hit the next gaslight right above the demon on all fours, spilling more flaming oil down on it. Both were towering infernos now, still advancing down the road toward me with malicious hunger in their eyes. One more shot was all I had, so I decided to make it count, aiming square between the eyes of the closest one. Breathe out, and pull the trigger.

POP!

The bullet hit it right on target, making the creature stumble as it walked. It tripped next to another lamp, cracking the glass and setting itself on fire with renewed force. It fell forward, shrieking in pain and clawing at its' skin. I took my chance, tossing aside the rifle and drawing my saber. As fast as my feet would move, jumping forward and swinging the saber high above my head, I brought it down on the first demon's neck, severing it clean.

Bathing in the most light I had seen since the battle of Gettysburg, I felt the heat of the flames licking at my coat. Keeping my saber out, I drew the pistol at my side, switching hands to accommodate my aim. Three shots left in the chamber. I flipped it back closed, taking aim at the next demon. It was still crawling toward me on all fours, staring at me with vacant eyes. I could see the abyss through it, Rachel's voice echoed in my head again, asking me to come to be with my family. I looked at the sky above, wondering if she was one of those pulsing stars out in the cosmos, in heaven, away from all of this nightmare we brought to earth. I hope she is. I hope I can join her there.

I could feel the wound on my leg stinging again, fresh blood dripping down as I reopened it by overextending my leg. I fired, steadying my hand as best as I could. The shot hit the terror in its shoulder, making it stumble.

Another shot. This time in the arm. My vision was starting to fade. I looked down to see blood quickly pooling underfoot, running from my leg.

Two more demons appeared on the street behind the remaining one, attracted by the sound of gunfire and screams of their kin. One bullet left, and it wasn't going to be enough.

Rachel's voice hit my mind again, this time even more loud and clear than before. Baby's laughter filled the air, making me smile knowing they were there. She spoke, "You can rest, Robert."

"Not yet," I said, shaking from the daze. I fired off one more shot, hoping to hit the nearest one just right to knock it down. My aim was true, hitting it right in the joint of its front leg. Unfortunately, the lamp that hit this one must have been low on oil, the flames burning low on it. I had to make my move, now. Tumbling down, I gritted my teeth and pushed through the pain of my leg, blood trailing behind me as my ankle throbbed. The saber again went for a wide slash, but my disoriented state threw the aim off. It sunk into the demon's shoulder.

Desperately, I pulled on it, trying to free it with my life still fading. The damned creature took the chance it had, shrieking and sinking sharp fangs into my side as it lunged toward me. My saber was trapped in its shoulder and half of my stomach was in its mouth. I knew this was the end. One more chance. Bludgeoning the creature's head with the pistol butt did nothing to loosen its grip. I needed something more. Reaching into my pockets, desperately searching for any ammunition I may have, I finally found my last resort to keeping these damned things occupied.

The flint was still in my pocket, along with the tinder box Peter had given me with it. I opened the box, finding a small burlap bag of gunpowder. The smell filled my nose, stinking as I tied off the end to close up the bag. Grabbing the blade of my saber, I ran the flint across it while holding the gunpowder close, hoping my last fleeting bit of fight would work. Blood loss was taking its toll on me, the demon still pressing teeth into my abdomen. Desperately, I kept striking the flint, sparks flying indiscriminately over me and the creature. It shrieked through the pain, still refusing to loosen the grip its teeth had on me.

Finally, my prayers were answered, the burlap taking light from the sparks. I gritted my teeth, pulling my arm back and feeling something tear in my stomach as muscles pulled against my teeth. No matter what, I knew I had to get this. I threw the bag with all my might, flames growing on the dry sackcloth as it flew.

It landed at the feet of the first demon, though it paid it no mind. Instead, its foot landed right on top of it, all but guaranteeing the flame would be extinguished.

Maybe Rachel was looking out for me, helping me do this one last task for someone before I faded. The creature began to step forward, the bag stuck to its foot, right into a pool of flame from one of the broken lanterns on the street. This was all the gunpowder needed, immediately igniting with a loud POP! The creature's leg was obliterated, white chunks of flesh flying out as it fell over, shrieking in pain. The other one tripped over it while still advancing, but my work was done. Sight fading, I pulled the saber from the demon's shoulder with all the might I had left, getting it free briefly before turning the blade and stabbing it through the skull.

Rachel was there, as it loosened its bite on me, letting me fall to the ground. I could see her kneel down in the street beside me, our baby still cradled in her arm, brushing a hand over my face with the other hand.

"I've missed you, my love," she said, standing and pulling me up with her. As we stared at each other, I noticed the light of the flames was replaced by soft, pulsating light. There were millions of stars shining around us, beckoning us closer in welcome. "Welcome home."

On the outskirts of Philadelphia, brother and sister fled the city's doom. Screams of demons pierced the night air, telling them to hurry away. As they found the road, a familiar one for Vincent, they looked back one more time to see the home they were leaving behind. It was only a moment before they turned, looking to the road ahead. There was a star that wasn't there before, shining more brightly than the others, beckoning them to safety. They continued onward, hoping to find a new home, or at least a peaceful life among the dark until they too, could join their loved ones in the stars.

WAR IS HELL

Gotta say, it was the last thing I expected to find going through all the crap in my grandpa's attic after he passed. He was never much for sentiment, and even though I knew his father, my great-grandfather, was a veteran of WWI, just like he was in WW2. Maybe he kept the journal out of some kind of soldier's honor, maybe a family obligation. Maybe it was just forgotten like he forgot all of us at the end. Probably would have been better had he tossed it.

My great-grandfather, Will Johnson—decorated lieutenant, fought at the battle of the River Somme in France, among others. The journal was definitely a snapshot of the time. Honestly, it's kind of sad, seeing the thoughts of a bright-eyed young boy who thought he was going to defend his country and come back to a loving, easy life go to a shell of a man was... harrowing. I'm honestly going to skip around the first few entries because it's sad to see. The worst thing is, he was becoming that empty shell long before the terrors started happening. Sometimes the horrors of war are just as bad as what we don't know.

Anyway, I'll transcribe what I can. I am going to do everyone the favor of making it a little easier to read though. He was definitely classically educated, and his vocabulary proved it. Even in the middle of a damn trench, the man was eloquent.

Oh, I'm also skipping around the love letter/entries he wrote to his wife, my great-grandmother. It just feels kind of wrong to share those, especially because I already felt awkward reading them. Alright, I'm going to get into it. Just a warning up front, the things he saw were pretty graphic, so... just be prepared. The movies don't capture half of what he saw in the field.

***

July 12, 1916

Today marks one week at Somme. The river still stands between us and the Germans, but we're advancing quickly. My British brethren here are hearty, with the hopes that this battle will be done soon so they can take a well-earned leave. I pray it's soon.

I've prayed to God as I go to sleep every few hours, taking my few free moments off watch or supply lines to shut my eyes whenever possible. Sleep came fitful at first, the sound of artillery shells falling around the trench keeping me on constant alert. We've lost a few good men in the past two days thanks to artillery. Paul, one of our British allies, was standing just feet away from me when he was taken out. An artillery shell came crashing down on him as he was setting up the razor wire atop the trench. One moment he was there, stretching coils out across the dirt and mud. I didn't even blink in the time it took for his insides to be scattered on those same coils of wire, a small boom deafening me. When I looked back up to see if he was okay, I could see part of his face hanging from the razor wire, a dangling eye staring right at me. I swear it looked like he was still there, pleading for help.

I couldn't even collect his tags. No idea where they ended up when there were parts of him scattered everywhere. I was clutching my rifle to my chest, struggling to breathe as I tasted the iron of his blood-spattered across my face. Another soldier nearby must have seen too, because his thousand-yard stare was worse than mine. I still had the faculty to do something, at least.

Sargeant told me to hit one of the bunks where I could actually sleep. He was unfazed by what I told him about the death, just a sigh and a confirmation that he would record it. Another in a long line. I'm going to sleep now, though I fear seeing Paul looking at me, begging with one eye for mercy every time I close my eyes.

July 13, 1916

I saw something last night, though I don't believe it was natural. We've had issues of course with wild animals coming into the field, but those are small. Foxes, deer, and yesterday a small bear, though all the poor creatures would often end up triggering mines planted in the no-man's-land to stop charges. I remember the bear stepping on one with a hind paw, setting it off, and blowing off its back legs. It was roaring in pain, legs bloody shreds almost up to the hip. After bickering over whether it would be a waste of ammo, one soldier finally hoisted up a white flag, running across the battlefield. He was hopping over mines like skipping stones until he finally got close enough. Two shots from his pistol and the screaming from the animal stopped. He came back without incident, our enemies likely taking pity on the animal just as we had. Guess we have something in common, despite their evil.

The body was left out there, nobody bothering to take it as we would our own dead. Maybe it was the rotting carcass that attracted the evil.

I was sitting near the battlement we had set up, a small line in the middle so we could see out without fear of taking a bullet, though it didn't always work well. The moon was out, full as well, so the entirety of the trenches and no-man's-land were lit with barely a lantern needed. A rain shower came by earlier, soaking the battlefield. Reflections cast from puddles made the field look like it was dotted with glowing orbs.

Maybe that's how it snuck in so easily, thanks to the glow of the moon reflecting. It was only the movement of it near the bear's carcass that gave it away. The bouncing of its ambient, white eyes was obvious against the backdrop of still, uninterrupted water.

It crawled from the river, stepping nimbly on long, nimble legs that were jointed in at least four points. It looked like a spider almost, the legs extending far before slanting down again toward the main body, a long, slithering thing that almost touched the ground itself. While the legs were spider-like, it reminded me more of the long centipedes we would see in our house during the summers, before the cat would gobble them up.

The eyes grew clearer the closer it got, to where I could see that they weren't actually solid. More like a fog that was taking consistent shape, moving with the creature. It was larger than the bear carcass it was moving toward, with the eyes turning a deep crimson as it grew closer, still glowing against the moonlight. What terrified me most was that even growing closer to the bear, its back end was still in the flowing river. At least two hundred meters, maybe more, still stalking toward the bear.

It finally reached the carcass, immediately ducking its head into the belly of the bear, like it was inhaling the scent of carrion. I could smell the thing beginning to rot from here in the humidity, even differentiating it from the stench of our own dead and wounded. This thing was taking enjoyment in it though, relishing the feast.

Don't think it took more than a minute. The damned thing reared its head, bear carcass in between two massive pincers. I could see a bristling opening just behind them, which it quickly used the pincers to push the bear into. With an assumed full belly, it slunk back down into the river, stepping around every mine as if it knew where they were. When it was finally back at the river, the twin moons disappeared, sinking back below the depths and blending with the full moon's reflection above.

I know not how long I sat there, breathless, as if watching something I shouldn't have seen. Something still gnaws at the back of my mind, a feeling that whatever this was is taboo from long ago. Ancient, maybe older than the river itself, is what this thing felt like. I remembered seeing some old artifacts that were brought around in a traveling museum, and watching this gave me that same primeval awe that those did.

I wasn't the only one to witness it, either. Later, when getting my field rations for the day, Jones, one of the newer privates joining our regiment, asked me if I was on watch last night. When I said yes, he asked me if I saw it. I suppose he thought I would what he meant, but I confirmed anyway to be safe, keeping myself subtle so as not to arouse suspicion. I've seen others get locked away for lunacy, the trenches getting to them a little too much, and was afraid it was happening to me now. I asked him if he meant the bear carcass, and he replied asking about the thing that ate it.

Our stories corroborated, lining up with the same descriptions, or in the same ballpark, at least. Though we still had no idea what it was, he believed it was a curse for all the blood spilled here. I don't know if I believe that, but do know I'll be praying more earnestly before closing my eyes to sleep again.

***

Hey, back to the present here. My head is killing me from trying to read his writing. The cursive he used was already super thin, but the pages had been water damaged at some point, so some words have me improvising with my best guess. I'll do some more transcription tomorrow, once I've had a chance to rest my eyes.

***

Okay, got a few more pages transcribed to upload. Going to go ahead and apologize for my fuckup in the last post—he was fighting on the Somme River, which is in France, not Britain. That's on me, I was tired. Anyway, the next few pages I've gotten here are a little more ambiguous in parts. I'm going with what I have, and I'll leave some notes where I wasn't able to transcribe what was written.

I know this sounds like a letdown, but this thing is in rough shape. It was stored in a little box in Gramps' attic, in the deep southeast where it's humid as satan's ballsack in the YMCA pool room. Some of the pages have damage from the ink bleeding. Others are literally covered in, what I have to assume, is blood. It's aged to a rusty brown color now, but the way it's spattered on the pages there's not much mistaking it.

I will say, the more I've read this and gotten to know my great-grandfather, the more I've understood what they mean by "war is hell". Saving Private Ryan doesn't have shit on what he saw in here. There're depths of hell that aren't enough for what some men have subjected others to.

July 14, 1916

I still know nothing of what the creature from the Somme was. Whether it may have been an apparition of evil or a primal force of nature, I can't say. I still see the glowing moons in my mind. Every time I close my eyes they haunt me, mandibles expanding to devour me. Strange as it sounds, I fear that I can feel the creature watching me. No matter what time of day, the feeling of dread doesn't leave my chest, a millstone weighing me to the bottom of this mud-ridden trench.

My chest hurts. We suffered many losses this morning when an attack took us by surprise. A gas attack, though we didn't realize these barbaric weapons had made it to this part of the line. An artillery shell landed a few meters down the trench from my lookout, hitting an unfortunate private hard enough to break his neck when it caught his helmet. For a moment everyone thought the shell just failed to explode. I'm just thankful I was far enough away that I wasn't caught in the real danger.

It was only a moment before some of the soldiers closer to the shell began to cough, clutching their chests in pain. It began to spread even further through the trench, a faint smell undercutting the gunpowder scent that had become so commonplace. It reminded me of grinding pepper for a meal, coarse and making me feel like I was going to sneeze.

The pain hit me immediately, like I had swallowed an entire pin cushion in one gulp. I could remember getting tangled in some swamp vines back home as a child, hunting with my father. The feeling of their thorns tearing at my skin now felt like it was being internalized. My mind worked quickly, praise be, as I was able to get my gas mask on relatively quickly. Unfortunately, I had already been hit with enough to be in pain, so the mask only prevented further injury. In the meantime, I ran, pulling a soldier nearby with me as I coughed and hacked, trying to get them out of range. Maybe twenty meters was all I made it before collapsing. I vomited in my mask from coughing so hard, blood mixing with mucus.

My breathing is still ragged, but stable now. The poor man I tried carrying out wasn't as lucky, with blood coming out ever thicker as he tried to cough the gas out. Every cough led him to gasp in for more air, desperately hoping this would be the one of fresh oxygen, but the gas was insidious, spreading through the trench. He died gasping in a puddle on the ground.

Explosions began to go off in the no-man's-land, loud and rapid. I lifted my head up to see if it was a bombing or an attempted charge while we were gassed, but what it really was filled me with more dread.

Our own men, the ones who were too late to put on their masks, had sought freedom from the gas in their oxygen-deprived terror. They climbed from the trench, venturing out into the no-man's-land before anyone could stop them. Many fell immediately, twitching on the ground as their lungs gave their last dying gasps. Others activated the mines without realizing it, bringing them a sweet release of death if they were fortunate. For others, it only increased their suffering, blowing off arms or legs. One fortunate soul fell face-first onto one, dying immediately. More mercy than the others could beg for.

Artillery shells fell not long after, likely already aimed by the enemy in the event this happened. All we could do was watch our brothers die choking in the mud.

I pray for their souls to find the embrace of heaven.

June 15, 1916

Jessica, I miss you. I hope you're well back home. I pray that the horrors I've seen are kept at bay here, far away from your innocence. The things I've seen here have left me changed, unsure of what may be real or not. My chest is pained even more, though I'm now feeling the effects on my skin and eyes even more so. It feels as though my eyes have been held open for hours against my will, dry and stinging with every movement. Even worse, my skin was blistered, red, and peeling even where my fatigues were covering me. The pain felt like an awful sunburn, though every time anything brushed me, it felt as though someone was scraping broken glass across my body.

Seeing some of the other men, I'm lucky. A soldier was brought by me, skin sloughing off in sheets from the chemical burns, screaming like a million demons were trying to escape his lungs.

Despite my injuries, I had to be on guard duty last night. The other man who was supposed to be on shift was currently scattered across the no-man's-land after the morning's attack. The night was bright once again, and from my cover, I could see much of no-man's-land, though clouds would occasionally bring darkness again.

Only a little before midnight, I was scanning the perimeter, keeping an eye to make sure no enemy troops snuck up on us. The wind tore through the trench, giving me a chill that only hurt the burns more. I was shivering when I noticed the movement, perhaps twenty meters away, and strained my eyes to see through the dark. As the moon finally broke cover, the perpetrator was illuminated. A soldier was staring at me, eyes twinkling in the moonlight, almost glaring right into mine. I caught my breath, straining to get up and take aim at him.

It only took me a moment to look through my scope to see that this soldier posed no danger. The bright, vacant eyes never blinked, staring into the abyssal darkness toward me. I could see that the lower jaw was missing, one of the many victims of the minefield. As fast as it appeared, another gust of strong wind came, turning it over face-first into the ground. Can't say I wasn't grateful for the breeze.

I wish that was the end of the horrors I saw last night. Those soldiers were still scattered about on the field, beginning to blend with the smell of death we were all so accustomed to already. I was keeping a keen eye on the river Somme, making sure that the moon-eyed creature wasn't going to appear to feast on their corpses. Reflections of the moon glimmered and played off the water though, leaving any efforts to pick out the creature pointless, if it was even there.

Eventually, sleep started to take me, but I shook myself awake by focusing on the river still. The rushing water was flowing, only rippling on the surface, but the strong current was undoubtedly carrying away anything caught under. Moonlight dancing off the currents was beautiful though, mesmerizing in the way every little ripple created a new pattern, dozens of new moons on the surface, leading down the river.

Clouds began to overtake the light again, the dark shadow quickly coasting over the field to cover us. When the shadow overtook the river, bringing darkness ever closer, I was hit with a sight that filled me with a pure terror that I've never felt in my life.

The moons in the water did not disappear with the cloud cover's takeover. Instead, they stayed teeming under the surface, swaying with the current through the length of the river. White, bulbous eyes were glowing faintly, with a few ascending from the water, moving those jointed spear-like legs nimbly over mines.

One came close enough to get the head that terrified me only a while before. I saw the mandibles pierce through the skull, sticking it on before lifting it to the gaping mouth. The pale moons turned a deep red once more as the decaying blood was fed on, this time giving a cemetery of orbs across the ruined battlefield.

I was mesmerized by them. The orbs went back to a soft glow, sliding back into the water with little sound or sign that it was ever there. Dozens of them, all slithering back into the dark, murky waters of the Somme.

In this moment, I know not if it was the shock of what I had just seen or my injuries. I fear it was far more real than I would ever hope though. As the cloud cover slid away from the moon again, revealing a battlefield now picked clean of the corpses there just moments before, they spoke to me. I know not if I was the only one that was spoken to, but the words have haunted me since, leaving me no rest as they repeat in my mind. I don't know if they're still speaking to me or if it's my imagination making me hear them. Even over the shelling though, like a deep, primeval growl of something that shouldn't be heard, I can still feel their whispers as I write these words.

"Bring us more."

———

Looking through the journal again, it's like these couple of pages are written by a totally different person. The difference is night and day in the man who was writing these words and the man writing the rest of the journal. I'm going to include a warning here because it will only let me use one flair, there is talk of a suicide in these next few pages. I know that's a bit much for some people.

June 16, 1916

The whispers haven't stopped. Nothing makes them cease, constantly muttering right into my ear their profane demands. It says to bring it more. Thousands of different voices, all clamoring to bring each of them more of the dead that already litter these fields.

I pray for them to stop in the night, crying as I whisper pleas to God for salvation. The words barely escape my ragged lungs, still stinging from the chlorine gas days ago. Nothing makes it stop. I would gladly take the gas again if it only made the voices stop. I fear for what they want me to do.

Sporadic artillery fire has been hitting closer today. Many of the others hit by the gas have already perished. I'm one of the few survivors, and even now it still feels that my skin is burning off. Even trying to use the pain to distract from the voices isn't working, as they simply get louder when I start ignoring them.

My belief right now is that others are hearing the whispers as well. Some of the other men around me have begun to act strange, more paranoid than is normal even for the trenches. Shell shock has set in among many of them, with most barely able to function. Many a poor soul has been carted out and back to base, ceasing to function after they just seemed to become overburdened by what they've seen.

I don't base this off mere speculation though, as Jones, the soldier who saw the first evil alongside me that night, confirmed my suspicions. In the night, he began screaming. From even further down the trench than I was, yet his screams echoed through the night, piercing the sound of bombs falling from heaven. The unmistakable sounds of a mine followed, with one more almost immediately behind, and his screaming stopped. I didn't realize at the time that it was him, but the news of what happened reached me only a few hours later.

Jones was muttering in his sleep about "feeding the riverbed", assumedly the same thing we had seen. When another soldier tried to rouse him to take his watch, Jones attacked. Before anyone could stop him, he had used his trench spade to behead the poor man. There were only seconds that passed when another soldier tried to get him off the dead one, the body still twitching, but Jones ran him through with the same spade.

Nobody was willing to approach him then, but they said he glowed in his eyes, almost like they were glazed over in sleep. They thought he was maybe having a fit, not quite awake, and believing their allies were enemies. Until he threw the severed head over the trench wall into no-man's-land, before starting to drag the rest up to the surface. When another soldier held him at gunpoint to question, all he said was that "he was hungry" and pointed to the river.

It's a wonder he wasn't shot right there, but instead, the story was that he got both of those dead bodies from the trench before hopping out himself. Once he was out, he kicked the head further into no-man's-land, stacked the bodies, and started dragging them toward the water. Made it maybe thirty meters before stepping on a mine, parts of him and the dead soldiers becoming unrecognizable from each other as they were scattered across the field. One of their pieces must have landed on another mine, making it explode as well.

The darkness of night was accented by heavy rains only minutes later, stopping anyone from trying to retrieve them. Sheets of sleet made a veil between us and the river, limiting our vision to only meters across the battlefield. Some of the watch last night believed they saw faint fires through the rain, but were disregarded. Their remains were gone by morning, though rationalized as being taken by the swelling river, engorged by the rain.

Right now it is still raining as I sit in this hole, praying to whatever god might listen. I don't know that the almighty lord of the bible is real anymore. If he was, this evil wouldn't be here.

***

June 17, 1916

He needs to feed. He's hungry. I don't know why I'm the one being told to do it, but I fear it's going to make me. Sleep has escaped me, I've been up for at least the past two days. There's no end to the voices. Does it torture our enemies as it does us? Is there someone on the other side suffering these same evils? Or is this evil on their side? I know not what to believe anymore. All I have are these whispers.

My prayers have failed.

***

(Editor's note—the following entries have no dates. I'm very likely missing a lot of information here, as the pages are covered almost completely in writings. Some I can understand, some are in what may very well be another language. Other pages are nonsense repeated. I've done what I can.)

It's rained for three days now. The river is invading no-man's-land, trying to reach our trench. I fear it's because they haven't eaten since Jones brought sacrifices. They will soon find us, turning the trench into a river of blood.

Their whispers grow louder as the flood rises. Whispers have become more demanding though, more aggressive. They threaten me if I don't feed them.

———————

Water grows near. The walls of the trench have been sloughing off as mud. There's no respite from the rain.

Voices of many are now becoming more clear as one. It sounds out like a chorus still, deafening me while nobody else hears. It demands to be fed.

———————

FEEDHIMFEEDHIMFEEDHIMFEEDHIM

———————

No God would allow such evil to exist. We are damned.

———————

IT SCREAMS AT ME TO FEED IT

———————

Last night I stole the corpse of a dead soldier. He was hit by a sniper bullet, right in the eye. The force of the bullet was enough to knock his helmet off the back, splattering brains over those near him. I don't know this young man's name, but I knew he could stop the demanding threats.

It only took a few moments for me to throw his corpse over the edge, out into the no-man's-land. The creeping flood waters were much closer now, rain still pouring in sheets. I pushed the body a little further, to the edge of where I knew the nearest mines were.

I was still standing there when it dragged his body into the current, pale moons glowing through curtains of rain. Eyes lit up red as it drained whatever dried blood was still in the soldier, sliding back into the depths where more glowing moons were waiting.

It still wants more.

———

Jessica, I'm sorry.

I'm sorry. I'm sorry. I'm so, so sorry. I have damned us.

———

Tonight I will throw myself into the current. Perhaps it will end this horror. It wants more. At least I will have silence if it devours me.

———

I will not be enough.

———

Water is splashing over the barricades of sand and dirt, desperately lapping at the trench. I swear I can see the glow of their eyes in the night, prowling the perimeter to choose their preferred meal. His whispers are louder now.

———

They are him. He is they. I fell asleep for the first time in days as water poured over me. These evils are only parts of the great terror below. It is greater than any nation can hope to fight, no matter our force. It demands to feed.

———

I will feed it. I will feed it as many as it needs.

———

It clouds my mind. I know that I cannot feed it. I cannot sacrifice my brothers in arms.

———

If it doesn't feed now it will take more.

———

A river of blood haunts my every waking moment. We are using what we can to stay above the water spilling into the trench.

———

Someone drowned in the bottom of the trench today. I found him. I... I believe I may have been the one to hold him under. His body disappeared under the waters and never came back up.

———

HE WANTS MORE

———

God is real. He is beneath us.

———

I will feed him. I will ascend.

———

I do not know who I am right now. I fear for these moments where I lose clarity. I do not know the man who wrote these pages. Someone is dead and I am to blame. Others will suspect me soon. I fear that the trench is only growing higher, and it is my fault. Others are despondent. Nobody acknowledges we may face our death of nature instead of the enemy. I cannot be the one to hurt more.

I will ensure I don't hurt anyone else.

Jessica, I love you. I'm sorry.

———

August 17, 1916

By the grace of God, I am alive. Though I am changed forever.

From what I have been told by the doctors, I will likely not walk again. Not on both legs, at least. My left leg is gone at the shin, while my right ends halfway up my thigh now. I will likely be in a wheelchair for the rest of my life, but I am alive.

I remember naught of the last hours I spent in the trenches. My allies tell me that one night I finally wandered into the no-man's-land of my own accord, stepping through the river and pushing up on us. I know not if I was following my own delusions or heeding the orders of evil. Before I was far from the trench, a shell hit in front of me. I was blown back to the trench, my legs being taken by the blast.

From there I was carted back to a field hospital where I lay even still. Recovery is a long road, and the pain is immense. I have heard that the line has advanced since my absence, finally able to move past the river. Now our only enemies are the ones we signed up to fight. I pray we are successful.

They have just delivered me more morphine. I grow weary, but it numbs the pain well. I hope to be back home soon, Jessica.

That's it. Nothing is mentioned again about whatever the hell he saw out there. The rest of the journal is basically a recovery process, learning to get around in a wheelchair and desperately hoping to get back home. Not sure who Jessica is, because my great-grand-mother's name is Meredith, but uh... I've heard a lot about her by now. Guessing she didn't accept what he came back as.

Gramps always told us he was an old bastard, with too much of a drinking problem and abusive as hell after what he had been through. Then again, that's how dad talks about gramps too. Guess seeing the horrors of war does that to people.

Maybe he just disregarded what he saw as just a part of hell on earth in the trenches. Maybe it was for his own sanity, unable to take the dissonance between what he saw and what he believed. He was a broken man in the end.

WE'LL ALL BE HERE FOREVER

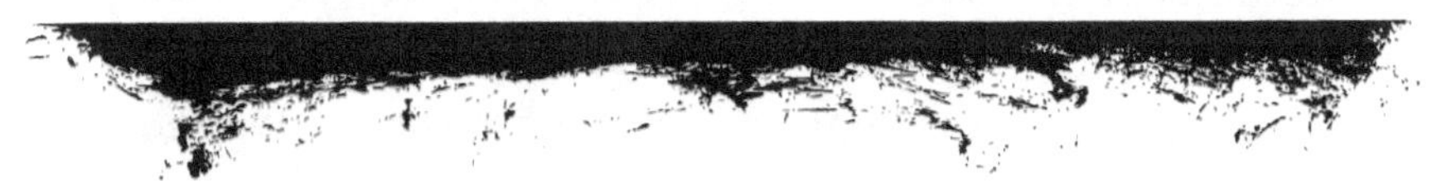

Michael Harrison walks into the small office we set up in. The man is going into his late seventies, but almost looked to be centuries old. We are in the CDC building in Atlanta, the date is July 7th, 2089. The temperature is at an all-time high and the small vent above the desk sounds like it is working overtime to keep a cool temperature. When Harrison sits down, he's cordial, almost excited to talk about our subject today, despite the negative impacts.

I apologize for being late. Traffic is terrible, miracle the interstate hasn't caught fire yet. Seems to be a summer tradition at this point.

[No worries, sir. Please, have a seat and we can begin the interview. I've had the room stocked with water and a few other drinks if you would like any.]

Yes, a water would be lovely, thank you. Now, how would you like to begin this?

[Well, the recorder is already set up and going since you stepped in. We just want to do a general overview of the beginnings of the outbreak. If you could please state your name and a bit about yourself for the recording, then begin your story.]

Great. Well, my name is Doctor Michael Harrison. I am the head researcher here for genetic anomalies at the Centers for Disease Control. For the last sixty-seven years, I have been assigned to researching the E2N6 virus, otherwise known as the Eternity Strain.

I had the misfortune of starting at the CDC one year before the virus became known to us. Before that, we studied various forms of cancer and other genetic diseases that cropped up here and there. None of that mattered once we started getting more and more cases of E2N6, though. We had to devote all time and resources to the virus once it took over twenty-five percent of the population. God knows it didn't do much good, though.

[Apologies, doctor. You are the first interview we are doing for this. Would you care to explain for the record exactly what the E2N6 virus is?]

Of course, all apologies. E2N6, the Eternity Strain, was a viral agent that made its way through the population starting, by our best estimation, in the year 2022. By 2040, my predecessors had determined that it had affected less than four hundred people, which explains how it flew under the radar for so long. Anyway, that's just the statistics part of it. Ninety-six percent of the population has it now, so it doesn't really do us much to think about those times.

The virus itself is a different story. It is found so far to be completely infectious to all but those with a natural genetic immunity. It is airborne, waterborne... everywhere. It's a fucking epidemic. A plague. The bastard is everywhere, pardon my French.

What happens is, the virus works its way through the bloodstream, reaching the spinal column. From there it completely rewrites the host's genetic code. Effectively, there's no way to explain it in plain English, but it prevents death from taking hold of the host.

[So it makes the host immortal?]

Yes... and no. We first discovered the gene in Charles Faron, who became what we dubbed Patient Zero. Faron, at the time in 2042, was a nine-year-old child living in Wisconsin. He was diagnosed two years prior with advanced leukemia, and was given a very grim outlook. He had been brought into the hospital one night by his parents when his condition had went into free fall overnight. He lapsed into a coma, and from the MRIs and tests the doctors performed, was effectively dead. The cancer was rapidly expanding.

Yet, he never flatlined. The cancer continued to spread, and his prognosis worsened, but he hung in there. They thought it was some sort of miracle. Eventually, the doctors told his parents they could try a much more aggressive treatment, but the survival rate was incredibly low. Knowing they would lose their son either way, they decided to go for it.

Lo-and-behold, the treatment was actually very effective. The child suffered some radiation sickness for about a year, but otherwise the cancer completely disappeared, and he had a new lease on life. Doctors simply believed it to be a one-off case, a child with an iron will to survive. Then the other cases started trickling in, and they took a closer look at him.

The real tell though, was when the more... gruesome cases started showing up. One was a car crash in Rhode Island. Poor bastard. Not so poor, of course, he was driving drunk and veered into the oncoming lane. Anyway, got split straight in half around his stomach. Entrails hanging, blood dripping, all the gory shit you see in the movies. EMTs thought they were pulling a mangled body out of the wreck to put into a closed casket funeral. Never expected for the fucker to start screaming in the body bag they had zipped him up in. Nearly made the ambulance driver need another EMT.

Do I need to stop cursing? It's a bad habit of mine, I'm sorry. Figure at this point though what's the harm, nobody's taking me to hell for it, after all.

[You're good, please continue.]

Yeah, yeah of course. They had to last minute reroute the guy from the morgue to the ICU. His vitals were still going, somehow. Still had brain activity, almost no heartbeat though thanks to the blood loss. Still coherent though. In shock, sure, but coherent. He was clawing at the poor nurse setting him up screaming at her not to let him die. {Harrison lets out a cold laugh here} If only he knew what he was asking.

Some other cases came in too. Suicide in Chicago, shotgun blast straight to the head. Poor lady missing half of her face but still walking around and gargling. She managed to walk right into the emergency room on her own, made it two blocks to get there with only one eye left in her skull. Doctors couldn't even fathom how she had the brain activity to think it through.

Naturally, as more and more incidents popped up, everyone started losing their minds. Can't blame them, of course. Seemed like the beginning of that old Romero film, everyone coming back from the dead. Except these folks didn't have a hunger for flesh. They only hungered for death's release. At this point, I honestly don't know if the former option would be worse.

We got a bunch of them together and did all kinds of tests. Nothing really showed until they did spinal taps on all of them. Spinal fluid came out looking like they had meningitis, we thought it was something we could pump them with some antivirals and fix up right away. Can you imagine a bunch of doctors sitting in a room discussing how they need to figure out a cure to life? Seriously floating discussions about how to kill humans again? So much for the Hippocratic Oath.

We've been working on this almost half a century, and we still haven't cracked the damn thing. Hell, all of our meddling may have just spread it around more. I know for sure I'm infected.

[At this point, he rolls up his sleeves showing me the myriad of scars running up and down his arms, crossing every way imaginable.]

Around twenty years ago, I had lost all hope we would ever fix this. Decided I was just going to take myself out of the equation and let someone else handle it. We hadn't even thought of testing anyone who wasn't a walking corpse, so I had no fucking clue the horror that was waiting for me. Wouldn't you know it... I was fucked too. Sat there in my bathtub for hours, warm water finally overcome with enough blood to overflow the whole thing. Fast as my body could make new blood, it left. Finally, the wounds healed, not that I was relieved about surviving a suicide.

We had hope there for a while that it was just an immunity from inflicted death, so to say. If we just let everyone live their natural lives, maybe they would pass on in their own time. We were quite a bit more naïve back then. As I'm sure you've seen in the past decades, nobody dies but those with the immunity gene. Those afflicted just continue to age, still being affected by the ravages of time. My poor mother, God help her, she's over a hundred years old at this point. She's had dementia since her late sixties. Doesn't remember who I am, who she is, half of the time she just screams for my father. He was one of the lucky few that was immune. Passed away back in 2054, God rest him.

So, here we are. No cure, no solution, humanity keeps on fucking and reproducing and we're running out of room since people aren't dying. Homelessness is at an all-time high, world hunger has skyrocketed, humanity as a whole is fucked. The worst part? It doesn't matter if it gets worse. Next to nobody is going to die from the awful conditions they live in. They're just going to keep on living, same shit circumstances, until they're just a bag of bones rotting away on the streets, not able to die, just trapped in their bodies fully aware of what's happening.

Would you say that there is any good that has come out of the Eternity Strain? Anything that could be construed as a positive?

[Harrison thinks for a moment, sipping at his water, before looking back and giving a wry smile]

Well, the murder rate dropped to nearly zero worldwide. Can't murder people when they can't die. If we have any kind of luck, the sun will explode and atomize us all.

[What about cremation? Will that actually cause death?]

If only. Even burnt to ashes, some kind of consciousness remains. We actually had someone volunteer to be the test for it, if you would believe that. Who the hell volunteers for the incinerator? Someone who's tasted more life than they can handle, that's who.

[Can you tell us what happened in this case?]

Screamed bloody murder a majority of the time he was in the incinerator. Eventually they died down, not sure if it was because of lack of oxygen or his lungs finally combusting. We gave it a little longer, of course, you know how they say you're safer overcooking than undercooking.

Opening the door, we had hope. Sure the process was painful and terrifying, but if it gave us the release of death again, something that many have lost the concept of by now, it would be worth it, right?

We were optimistic. Too optimistic, really. Opened the door, pulled out the tray with all the ashes. As much as a human body contains, we make a surprisingly small amount of ashes. Did you know that? Well, color us surprised when the still smoking remains on the tray were moving. Flowing, pulsating like they were trying to regain their human form. Even scattering the ashes didn't do anything. Every small particle, every minute cinder of that man, gravitated back together over the course of a day. We found the pile of ashes on the ground like someone had swept it up neatly.

I honestly believe this disease didn't just rewrite the genetic code for immortality, but for hanging on to the very soul of those it infects. Maybe God has damned us. Maybe it was our own hubris that brought this about. All I know is we have plenty of time to figure out a cure, if there is one.

You can actually visit that man if you'd like. There's a large glass urn in the lobby. We don't really know what else to do with him. We've tried communicating, but it's just lethargic, lost all will to live, but it can't fucking die. Life's greatest prank on humanity.

[Thank you for your service and your time today, Professor. Last thing, do you have any kind of advice for those dealing with the ramifications or challenges of their immortality?]

Get used to it, get used to each other. We'll all be here forever, after all.

NIGHT SHIFT

"Another night, another unit," I said, pressing the button on the screen as I hopped in the passenger seat of our medical transport pod. Merv hopped in next to me, taking his place behind the driving console and setting the coordinates. He offered me a steaming metal cup full of a dark liquid with a bitter, pungent smell. "God, how do you drink that stuff."

"Like this," Merv said, taking a massive gulp and audibly swallowing it. I could just shake my head, turning on the task screen in front of me. As Merv punched in coordinates on his side, I scrolled through last night's intake list, seeing what the other shift dealt with while we were off. Merv looked over as the pod rose, hovering briefly before ascending to a high point above the hangar, taking a lookout in the night sky. "They have a busy night?"

"Hell no! They only logged three and one was dead on arrival, so they just left it for the morning. Lazy sons of a... ah crap, of course we can't get an easy night too. First call is in." We started zipping northwest, speeding through the sky just below, creating a sonic boom in lower airspace. I opened the call notes and read them out loud. "Fifty-three-year-old male, history of heart palpitations and prostate issues. Requiring sample collection. Oh, come on!"

"Barely dark out and that's what we get. Gonna be a long night," Merv mused as the ship flew closer to our destination, finally coming to a rest hovering just over a small house in the middle of the suburbs. If anyone saw them, they paid no mind. Merv looked to my screen again as I further muttered the notes to myself. "They say what the sample is we need?"

"Guess," I said, looking him dead in the eyes. He sighed, letting out a curse.

"Fecal?" He groaned.

"And semen," I mentioned, throwing in the worst part last just to try and soften the blow. He punched the ceiling of the pilot cabin, cursing. "Flip for it?"

"No. This makes up for you covering me last week though, got it?" Merv pointed a finger at me as he crawled to the back, maneuvering the intake doors open and pushing the lever down on the platform. I waited a few minutes while he rode the platform down into the house, taking the sample there instead of bothering to load the patient up. After a moment he came back up, intake doors closing behind him as he put canisters into a nearby cooler and snapped gloves off, washing hands in the nearby sink. "God, I hate this job."

"Eh, it's not the worst job I've ever had. Sanitation? That was a bitch. Long days going and cleaning up other people's messes. You know who's the worst though?" I said as he took his seat back, swiping away the call log on his screen and confirming this task was finished. He looked at me, already knowing the answer.

"Veterinary?" he deadpanned.

"Jackpot. Those bastards once left an entire pile of cows for us to clean up. A pile, Merv. These were massive cows too!" I was pissed just thinking about it, the eighteen-hour cleanup and cows baking in the hot New Mexico sun was a smell I would never forget. The screen popped up another assignment. "Ah, crap. There's another one."

"Something other than stealing some guy's poop I hope," Merv mentioned, taking a big sip from his container, still steaming with heat. He punched a button on the console, zipping them high into the air again and off toward the next patient.

"Routine check," I said, scrolling through notes on the screen, scanning the notes for what was needed. "Says patient has possible growth on lungs, requesting biopsy. Then there's something about an enlarged heart they also want us to see about?"

"The hell are we supposed to do about an enlarged heart? Do they want us to slice it down to size or something? Sure, let me just trim off these little tough bits and that'll make it fit easier. I swear to God the people making these orders don't know what we even do down here!" Merv was almost shouting now as the cities zipped by below us, small masses of lights and sound teeming with nightlife. They must have been approaching the destination because the pod slowed to a stop just over a small clearing where a tent was set up. "Alright, who are we looking at?"

"Thirty-three-year-old female," I said, consulting the screen again. "You need help? We're gonna have to bring her on."

"Yeah, my back is killing me," he replied as we both clambered back to the exterior door, dropping it out and riding the platform down in front of the tent. Merv walked across the grass to the tent opening, unzipping it and peeking in. "Oh, come on."

"What?" I said, elbowing past him.

"There's two of them!" Merv whisper-shouted at me, holding the flap open to show me two women snuggled tightly together in the brisk night. "Which one do we need?"

"I don't know? It just gives the age and sex! There's no other identifying information!" I whisper-shouted back to him, getting frantic and not knowing which patient we were assigned to. "What do we do?"

"Just grab one and hope it's right?" he offered, stepping back from the tent and looking at me just as anxious.

"No! You know what happens if there's a mixup, remember what happened up in Vegas a few weeks ago with Pell?" I asked, remembering our coworker who had recently been demoted. "He's on sanitation now! He's got the shitty job! We're just going to have to take both and scan them on the ship!"

"How are we going to get both?!" Merv was almost shouting at me now, making me raise my hands and shush him quickly. "How the hell can we explain two patients in one call? They're going to get suspicious and fire us!"

The tent unzipped further, one of the women stepping out and looking at them, bleary-eyed. She blinked a few times before widening her eyes, staring at us in front of her. She simply nodded, muttering to herself as she stepped out of the tent and grabbed a roll of toilet paper, making her way to the edge of the clearing blissfully ignorant of us. I looked to Merv, who just nodded at me. We waited for her to come back, crouching behind the tent from view before Merv sprayed a small spritz from a canister on his belt. She walked right into it before being able to reach the tent flap, almost collapsing when I popped out and caught her, carrying her back to the loading lift.

"See? That was easy," I said, panting as we each heaved her on the table. "God, she's small. You would think she would be easier to carry."

"No way, these small ones are like concentrated mass. Once they go limp it's just dead weight and they become boulders," Merv muttered to me. I don't know how he thought that after all this time working medical, but I wasn't questioning at this point. "I thought they only sent us singles? They could have told us she had a roommate or something."

"Don't think they were roommates, bud," I popped back at him, examining the girl now resting peacefully on the exam table. I grabbed the incision laser nearby, holding up an X-ray screen with my other and searching over her lungs for the lump. I sighed in relief as I found it, immediately tracing a smooth line with the laser scalpel to reach it. The laser cut through with no issue, cauterizing the wound as it went. I saw the mass now, sitting large and discolored against her lung.

"Damn. That's definitely not good. They just wanted a biopsy? Like this needs to be removed," I mentioned, looking over the notes again before glancing back at the hole in her chest. "There's cancer there for sure. Well, they didn't say how much they needed for the biopsy."

I cleanly trimmed the tumor off with the laser, leaving no trace of discoloration behind before spraying in the sterilizing agent to heal and seal the incision. I plopped the lump into a canister and handed it off to Merv, who observed it briefly before setting it back in another cooler. "Think they're gonna have an issue with that?"

"I'll take it if they do," I mentioned, now bringing the X-ray screen over to the other side of her chest and seeing her heart, pulsing as it rushed blood through her body. I pushed the option for measurements and compared them to her size references "Normal-sized heart by all counts. Looks like that lump was the problem. Either way, cancer is a bitch and they don't deserve that. Just don't put it in the call notes and we should be alright."

Merv shrugged, pushing a small pen into the woman's arm, making an identifying mark for any other calls that may check back on her. He hoisted her up, moving back to the platform and lowering himself down to the ground once more, quickly taking her to the tent and plopping her through the flap. He heard a muffled groan of pain as she landed on the other woman, and came rushing up the platform again, whispering and making motions for me to move. "Start the damn engine! Take off!"

He hopped in as I approached my seat once more, pushing the takeoff button before also putting in the command for the medical station to self-sanitize. Merve made it through into the pod just as steam came zipping through it, bathing all the medical equipment.

"Could've waited!" he shouted at me as he took his seat once more, punching in notes for the call as he turned back to the screen dand we took off, leaving two very confused women below in the tent. I just looked back at him, shrugging. He started getting louder, "You would've cooked me!"

"Oh come on, that's early retirement at best and a nice workplace safety payout for you at worst. I was doing it with you in mind." I smiled at him as he rolled his eyes, going back to his console once more as we zipped high into the night now, assuming our place between the stars of the sky above and humanity's light underneath us. He shook his head at me as another notification popped up on our screens, reading 'Biopsy Sample Too Large'. I adopted my sarcastic surprise voice, "Oh no! Override it."

It was swiped away as the override went through, replaced by the next call for the night. I groaned as I looked at it, the list extending into a novel of problems the patient was having. "Oh come on, this one is going to take the rest of the night. They want an entire full organ check."

Merv groaned, tilting his head back, looking to the sky in frustration. "Just do it. Tell me everything they want. Let's get this over with."

"Ah hell. Well, we have the full organ check, a cerebral capacity test, and... oh come on!" I shouted, feeling like last night's shift got off easy compared to this.

"The one?" Merv asked, now flopping his head down on the console in front of him, causing the pod to alternate air temperature and various other settings. He was rocked back by his chair leaning, looking at me and just waiting to take the blow. I nodded, and he screamed in frustration. "Fine. Fine, but I'm so over this."

"Me too," I sighed, tapping a confirmation on the screen and bringing up the call sheet. The pod zipped us through the air once more, heading northeast this time as I scanned the sheet and figured out where we were heading. "Ah hell, it's a rural one too. Those are the worst."

"That's the best. Means nobody will be around to bother us and we can get things done quickly," Merv mentioned as the pod finished zipping through the air, slowing to a stop once more over a small ranch house in the middle of rolling fields, isolated and alone under the stars of the night. "Sweet. We'll pop him up, get what we need, then pop him back out. No problem!"

"Hate when you say that," I muttered as we both stood up, making our way to the loading hatch and pulling the lever. The lift descended right to the patient's window as we walked in, making as little sound as possible. The first thing to hit was the smell of alcohol, heavy and stale in the air like he had bathed in a thirty-six pack of the cheapest beer he could find. The older man was laying in the bed by himself, drool puddling on the mattress by his mouth as he sprawled in every direction. "Always ends up being some kind of problem..."

"Doesn't look like much of a problem here. He's already out, so that helps." Merv brought out a remote, pressing a button that materialized a hovering stretcher. We heaved to load the man on, moving him quickly back through the window and into the ship. The side of the stretcher hit the window frame, causing us both to stop dead in our tracks and wait for a moment to hear if he awoke. Snores continued as we both sighed in relief, bringing him up to the examination table and setting the stretcher down on top of it. Merv pressed his button again, making the stretcher disappear. "Alright, top-down?"

"Yeah, I'll start at the head, you go ahead and get the chest." I sighed, pulling scalpels and measurement tools from a nearby drawer under the exam table. I began cutting into the skin around his head, working my way down into the skull to look at his brain matter. "I'll never understand why they call us in for these. Like they live out in the middle of nowhere, what could there be to observe? Not like their social skills are usually great."

"Hell, not like anyone's social skills are great," Merv chortled back, cutting into the man's chest and fishing around for something. He pulled out a small handful of organs, plopping them on a scale nearby. "You hear about Tae?"

"Didn't he get moved to vet?" I asked, not looking over from the grey matter. Merv laughed again, plopping the organs back down into the man's chest before spraying the incision, making it close up almost immediately.

"Sanitation. Poor guy's been down there cleaning up cow guts for weeks. Apparently, his wife left him for his brother," Merv mentioned, giving a solid whistle to finish it off. "Alright, no abnormal organ weight or anything, so that's good. How's the brain looking?"

"I've seen worse. Some spots in the prefrontal are hardened, probably stopped development somewhere in the mid-teens. Parts around it have a few soft spots, probably a couple of untreated concussions in here too. God, they really did a number on people using lead for fuel." I kept examining, poking around through the man's brain as I went. "Poor guy. Sanitation was a bitch back in the day, probably hasn't gotten much easier since we have to be more low-key than the old days."

"Yeah, he messed up big time though. Like, fucked up with a capital 'F'," Merv replied as he moved down, looking into the man's abdomen now and examining the organs therein, "Oof. My liver is in rough shape down here. Tae was on one of the tapes that got released a few months back though, and you know how the suits took that."

"Seriously? It's been what, almost a hundred years since that old asshole crashed in New Mexico and got off with a slap on the wrist and paid suspension for a year, but we get moved to the literal shit shift if we get caught by one of these water bags with a camera that barely gets their lowest quality video?" I could feel my anger rising, I kept the rant going, thinking about my own time back in sanitation and the entire mess that came with it. "Am I being crazy about this? Like, nobody in charge knows what it's like to be in the field these days. They haven't done a probe since the sixties! Remember when they got an entire committee made to look for us?"

"Uh," Merv stuttered as I kept poking at the man's brain, taking a small sample and placing it in a jar.

"Doubt they've even used the new tech. Hell, their ships didn't even cloak! These assholes flew around with bright ass lights all over the damn place because they liked fucking with the locals! It was just a practical joke to make them think they were gods or something." I finished poking the man's brain, flipping the top of his skull back on his head and lasering the scalp back on. "Look, let them come do a round then they can bitch at us. I'd like to see them try."

"WHAT THE HELL ARE YOU?!" The shout scared me, making me look at Merv before realizing his eyes were wider than normal, staring at the patient. "Jesus Christ! Lizard people!"

"Why is it always lizard people with these guys? Do we look like lizards?" I asked Merv, calmly reaching over to grab a needle, moving to a cabinet, and searching for the sedative. "Oh, shit."

"ALIENS! ALIENS! HELP ME!" The patient was still ranting and raving, eyes wide as he tried to fight the straps holding him to the table. "I KNEW IT! YOU WILL NOT TRIUMPH HERE, SATAN!"

"Stereotype checklist is going strong..." I muttered, finally finding the sedative and loading it into the syringe. "That was probably my fault, I'll take the probe."

"Oh, thank god," Merv said, making the patient's eyes grow wide at the expression. Merv looked at him before he could start stammering out more exorcism liturgies at us. "You don't have a trademark on the word 'god', buddy. Been a lot of them over the years."

"Doubt that's what he's gonna take away from this," I mentioned, moving back to the table and jabbing the syringe into his neck.

"You will not prevail, demons! Our Lord Jesus Christ will vanquish you and bring you to light!" The man ranted and raved, slowly losing steam over his babbling, "Our president will expose all of you damn Illumin-"

He trailed off and passed out, lightly snoring as his eyes rolled back before closing. Merv moved down to his legs, taking a small reflex hammer and testing on the patient's knee before looking over to me. "You gonna do the probe?"

"Yeah, yeah. Getting to it." I waved him off, moving over to the tool shelf on the wall and picking up the old faithful, used since the early days when we first came to the planet and began studying these strange, primitive people. Before I could get to work on it, the man began convulsing on the table. "Oh, hell."

We grabbed a neutralizer, holding it to his chest and zapping a few bolts to stabilize him. Nothing. The convulsions kept on, foam beginning to exude from the patient's mouth as it went. After a few more shocks from the neutralizer, he went still, eyes rolling back and breathing coming to a halt.

"You gave him the right sedative, right?" Merv asked me, staring at the now dead body on our exam table. "Like, measured right and everything?"

"I've done this a thousand times, of course I gave it right." I was pacing, poking the patient and taking a blood sample before placing the small drop in one of our scanners. The mechanism whirred for a moment before popping out a list of chemicals and medications found inside. "Of course. Of course, they wouldn't do a habit search and maybe some basic investigating before they sent us the call. Wouldn't be important or anything to know the guy has enough methamphetamine in his system to kill a rhino. Definitely wouldn't be important to have a 'No Sedation' note."

"How are we supposed to do a full workup without some kind of sedation? That makes no sense." Merv looked at me quizzically before seemingly understanding. "Yeah, no. Looking at it, it makes total sense."

"Of course it does! They never had to deal with this shit! Why should they make sure they're sending the correct information in 2019? Not like things have evolved over eight hundred or so years. They only had to worry about natives smoking hashish and thinking they were deities!" I was worked up now, trying to fight between my infuriated side, wanting to throw the higher-ups in an airlock and press the button while my other side was near a breakdown over the implications this might have on my job. "Can't we just put him back?"

"No, we can't just put him back! Look at him! They're going to find traces of Roxar-6 in his system, then you know what that's going to mean. There'll be a whole thing while the humans figure out if it's some new drug they invented, then it'll go into the conspiracy theories because this guy was obviously off his damn rocker, and they'll probably think he was silenced. Don't even get me started on when the chem tests move past the higher-ups and those guys in the black suits get involved. Bunch of damn pricks thinking they're the ones monitoring us..." Merv was ranting now as I watched him, wondering where all this sudden knowledge of Earth society came from. He shrugged back at me, "Earth news is probably the best entertainment I've seen since they thought that radio broadcast was real, alright? Don't shame me for my interests."

"So what should we do with him?" I asked, putting my head in my hands and massaging my temples. We couldn't just leave him in his bed because he would be discovered, but if he goes missing, that's a whole other issue.... "Think I've got an idea. We need to check his house though."

"Oh god, please don't tell me..." Merv groaned, looking up and holding his head now. "Look, just because he was on the stuff doesn't mean..."

"Shhh... let's just find out," I said, hopping back to the front of our pod and zipping us back down near the former patient's home. I stood and moved to the intake hatch, turning back to Merv as the lights went off and I left the pod in cloak mode. "Come on, help me out."

"I need to retire," Merv muttered, following behind me as I jumped through the open window we had originally lifted him through. The house was two stories, so we immediately made our way out of the room in search of stairs, following them down before scanning and checking all the doors of the bottom floor. "See a basement door anywhere? That's the best bet."

"Hold on..." I said, moving aside a tacky painting of Jesus standing behind the president in the oval office. "Gotta be honest, I don't feel so bad after seeing all the wood paneling in here. Imagine being a tree and growing for a millennium before some asshole turns you into paneling in a neo-Nazi's house? How long do you think before humans find out about sentient nature?"

"Doubt it's coming soon. They're barely sentient," Merv snorted back, opening another door near the back of the house and staring down. "Basement over here."

I hurried over and we descended the stairs, trying not to fall as our short legs made the downward climb rough. We finally entered a small basement space, flipping on a nearby light switch and almost being blinded as bright fluorescents began to shine off all white walls. Merv turned to me and shook his head.

"You're either a genius or really lucky," he mentioned, moving forward and beginning to tinker with various lab equipment and beakers that lined the walls and tables. A steady flame was running under one, making something evaporate and drip through a small spout into another liquid that was slowly forming.

"I could be both," I said, moving forward and pulling cabinets open before finding my prize. A small rubber hose was being fed through under the countertop, providing gas for the small flame. I punched a small hole in it before turning the flame burner to its lowest setting, ensuring the maximum amount leaked from the hole instead of the burner. "Anything else good and flammable?"

"There's an entire bottle of methane gas in here. I'm just gonna tweak the nozzle a little," Merv shouted back to me before we regrouped by the stairs. "Alright, let's load him back in and get out of here before it all goes down."

We began to head toward the stairs before the closing of a door and footsteps above before a voice cut through. "Joey! Joey, you awake!? I need a re-up."

"Shit," I muttered, assuming Joey was the one lying dead on our table right now. I heard more stomps, heading in the direction of the door we had entered the basement through.

"Aight I'm just gonna grab some and leave money on the counter, okay!?" The door opened, footsteps now thumping heavily down the stairs. Merv looked around wildly as he tried to find anywhere we could hide. He opened a nearby cabinet under the counter, finding only graduated cylinders and glassware full of various chemicals awaiting their turn to be mixed. He grabbed one with a label on it reading Cl. The man rounded the stair corner and stopped about ten steps from the bottom, rubbing his eyes before looking back at the sight before him. "Damn Joey, you gotta stop getting all this weird stuff to decorate. Little green men seem kinda cliche out here."

He moved down the steps as we stayed completely still, hoping he would hang onto the idea that we were just terrible decorations. I could hear Merv grasping the bottle more tightly, and smell the gas getting stronger by the moment. If the newcomer smelled it too, he made no sign. Instead, he moved to the counter near him and picked up a small back full of crystals, rattling it around in front of his eyes before sticking it in the pocket of his jacket. He stopped in front of us as he went to leave, coming down to our level to inspect.

"Must be more of those little props he buys. Looks like it could be in a movie though. Really nice quality." He poked my forehead, prodding around my body as I desperately tried to stay still and act like a prop. Tried, until he poked me, "Damn, the eyes almost look like they're looking at me."

He poked hard, making me reel back and hold a hand to my eye. He screamed as I shouted, Merv quickly taking advantage of the situation and running up to the stairs, dragging me behind him as he did. He finally twisted the cap off the bottle completely, tossing it back at the man's feet as I came to my own senses and began climbing the stairs with him. The bottle burst into glass fragments as a yellow haze sprung forth from the spot it landed at, quickly rising into the air and enveloping the man. He fell to his knees, coughing and trying to rid his lungs of the chlorine now stabbing needles into his chest as he breathed.

"I'm quitting. I swear I'm quitting. I'm done with this shitty job, on this shitty planet, with these shitty bosses," I ranted, running back up the next flight of stairs and trying to reach the window we jumped through. I could still hear him coughing and hacking from behind us, desperately trying to evacuate the gas's excruciating pain. Merv finally reached the window, hopping through before reaching back and helping me in. We moved over to the exam table quickly, grabbing onto Joey's rapidly cooling body and throwing it through the window haphazardly. Merv barely hit the button to close the hatch before we were in our seats, frantically trying to zip away from the house.

"Yeah, if they don't fire us then I quit," Merv said through labored breaths. "Haven't run that fast since the Phoenix incident."

"That when you forgot your lights were on before you left the ship?" I replied, chuckling as we finally heard a massive explosion behind us. Merv turned on the rear camera, showing a massive fireball shooting up from where the house was just moments ago. "Thank god that's over."

The explosion only took moments to hit us, the pod rocking slightly as we looked back to the flaming pyre we had created in the night. Blue and orange flames licked at each other as the rest of the house caught, incinerating the evidence of our botched abduction.

"Yeah. Forgot the damned things were on. In my defense, they had just switched to the new lighting system, and I told them it was a bad idea to fly over a city metro, but noooooo why would we listen to the person actually doing the job?" Merv started ranting. I chuckled, bringing up the call log and beginning to input the falsified notes for our failure tonight. Merv looked over, reading as I went. "Don't tell me you're notating all that."

"Hell no. I'm putting in that we pulled everything off safely and noted that there was the smell of natural gas in the house so that may lead to further follow-up exams," I said, finishing out the results of our investigation and signing off before closing down the scanner. "Call it?"

"We're on the same wavelength," he replied, picking up his tin and giving a small toast as he downed the remainder of its liquid. "You should really try this stuff. I can see why they like it down there. Especially when they mix it with milk. You ever wonder about the person that discovered milk?"

"Can't say I have," I sighed, punching in our home coordinates. The ship zipped off into the sky, heading for the moon.

"Like, who saw a cow's udder and thought 'I can drink this'? Where did that cross anyone's mind? God, these humans, I swear what they do makes no sense." He rambled on as we began breaking free from Earth's atmosphere, heading into orbit and past a roaming defense satellite. "Tell you though, they ever get back to space and that's gonna be a whole other fiasco. Higher-ups had enough of a time getting them to stop the first go around. Hell, remember when they had all those guys shoot each other in Dallas? Still didn't throw them off! Jackasses didn't stop until they hit the moon. Now they've got these stupid robots on Mars too. Ever wonder what it would be like if we just stopped replacing the video feed it sends back?"

"All hell would break loose, and humans would probably cease to exist," I replied, pod zipping ever closer to the moon's surface as a small hatch opened to welcome us in. "They can't stand the idea of a thriving civilization on their own planet. Why would they accept it from a whole other one?"

"Got a point there. Hell, we still have problems of our own to work out. We may not be as behind as them, but we're nowhere near finished," he answered back as the pod landed in the small docking bay of the moon, an attendant coming over as they stepped off to service and sanitize the interior. We disembarked, Merv giving a wave to the attendant as he passed them. "Mornin' Sev."

"Morning. Anything fun out there tonight?" Sev asked them back, moving in and examining the rear pod. "Heard there was an explosion at one of the places you left not long ago. House and the patient went up in flames. You two happen to know why that came to be?"

Uh oh. Merv and I shot each other a glance and desperately searched for something, stalling as we went. I offered up, "You know, I think we felt a little turbulence heading back up. Thought we smelled gas in there when we were putting him back, right Merv?"

"Yeah, yeah, it definitely smelled like there was gas in the room. Could have left his stove on, maybe? We did notice a car was there when we put him back that wasn't there before, but there wasn't anyone in his bedroom when we put him back," Merv spat out. I could tell he was trying not to crack, not to make the slightest nervous hint as Sev stared us down. Finally, he looked away, moving into the pod bay.

"Ah, well. Not the first, not the last." I could hear him say as he began his sanitizing and inspection process. Merv and I simply shook our heads at each other, turning to walk back toward the employee barracks.

"Why did we sign up for this again?" he asked me.

"I recall something about civic duty and helping to further other civilizations to avoid our mistakes. At least that's what I had to swear when I signed up," I replied, letting out a heavy sigh as the massive doors opened. "Either way, only a few more decades. They'll either destroy themselves or figure their shit out here in the next few decades."

"Heard that one before." He rolled his eyes as we entered, stepping up to our respective rest pods. "Guess you're more optimistic than I am."

I thought back to the things I had seen in Earth broadcasts recently, from the civil unrest to the seeming regression in sociological and ecological use. There were bright spots in it though, and those were the parts I kept replaying when I asked myself why I kept going. The brief flashes where I could tell they were beginning to shine through and transcend beyond their individual selves. The togetherness, celebrations, mourning, and even riots that had unfolded all held a single goal of unity.

"Yeah, we were like that once too, though," I replied, smiling as I hopped into my rest pod for the night, knowing as much as I grumble and moan about it, there was a brighter future in mind.

"So if anyone asks, we know nothing about what happened, right?" Merv said, again giving me a nervous look from his pod.

I could only chuckle, making a zip motion across my narrow mouth, "We know nothing."

MOONSTRUCK

"**W**ake up Collins." Sarge's gruff voice roused me from my sleep, making me shake the exhaustion from my bones. The AR was still resting on my knee, hand around the grip and at the ready. "Prisoner's comin' in. We're making the jump soon."

This was the third jump I've been on this month, and it was getting exhausting. Ever been molecularized through a teleporter through space? Yeah, not a fun experience. Not to mention having to stay for a few days in Cerberus is going to be a bitch. The gravity change alone is going to wreak havoc on my stomach.

"Alright folks, we've got a big one today." The Sarge stood at the front of the briefing room, looking us all down. "Real goddamn monster. The Blackwater Ripper killed seventy people in the span of one night."

A picture flashed up on the screen, just a scrawny little guy, bags under his eyes. Didn't look like he could hurt a store mannequin, much less seventy people in one night.

"Oh shit, I heard about this guy," Perkins said from another seat. His eyes narrow, looking closer at the picture of the man. "Asshole looks like he never left his basement."

"Yeah, you would think. A lot of people with their insides shredded say otherwise. Almost half of 'em kids. This damn monster went on a killing spree at a birthday first, then made his way through most of the neighborhood he lived in. All ripped out like a damn animal was eating 'em," Sarge continued, shouting and red-faced. Wasn't often that we got a transfer that riled him up, but this guy touched a nerve.

"Thought they said it was a shooting?" Matthews asked, but Sarge shook his head.

"No. They were torn apart. Called it a shooting to keep the public from going crazy with the details." Sarge was more on edge, with a steel in his voice that I had only heard in the most tense situations.

"Hey Sarge, you're awfully pissed about this guy," Perkins spoke up, noticing just as I did. Sarge shook his head, looking down for a moment.

"That happened back home. I knew some of those people. Went to school with them. Seeing those crime scene photos is one of the few things that's gonna haunt me," he said, before composing himself once more. "Alright, they're bringing him in now. We've got a quick jump up there then a twenty-four-hour security hold to make sure he doesn't just croak when he goes through the diffusion."

"Would that really be so bad?" Matthews said, from his corner of the room. He was leaning forward, gun off leaning against the wall. Eyebrows raised, he just shrugged his shoulders when Sarge glared at him. "Just saying, an airlock wouldn't cost as many taxpayer dollars."

"I want to as much as the next person, but we're sworn to our duty. You know with your clearance we can't just do that kind of shit," Sarge replied.

"Even the dumbass president doesn't know we exist, you think someone's gonna be mad for murking a murderer?" Perkins spoke again, chuckling. Another glare shut him down, but he was still breathing out of his nose, laughing to himself.

"Collins, I want you and Matthews on rear guard, standard formation. We're going the two-by-two system, me and Perkins first, then the perp, then you two. From there you know the walk toward the main facility, all the standard shit. Just another routine transfer as far as we're concerned." Sarge finished his orders, looking at all of us for confirmation we understood.

"Yes, sir!" All echoed at once as we filed out of the room, toward the transport station.

The prisoner was standing by the door, chains on hands and feet. Nobody knew what the hell he could do, or how he did the murders. I heard the story from Sarge, but there wasn't any way someone this scrawny could have done it. Hell, covering it up as a shooting is the new norm for a lot of fuckers like this guy. Not like it isn't a plausible situation everywhere these days.

"Phillip Kent," Sarge said, stiff but loud so the little man heard. He jumped, frightened by the loud voice as his glasses almost fell off. Brown hair, shaggy down to his neck almost, with a massive pair of old Coke bottle glasses. The guy looked like a Dahmer for the new age. "You understand that you have been waived trial rights due to the nature of your crimes?"

"Please, where are we? I don't even know what I did!?" He was almost in tears, begging and pleading. The bags under his eyes were more exacerbated than the pictures, and the eyes themselves were almost bloodshot. "I just woke up in blood. I don't know how I got there. They told me I killed people but... I couldn't kill people. I wouldn't! Please, you believe me, right?"

"Shut up. Do you understand that you will be effectively a dead man when it comes to any record of your life? You, as a person, no longer exist," Sarge continued. "Everything from here on out is off the books, does not exist, and that includes you. You are being transferred to Cerberus, where you'll be locked in and promptly forgotten by the rest of the world."

At this point, he was just streaming tears, close to falling to his knees. I started to feel sorry for him, but then remembered what Sarge had said about those people he killed. There was something this guy was hiding behind the pitiful act.

Sarge pushed Kent into the diffusion room, where two techs stood on standby in front of a console. Sarge situated Kent in the third silver pod on the wall, sealing it shut while the prisoner just kept crying. Then, Sarge climbed into the first, while Perkins took his spot in the second. Matthews and I climbed into the last two on the other side of Kent.

"Diffusion initializing," one of the techs said through a small speaker in the tube. It was cramped, with only the small window to see outside through. I took a deep breath, knowing it could be a couple of minutes before it sent me up. The metal they use to make the pods smelled like an old jewelry store, making me wish for times when I didn't have to go to the fucking moon. All I could do was sigh, though. These things might be cutting-edge tech, but the transfer rate is slow and has to be done one by one so we don't fuse or some crazy science mumbo jumbo. I fell asleep during the presentation on it.

I closed my eyes, letting myself forget I was in a tube about to get broken down to a genetic level and sent through space. When they told me I was getting a promotion from being in spec ops for so long, telling me that it was an easy, cushy job with very little work, they really should have elaborated. Would've been nice to know ahead of time if it involved being broken down into the void of space, y'know?

"Collins, you're up," the voice came through again. I felt the lights go down and saw the darkness creep in. The feeling started from down in my toes first, everything coming apart as I broke down. It was an odd sensation, kind of like when a limb falls asleep.

Everything started coming back together, even as I felt my consciousness drifting through space toward the moon. I felt the weightlessness take hold for a moment, and then I was grounded again, though a little bit lighter than before. My gun was still firmly at my side, with nothing out of place. I made these jumps dozens of times, but it still felt really odd to go through this.

"Go back!" I heard the scream before I could see the scene outside my pod window. Crimson was everywhere, even across the plexiglass that covered my own pod opening. There were sprays of blood and through the corner, I could see a body. Blood was pooled in all around them, and there was way more than any one human body could hold. "Get the hell out of here, dammit! Tell them to stop sending people!"

The blood sprayed again before I could hear a gunshot, followed by a massive, guttural roar. I saw Sarge backing up toward my pod, holding on to his pistol while aiming at some massive creature moving closer toward him. I could see blood shimmering off of it in the reflected sunlight off the moon as it stalked closer, Sarge firing off more bullets as it did. Nothing seemed to work, and he just kept coming.

"Sir, I'm not just going to leave you here, what happened!" I screamed through the window. He grunted back, firing again, but this time at the thing's feet. There wasn't any sign it had an effect, and the creature just kept coming towards us with no regard. The other tube finally beeped, and I could see the door open while Matthews stepped out.

"The hell, Sarge?" he said, before the thing grabbed him, biting hard on his neck. I had to do something, so popped open my door and hefted the rifle to my shoulders, aiming straight for the thing's head. A three-round burst flew out of the chamber but bounced off and pinged on the floor after hitting the thing's skull. I could see it more clearly now, fur matted with blood from the techs. Perkins was lying in a corner, hand to his neck as it was oozing blood. He was still alive, but there was no way he was fighting. Matthews was in the same spot now, with a gaping wound in his neck. Perkins started to stand up as Sarge shouted him down.

"Stop before you bleed out, idiot!" Sarge fired more rounds into the beast, again bouncing off without harm. Its eyes were glowing red, with fangs dripping deep scarlet blood, shining in the pale fluorescent light. I stepped back, not sure what to do when Perkins began to change.

It looked like he started seizing, but after a moment, fur began to sprout. He screamed in anguish, face contorting as something happened. The bones in his face looked like they were breaking and reforming, reconnecting into some new species. The teeth in his mouth grew to massive fangs, bones bursting forth from his fingertips into sharp claws. I could see Matthews beginning to undergo the same thing.

"RUN!" Sarge shouted at me, pushing me toward the main corridor to the prison. "Get the hell out of here, hide."

We both ran through the tunnel, only the occasional fluorescent light every few feet to light the way. Plexiglass windows, thick to keep up from depressurizing, gave a view of the rocky moon's surface outside. The earth sat far on the horizon, like a distant dream of safety. The blue water looked like the safest place in the universe, but the moon was thousands of miles away from any haven. I could tell Sarge was hurt, limping as we ran.

"Fucker got my ankle when I unlocked his pod. Don't know what the fuck happened, but soon as he was up here shit went south," he grumbled as we kept our pace down the tunnel. The airlock was ahead, a guard standing behind it waiting for us to reach them. The look of surprise on their face told me they weren't prepared for anything that was about to go down. "Open the damn door!"

The man scrambled, hitting the button to let us through. The noises behind us were unworldly, like howls from the jowls of hell. They were getting closer, rounding the curve right along a blood trail left by Sarge. We got through the door, repeatedly mashing the button to close it before turning around and hefting my gun.

"No, hide. This thing isn't something we can just fight off," Sarge said, ushering me toward one of the large storage lockers in the corner. I opened the door, flinging things to the side and stepping in before closing it. I tried to keep my gun where it could be aimed and shot immediately, but there wasn't any guarantee it would happen fast enough to save us. "I'm going to lead them away. Once they're gone, you go back to the teleporter."

"The fuck is happening down there?!" A yell came from the upper part of the base, where the cells were lined up above. The other guards must have been in the monitoring station on the other side.

"Get the warden!" The airlock guard shouted back. A clamor rose up among the cells above, most with the resounding sentiment of 'fuck the warden'. "Jackasses. Jerry, run and get the warden!"

"No. Best you can do right now is barricade until everyone can get to the pods. These things ain't hurt by regular bullets," I said, still watching them through the locker slats. The beasts finally reached the door, slamming against it with tremendous force. I'm surprised it didn't give then and there, but they kept slamming through it. "Sarge, what are we going to do?"

"Fuck. Alright, you go warn the others to barricade themselves. Collins, once they're past here and you can get out, go back to the pods and get a message back home," he said, backing toward the next hallway as the airlock guard took off running down it. "You get out of here. That's an order."

"Yes, sir," I said, keeping my eyes trained on him as the plexiglass finally gave a resounding crunch. The entire door shattered, leaving massive shards everywhere on the floor. The three came through, Perkins and Matthews now both hulking beasts, just like Kent became.

"Come on, bastards!" Sarge said, firing off a shot at one and leading them into the hall. They kept running after him, gaining quick as he limped. Prisoners along both levels in the hall started shouting, some screaming in fear. The beasts seem to have gotten distracted by the new canned food all around them, because one turned to the nearest cell right through the door, reaching through to grab the inmate inside before he could move back far enough. Crimson bloomed forth on the white prison jumpsuit, and the man fell back screaming in terror as the beast again pulled him toward their jowls. Their snout was narrow enough to get through the bars, biting the man inside.

I had to put a hand over my mouth as they began making their way, the newest bitten now turning like the rest. The howling just kept growing as they increased their numbers, and I could hear useless gunshots going off over the chaos. We'll be lucky if someone doesn't break a hole in the pressurized system. Then again, it may be a mercy if all of us are just sucked into the vacuum of space, never to speak of what happened here.

When the coast finally seemed clear, or clear enough where I could get through without being seen, I slowly made my way out of the locker, making sure to keep my head on a swivel for any beasts that may be lurking in wait. Nothing I could see, so I started off down the corridor, making my way back to the pod bay. The blood trails were still fresh, and the three had only sprayed more around during their rush after us. I finally got to the pod room to see the floor almost completely covered in blood in the cramped space. It took me a moment, but once my footsteps from the hall stopped echoing, I could hear muffled breathing.

"Oh my god, is someone alive in here?" I said, trying not to be too loud just in case. Suddenly a head popped up from behind the tech station, fur and snout covered in fresh blood from a corpse on the floor. They must not have turned immediately like the others. "Shit."

I tried my best to duck, barely managing to sidestep it but slipping in the blood. I somehow kept on my feet, making my way over to one of the pods. If I could get behind the pods, there may be a chance it's too big to get back there. At least I'll be safe until someone else gets here. Lunging through, I made my way in just as the beast reached an arm between two of the pods to grab me. Instead, it got stuck, too big to fit through. The creature screamed in agony, and I could see smoke rising from the arm that was stuck.

"Holy shit," I said. Of course! The pods were made with an outer shell of silver because they conduct one hundred percent of electricity. Something about keeping the techs safe from the energy diffusion going on inside. All I could think of were those old Wolfman movies I watched as a kid, though. It always took a silver bullet to kill a werewolf, but nobody said it had to be a bullet, right?

I shot my pistol at one of the electrical tubes running from the last pod. It would put us down one for escape, but if I'm right we can fuck these guys up and get home. The tube severed at the bullet, and I tore it off the rest of the way. The beast was standing back, studying the pods like it was trying to figure out how to get through without injury. Slowly... slowly I made my way back toward the first pod, hoping it would mirror me. It did.

"Okay..." I whispered to myself, finally going past the last pod before quickly ducking back in as it lunged. Instead, I stuck the sharp end of the tube out, catching the beast right in the chest. It let out a final, ragged howl before slowly shrinking, turning human again before letting out its last breath. "Holy shit, it worked."

"Collins!" Sarge's voice again, coming down the corridor back to us. He fired off a couple of shots behind him and shouted ahead. "If you're in there, you better be ready!"

"Sir! Sir, they're werewolves!" I met him at the door, brandishing the tube so he could see. "Silver kills them, look!"

He looked at the dead body on the ground, snatching the tube from me before pushing me backward into the first pod, the door still open from when he got out just minutes ago. Before I could protest, he shut the door, securing the pressure lock from the outside.

"That means they can't get out of here," he said, running over to the console and slipping on blood, using the momentum to swing around. I beat at the window on my pod, screaming at him to let me out. "Get home, tell them don't come back up here. I'm destroying this thing."

"No, sir! It's just the moon, they'll turn back!" I was shouting at him over the comm speaker. He just shook his head.

"It's overrun, Collins. We're the only humans here now. Only ones with any way out anyway," he said, hitting buttons on the console and starting the diffusion sequence. The beasts were howling loud again, coming down the corridor after Sarge. "I set a fire back there hoping it would keep them busy. Guess that was wishful thinking."

"Get in! You can't just stay here!" I shouted. Sarge smiled at me, throwing down the rifle he was still carrying along with the silver tube. Instead, he reached onto his back, holding up a grenade.

I could feel my limbs turning tingly, things beginning to break down as I was being transferred through space. The last image I got of him was a flood of fur and blood coming through the door. Fangs tore into the Sarge as he smiled at me, pulling the pin and backing into the wall. My vision began to black out, phasing between up here and back on earth. I could see the wall where Sarge was standing suddenly splatter red with blood, not exploding like he hoped.

The next thing I knew, I was on my hands and knees barfing back on earth. The pod techs were horrified, afraid to touch me because of all the blood. They took me for questioning, but all I could tell them was to watch the feeds. As far as they can see, everything is still functioning, but the beasts are now just aimlessly wandering the halls. They said some people were still up there... but I think they're just going to leave them. There's no way anyone is going to go back up there, and Sarge did enough damage to the diffusion console that it won't work on that end.

I think they're going to discharge me. Probably a nice pension somewhere, out on the coast. I'm definitely taking any kind of retirement they throw my way. They at least owe it to me after that.

RUN THROUGH THE JUNGLE

Vietnam, April 1973

"Who the fuck decided to put you in the army, son?! Did they not realize what a fucking waste of space you were?" Col. Danvers was screaming at one of the new arrivals. Typical initiation for fresh meat. Poor kid looked like he was fresh out of high school. Skinny, with big horn-rimmed glasses and a look on his face like he would rather disappear into the earth than go through this.

"I'm sorry, sir!" The boy said as he tried to gather items from his pack. The strap had broken as he was picking it up, causing it to fall and unload the contents all over the jungle floor.

"GODDAMN RIGHT YOU'RE SORRY! PICK THIS SHIT UP NOW!" Colonel was in a bad mood. He usually just yelled at the new kids once, then let them walk away, fresh shit in their pants. This time, though... something had him on edge.

Gerald walked over and stooped down, helping the kid clean up. Bad enough he had to come to fucking Vietnam, now he's getting screamed at when he's fresh off the plane. Gerald remembered what those days were like. They seemed so long ago.

"I'll take it from here, Corporal," Gerald told the older man as he picked up the last item from the ground, stuffing it in the kid's pack.

"Is this weak piece of shit yours, Sergeant?" Danvers asked Gerald, still at attention, staring the kid down.

"No clue, sir. What's your name, son?" Gerald turned to the kid, noticing the scared look on his face. He wouldn't last a week out here.

"McCoy, sir." The boy straightened up and saluted, realizing that he had two higher-ranking officers standing in front of him.

"Well, I better not catch you fucking up again, McCoy!" Danvers yelled at him one more time, then turned on his heel and walked away, looking for someone else to scream at.

"You caught him on a bad day, kid. Try to lay low for a while," Gerald told him as he walked away. McCoy looked after him, not knowing whether to cry or run back onto the plane. The only thing he knew was that this was going to be awful.

Gerald was woken by the sound of someone yelling at him and shaking his bunk.

"Get up, asshole. We've got orders. Hotel squad ain't come back from their patrol yesterday. We're supposed to go find 'em."

It was Fox waking him up. Fuck. Gerald thought to himself, Colonel probably assigned the whole peanut gallery to go look for them.

Gerald rolled off his bunk, landing lightly on his feet. He had been in Vietnam for four years now, starting out as a low ranking private. Now, he was a Sergeant, which typically got him out of the grunt work and more dangerous runs. Something bad must have happened if they were sending him with a patrol.

He walked into the officer tent, and saw Col. Danvers waiting, along with five others. He looked around and took note of his squad for the day.

Fox, the asshole that woke him. Guy had been here longer than Gerald, but they knew he was too unstable to hold any kind of rank.

He got off on killing, and volunteered for the dangerous missions whenever possible. If this war ever ends, the army is going to have to drag his ass back home.

Harris was there too. No surprise, he was Fox's lackey. Did whatever he said and seemed to enjoy the killing just as much. Gerald knew he would have his hands full with just these two alone.

The Samson twins. They were good kids, Derek and Darren, but the other soldiers around camp typically just referred to them as Samson One and Samson Two. Only way they could be told apart was that Darren, Samson 2, had part of his left ear missing. Lucky son of a bitch managed to be far enough away from an enemy grenade to only lose half an ear instead of his whole head.

The last one in the lineup was the new kid, McCoy. He looked even more nervous than he had when he dropped his pack, and Col. Danvers was eyeing him. Danvers knew fear when he saw it. He lived for it.

"Hotel Squad went on patrol yesterday and has yet to return," Danvers started in, wasting no time on the briefing. "They were due to hit a small village northwest of here, and radio in once they arrived. We never received any transmission from them. ETA for their return is going on twenty hours at this point. We need you to find them."

"Do we think it was someone in the village or VietCong?" Gerald asked the Sergeant, pressing for more details on what to expect.

"Don't fuckin' matter. We'll blow them right back to hell no matter who they are," Fox chimed in from the corner he was sitting in.

"You are not to engage unless provoked." Colonel Danvers glared over at Fox. "I'm warning you. If Sergeant Farron tells me of any bullshit you try to pull, you'll be locked up stateside before you can make some smart as comment."

Fox glared over at Gerald. They hadn't gotten along since the first day he arrived in camp. Gerald had been a critic of the war all along. He was only here to get his time out of the way and get some money to go to college later. Fox was here because he belonged in this hell.

"You are to leave immediately. Radio in and make a full report once you reach the village." Danvers dismissed them with a wave of his hand.

"Yes, sir," they all said in unison, walking out of the tent. Gerald didn't have a good feeling about this. At best, Hotel squad was lost in the jungle. At worst, they're either captured or dead.

They had been walking through the jungle for at least five hours. The sun was setting, and they hadn't found anything. Gerald was leading the pack, with Fox, Harris, and the Samson twins behind him. McCoy was bringing up the rear of the group, twitching at anything that moved.

"So what we gonna do once we get to this village, assuming we don't find them?" Harris asked.

"We beat some Charlies until they tell us where the hell they are," Fox said gleefully. Gerald could tell he was itching to kill someone, and he didn't like it one bit. Why would Danvers give him the most trigger-happy bastard in camp for this?

"You ain't beating anybody long as I'm here," he said back to Fox. Gerald didn't look, but he could feel Fox's eyes burning into his back.

The village was up ahead. Gerald motioned for all of them to lower their weapons, and turned his light on to cut through the creeping darkness. A grisly sight met him.

"Holy fuck," he whispered.

"God help us," Samson One said, crossing himself.

It looked like a slaughterhouse at peak time. The ground in the middle of the clearing was red, with blood pooled wherever it could collect. Off to the side, they could see a small pile. An arm was jutting out of the top, fingers outstretched to the heavens, warning them away.

As they stared at the carnage that met them, a small man walked out of the nearest hut. He was ancient, long silver hair falling down his back in a ponytail, and a scraggly beard reaching almost to his waist.

"Go," he said to them as they approached. Others stepped out of the huts around them, clutching makeshift weapons. A couple of them held the assault rifles that were likely taken off the dead soldiers.

"We just want to know what happened. Then we'll leave you alone," Gerald said, holding his hands up in a gesture of peace. "We were sent to find our people. How did this happen?"

"They attack. We defend," said the man in back.

"Fuck that. What kind of monsters could do this? They're torn limb from fucking limb!" Fox was spiraling quick. Gerald could tell his bloodlust was rising. He already wanted to kill something, now he had his excuse.

"Calm the hell down, Fox. We're going to find out what's going on," Gerald said back to him, putting up his hand in warning.

Thunder rumbled ominously in the distance. A storm was moving in, and the sun was going down. Gerald knew they needed to diffuse the situation and get back to camp, quick.

"At least let us get their tags. Please. Their families deserve to know they're gone," he appealed to the old man, pointing at the tags hanging from his neck, hoping for some sense of mercy for the poor souls.

The man threw a bundle of tags to the ground at Gerald's feet. They clattered together, their chiming adding to the animosity in the air.

"Now go. Tell your leaders to stay away, or else," the man said to him, waving them away.

"FUCK. THAT," Fox said, grabbing a woman that was standing near him and pointing his gun at her. "You tell us what the hell happened here. I'll be adding a fresh corpse to that pile every minute you don't answer."

"Fox, let her go," Gerald said. His voice was low, menacing. His laid-back nature was gone, replaced by the cold steel of someone who had already seen too much bloodshed.

"Don't think I fucking will," Fox said, pressing the barrel of his gun against the woman's temple. "Boys, take your pick"

Harris and the Samson twins each turned their rifles on a different villager. McCoy looked on, hands at his side, mouth open. He hadn't been here for a week. What kind of hell had he been dropped into?

"All of you, put your goddamn guns down!" Gerald said, screaming at them. "That's a fucking order!!"

A villager moved to attack Fox. Gerald couldn't tell if it was lightning or the muzzle flash that he saw. Thunder boomed along with the gunshot, and the woman fell dead at Fox's feet.

"YOU GODDAMN IDIOT!" Gerald screamed, rushing at Fox. Fox raised his gun and fired once at Gerald, hitting him in the stomach.

"FUCK!" he screamed, the bullet tearing through his belly. "You bastard... I'm going to make sure you fry for this."

"You won't be doing anything," Fox sneered, leveling the rifle at Gerald's head.

There was a crash as lightning hit feet away from them, blinding them all, the shockwave making them stumble. McCoy was knocked back into the trees, sprawled on his back. He sat up in a daze.

Where the old man had been standing, there was a large scorch mark. The old man was nowhere to be seen. Gerald looked back to Fox, who was bringing his rifle back up to aim at Gerald's forehead.

"Well, if that ain't the weirdest shit I've seen," Fox said, looking at the burn mark. "Serves the old fucker ri-"

His boasting became screaming as he was flung into the air by what looked like another bolt of lightning. He flew up at least fifteen feet, coming back to the ground on his head. McCoy looked on, still on the ground where he landed, frozen in fear. He heard the crunch as Fox's neck snapped.

"What the hell..." Harris said, jabbing at his captive villager.

Lightning flashed by again, but McCoy noticed this time that it wasn't coming from the sky. The bolts seemed to be streaking across the clearing, from one side to the other. Occasionally, it would arc upwards, coming back down and settling in the trees. It was almost a solid mass, moving and stopping as it pleased.

Harris gasped, dropping his rifle and clutching at his midsection. He had been ripped open when the bolt streaked past him, entrails spewing out in ropes onto the ground.

"Shit," Samson One said. He looked over at his twin, silently communicating the idea to run. They both dropped their hostages and fled in opposite directions toward the tree line. The lightning streaked by again, running a loop around the both of them. McCoy saw Samson Two's head disappear, and a geyser of blood spray from the stump that was left.

Samson One looked back and screamed. They had come into this world together, now they left it together. He was shorn in half by the bolt, falling to the ground and briefly clutching at the entrails coming from his waist where his bottom half had been moments before. Letting out a silent scream, he expired.

Gerald wasn't sure what he was seeing was real. He knew he was dying. The bullet would have done a lot of damage, and his blood was mixing with the viscera and dirt of the jungle. He must be imagining all this.

The lightning stopped in front of McCoy, hovering in the air. That's when he was able to see it for what it was. A serpent, at least twenty feet in length, coiled around itself. It floated in the air, electricity crackling and arcing off its scales as it studied him. It had small arms coming out of its front, and more spaced out as the length of its body went on. The head was gruesome and majestic all at once, with sparkling blue scales, the color of lightning itself, as if it had harnessed nature. No, it was nature. This was something older than humans. This was the planet itself. This was what had killed the other squad, and it was going to kill him next.

"Don't hurt him. Please. The kid is innocent. He didn't ask to be here," Gerald pleaded with the serpent. It turned around, looking from him to McCoy, as if deciding their fates.

Lightning struck from the sky again, and the serpent was gone. The old man stood in its place. He moved toward Gerald, picked up the bundle of tags he had thrown earlier, and handed them over.

"Go," he said, nodding to McCoy to take Gerald. He scrambled over, leaving his gun on the ground, and helped the injured man to his feet. Taking one last look back at the old man, he nodded and began helping Gerald away.

They walked in silence for a few minutes. Finally, McCoy had to speak.

"Sir, what the fuck was that?" he asked, stammering and tripping through the darkness. The storm had descended among them the same time that the serpent had, and every flash of lightning made him jump. He could feel Gerald next to him, his breathing becoming more labored.

"Don't know, kid," he answered. "Fuck. Set me down over here. Get back to camp. They can come back for me later."

"You won't make it until they can come for you!" McCoy said, not fathoming leaving the only decent person at the camp for dead.

"I ain't gonna make it anyway. Much of a bastard as Fox was, he's a decent shot. I'm fucked," Gerald said, his breathing becoming more shallow with every word. "Go. Get the fuck out of Vietnam. Tell them exactly what you saw, and they're bound to let you go. They'll definitely think you've lost your shit."

"I can't. I can't just leave you here to die." McCoy started to cry, his tears blending into the rain falling on his face. He never wanted to be here. This goddamn war was supposed to be over. He was supposed to be going to college, doing all the dumb shit that college comes with. Getting drunk, chasing girls, partying... not sitting in a jungle watching the man who saved him dying.

"Tough shit. Go." Gerald brought his pistol out of its holster, waving him off. He knew what he was getting into coming out here. He wanted to serve his country. He didn't think he would see half the things he had experienced. There were bigger monsters back home in Washington than that thing back there, and he wasn't going to let them have McCoy's blood on their hands, along with the countless others they already took.

Gerald lifted the pistol to his temple.

"NO!" McCoy shouted, leaping toward him. He managed to knock the pistol out of Gerald's hand. It discharged as it hit the ground, hitting McCoy in the left ankle.

"Ah, Jesus Christ," Gerald said. This kid was too goddamn stubborn. Gerald wanted him to get back to camp, but the kid couldn't leave well enough alone. "Guess we're going back two cripples."

He leaned over, picking up McCoy on his left side. McCoy was still screaming, the pain tearing from his ankle up into his knee. He leaned on Gerald, hopping on his right leg as they moved forward.

"Alright, McCoy. Let's get through this so once you're re-covered I can kick your ass for injuring yourself." Gerald gritted his teeth. Adrenaline was surging through him now, giving him a second wind. They were at least two hours from camp, and he knew the weather would only make them slower. He had to get the kid to safety.

"Only if I can kick your ass right back for trying to off yourself back there." McCoy laughed through gritted teeth. They began the trek, two broken men supporting each other on their journey back from hell.

By the time they arrived back at camp, dawn was breaking. They both collapsed at the edge of the main campsite and were quickly put on stretchers and run into the medical tent. Gerald went into emergency surgery to have the bullet removed from his stomach. McCoy was taken to have his ankle cleaned and disinfected. He floated away on a wave of exhaustion and morphine.

Lightning flashed, waking McCoy from his fitful sleep. Sitting bolt upright, drenched in sweat and tears, he screamed.

"Easy, easy. You're okay now," a voice said near his feet. A man in a doctor's coat was sitting there, looking at him with an expression of worry.

"Where's Gerald, is he okay?" McCoy asked. Please don't be dead. Please, God. He prayed silently.

"He's resting in a private room. It's going to be pretty touch and go for a few days, but I have faith he'll pull through. Gerald's been here longer than I have, and he's a tough son of a bitch. You, on the other hand, weren't so lucky I'm afraid."

McCoy pulled the sheet over his legs back, looking down at his foot. It was heavily bandaged from the ankle up to the knee, mummified almost.

"The bullet completely shattered your ankle, and managed to sever your Achilles' tendon. I'm afraid they're going to have to amputate. You're both going back stateside."

McCoy looked at the doctor, not comprehending his words. His leg felt fine. Hell, he could get up and walk out of here right now.

"I know this is tough to take, son. They're doing great prosthetics now though. You can get a brand-new leg, no problem at all. Uncle Sam will foot the bill, of course."

"Foot the bill..." McCoy repeated after the doctor. He chuckled to himself, which eventually turned into a full-on belly laugh. The doctor didn't seem to catch on to the joke.

MORE CHILLS FROM VELOX BOOKS

MORE CHILLS FROM VELOX BOOKS

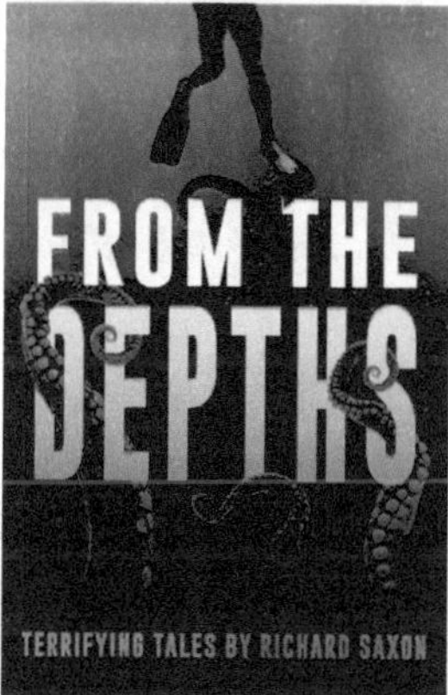

MORE CHILLS FROM VELOX BOOKS

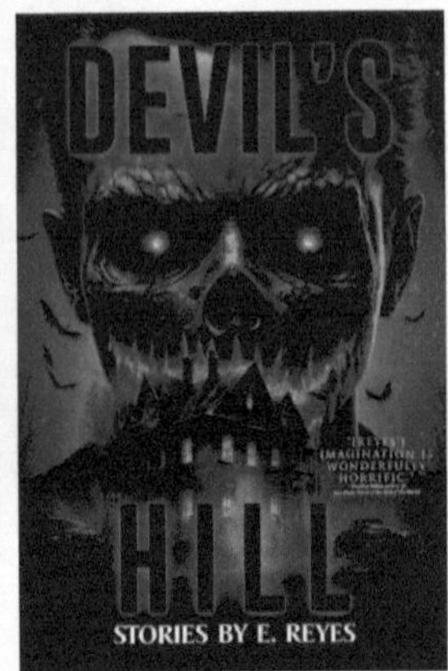

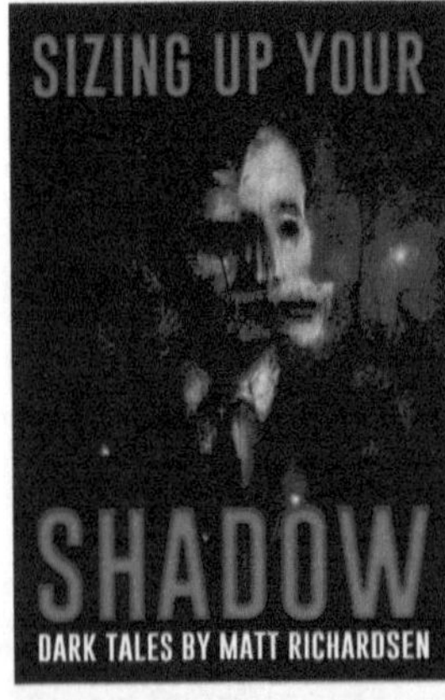

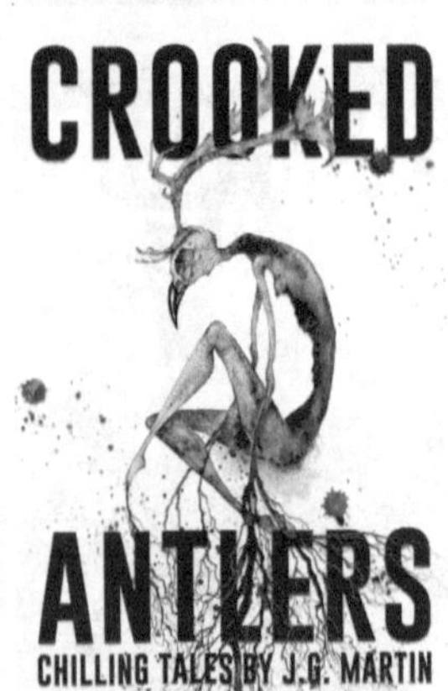

www.ingramcontent.com/pod-product-compliance
Lightning Source LLC
Chambersburg PA
CBHW021045310726
48969CB00006B/1819